HAUNTED

STATE V. SEFORÉ - BOOK ONE

HAUNTED

CHARITY TINNIN

Summary

In a dystopian future, Noah State, a guilt-ridden government enforcer, tries to save the resistance he's been tasked with eliminating.

To Mom:

This book would not exist without you.
You taught me how to read and write and
showed me how to fall in love with both.

I am grateful every day.

CHAPTER ONE

NOAH HAD KNOWN he wouldn't live to see twenty-one. And until this moment, he'd considered himself prepared. Turns out, facing death wasn't the same as contemplating it.

If it weren't illegal, he might've sent up a silent prayer. Not that he was religious or anything. But desperate times and all … His heart beat a crazy rhythm that rivaled any of the top-ten pop hits on the airwaves. It echoed in his ears.

Sweat beaded on his forehead as though he were still outside in Coastal South West's hot desert air. The metal chair back dug into his ribs. He allowed himself to straighten but not fidget. He might be dead in a couple of hours, but he would go out on his own terms, and those terms allowed for no evident traces of fear or weakness. He wouldn't display a hint. Not to them, not to their cameras.

His gaze landed on the wall opposite him. Six-inch letters hung at eye level. *It is a fact of nature that the fittest will always survive, but if those with the highest intelligence and best abilities seek to serve and protect, society will also survive. This is the Elite's privilege and burden: to carry the weight of Patrisia on their shoulders.*

He fought to keep his face impassive. The propaganda might fool some of Patrisia's more gullible citizens, but he knew the Elite protected Potentate Marcioni and themselves alone. His resolve to be different was no doubt what led to this moment.

"Noah State? Harrow will see you now." The dark-haired receptionist held the door open to his right.

He stood, his palms sweating. Were these the last steps he would take? He cleared his throat. "Thank you."

She nodded and led him forward, wafting rose water with every step. The perfume invaded his senses, a failed cover-up for the faint smell of curry and garlic seeping out of her pores. Her own enhanced senses had to tell her it wasn't working. Why bother?

She motioned to an open room complete with vidwall, table, and six chairs. Five of the chairs faced him. His knees threatened to give out, but he locked the traitorous joints and forced himself to take in the other details.

Darkened windows lined one side of the room. A camera was mounted in the far left corner facing the door, another in the near right facing the table. Several compads and one empty glass lay on the table.

"That'll be all, Marcy."

Noah spun. Regional Liquidator Doug Harrow stepped into the doorway, his arms clasped behind his back. His eyes, almost the color of desert khaki, studied Noah through a squint. Everything about his appearance screamed military, from the bald head and lines around his eyes to his trim physique. Had he served before Potentate, then President, Marcioni disbanded the Pentagon and armed forces?

"Have a seat, Noah." Doug Harrow's gravelly tone registered just above a whisper. Calm confidence seeped out of the man. Noah sat and hid his trembling hands under the table.

"You can relax, kid. This isn't a tribunal."

Noah allowed himself one small sigh. He might live to see tomorrow? Then why had he been summoned? Nothing good came from a one-on-one visit with a regional liquidator.

Harrow sat opposite Noah and leaned back against one arm of the chair. "You've finished your second year as a liquidator."

"Yes, sir."

Harrow slid a compad from the table into his hands. "Six months in Coastal South East, almost a year in Coastal North West, and the last several months under my authority. Your caseload is light for a free agent, even for one fresh out of the Academy. You've closed eighteen inquires, but you have only five liquidations on your record. Care to explain?"

Noah's hands curled into fists. Explain that he didn't consider death a just punishment for petty crime? No, thank you, he liked continuing to breathe. "I prefer to be exact with my rulings, sir."

"Hmm." Harrow tapped a callused finger on the table. "We left the justice system behind for a reason, kid. Punishments that fit the crime weren't effective deterrents. Fear is more useful. When we all understand that there are no second chances, we give our choices more weight. You're doing no one any favors with your do-overs—not the criminals and not their next victims."

A bullet straight to his heart. The assault reactivated pain in the fresh wound. Blonde, cherubic faces flashed before Noah's eyes. But no, not a flashback. The vidwall's surface displayed their faces. The girls were orphans now because Noah gave a thief a second chance. A second chance the man had used to rob another convenience store—and kill the thirty-year-old female clerk with three little girls at home.

"You didn't do these girls or their mother any good." Harrow leaned forward but didn't raise his voice. "It's past time you got with the program, kid. Followed in your brother's footsteps. He's got a liquidation count to be proud of."

The vidwall's contents shifted to Daniel's profile. The numbers turned Noah's stomach. Eighty cases and seventy-six liquidations. The numbers would've been equal had Noah not stepped in those four times. Too late for the others. Always too late where Daniel was concerned. Not that Daniel cared. Not that anyone cared.

"If it were up to me, you would be facing a tribunal today. We have enough trouble on our hands without having to babysit liquidators who've taken our time and resources but think they're too good for our system." Harrow's eyes drilled into Noah's for the space of ten heartbeats. "Lucky for you the Council has made a unique request." He sighed and keyed a sequence into the compad. "I'll let Regional Liquidator McCray explain."

Lawson McCray appeared on the vidwall, his shoulders filling the frame. If Harrow was a military sniper, calm and cool under pressure, McCray was a blustering general with a sandy blond buzz cut and a five o'clock shadow. A smoking cigar lay in an ashtray between McCray and the camera. "You fill him in?"

Harrow shook his head. "Your turf, your details."

McCray narrowed his eyes, dissecting Noah with his stare. "Yeah, we all know how I feel about this objective on my turf...."

A noose tightened around Noah's neck. He might as well be at a tribunal.

"Nevertheless, the Council has already handed down the order," Harrow said.

McCray cursed. "Okay, State, let's hope those enhanced ears of yours are at a hundred percent today 'cause I'm not going to repeat myself. I don't want you and your old-fashioned ideals in Coastal South East. I don't think you'll succeed at the objective either, but then I guess I get to kill you." He took a long drag of the cigar. "So, maybe there are some perks to this arrangement...."

Harrow cleared his throat, and McCray scowled again. "In the last three months, a terrorist group has made its way onto my radar. My stationary liquidators have questioned and liquidated anyone we considered connected to the activity. But, if anything, the activity has multiplied. Clearly, I've been assigned a group of idiots for liquidators. I'm in favor of purging the region, but the Council is worried about bad press. How maintaining power could be misconstrued as bad press, I have no clue. Anyway, the Council has ordered an undercover investigation."

Noah's pulse quickened. An actual investigation? That he could do. Maybe he had earned a reprieve.

McCray rolled his eyes. "The Council suspects the terrorists are a vast network—a group of well-sourced obsessive-compulsives. I think it's a bunch of crackpots who've been lucky, but nobody's seen fit to ask my opinion. The Council's called for a Hail Mary before taking drastic measures. Since they like you and your meticulous record, seems you're the man for the job."

Where was his vidcom? Pocket. Noah reached back, opened it up, and began making notes, his fingers flying across the keyboard. "Where will I be stationed?"

McCray let out a puff of smoke and typed on a compad with one hand. "Metro Area Four in Coastal South East. You should have the details now."

Noah's vidcom vibrated. He opened the downloaded file and began reading. Cover: Noah Jackson Seforé. Age: Twenty. Description: 5'11", Brown Hair, Green Eyes. Occupation: CNA at MA-4 Hospital D. Background—

"Hey, I'm not done with you yet. You can study the fascinating details later." McCray leaned closer to the camera. "Let me make this abundantly clear. Your objective is to uncover, join, and then liquidate these terrorists. Every last one of them. By, let's say, mid-February. Five months should be more than enough time for a wonder boy like yourself, right?" McCray smirked. "Oh, and Doug might've let you get away with slapping criminals on the wrist, but I don't work that way. If you fail to uncover the group, I liquidate you. If you fail to gain their trust and identify every party involved, I liquidate you. If you don't liquidate every single one of those scumbags … well, you get the idea."

Wet cement dripped into Noah's veins, clogging his brain, his lungs, his limbs. No reprieve then. "Yes, sir."

"Study up, State." He disconnected, and the vidwall went black.

Noah swiveled to face Harrow. "Study up?"

"You have CNA training to complete. It's all in your file."

Noah glanced at his vidcom again. Sure enough, there it was. Private training tomorrow at 7 in the morning. "They suspect some of the hospital employees?"

Harrow nodded "Rumors tend to spread quicker there than anywhere else. Plus, it hasn't been targeted."

Targeted? Noah scanned the file. "Hacks."

"Someone found a back door into the government networks. Embarrassed McCray, but the man's a sleeping bear. Once riled … Well, you know the saying. He's taken these attacks very personally. Some of the Elite's best programmers are working on potential entry sites, but it'll be your job to locate the group responsible before they stage another attack."

Noah took his time looking over the illegal video, audio, and text messages. He clicked on the file behind one text message reading "Back to Democracy." The message had been online for five minutes before detected. The suspect initiated the hack at a public information booth in Metro Area Six. He opened another file, finding a hack from a grocery store mainframe in MA-3. One in MA-2. The final hack took place in MA-5 at a computer in the Regional Classification Office.

No wonder McCray was foaming at the mouth—somebody in his region pointed out the areas he hadn't secured. Whoever instigated these security breaches was intelligent, well sourced, and aware of the identities and routines of the stationary liquidators. Instinct told Noah the hacks were likely the work of one very detailed individual. One person who could slip in and out of most places without being flagged. Not to say that the individual was acting alone—someone was funding the hacks. He'd just have to figure out who it was … and who it wasn't. He might have only five months to live, but that was enough time to minimize the collateral damage. After all, it was what he did best.

"I'd recommend you channel your brother, kid." Harrow rose and pushed his chair under the table. "You're all out of second chances."

Better make the most of this one.

CHAPTER TWO

MADDISON HATED ALL Sundays, but this one in particular conspired against her. Throwing her messenger bag over her shoulder, she raced for the front door. "Disengage lock."

She grabbed her remote from the bowl on the table and bolted toward her navy blue Chrysler 8, deactivating its alarm as well.

Footsteps pounded behind her. "Wait up."

"Don't you know what time it is? Why didn't you tell me?" The sharp words bounced off Jakob, who shrugged as he dropped into the passenger seat. He tossed an apple into her lap.

"You might get hungry later."

"Start ignition." She tossed the apple into the console as the seatbelt locked into place. The strap rested at an awkward angle along her collarbone. She resisted the useless urge to tug it back.

The autopilot computer came online. "Identify passenger and destination, please."

"Jakob James. Destination: PS 124."

"Passenger and destination accepted." The dash lit up, the clock displaying 7:38 a.m.

She tried to swallow the panic crawling up her throat, but it leaked out. "We're never going to make it."

"Well, then your car better step on it." Jakob grinned.

The glare she shot his way didn't make a dent. Her brother—unflappable in the face of fear. That used to be her.

She stomped down on the memories as the car shot out of the driveway and toward the corner. The computer's GPS registered the time and replaced their normal route with a quicker but less maintained way. Her fingers curled around the steering wheel. She formulated acceptable excuses for their lateness.

She knew better than to be late for school and hadn't been, not once, since the day after her parents … Well, the teachers had understood. She had no such excuse today. This morning's noteworthiness lay in nothing more than being the beginning of another school week. No, the fault lay with her alone.

She found herself hitting the snooze button more and more, clinging to every moment away from school. The attendance panels, boring teachers, and a dwindling senior class trapped her in a rapidly tightening net.

"Look, the GPS already cut ten minutes off our route. We'll be there in no time." Jakob drummed his fingers on the door. "Radio on."

"Radio off." She shot him a glare. "Be serious, would you? I don't want a visitation."

His mouth tightened, and his hand stilled. "Neither do I, but we'll be fine."

Her eyes returned to the road as they pulled into the school parking lot and her assigned space on the far end. "You don't know that."

"We'll run. It'll be okay." As soon as the car finished parking itself, he hit the manual seatbelt release, alarms blaring, and darted out. He sprinted toward the tenth-grade building, a blur of sandy brown hair, red t-shirt, and distressed jeans.

The clock read 7:57 a.m. Three minutes.

"Power off." The alarms silenced, and her seatbelt flew off. She grabbed her bag from the backseat and swung around to open the door, activating the alarm even as she made her own dash. The cars in the lot stood alone, devoid of their usual groups of lounging students waiting for the first bell.

The trees and flowers along the manicured paths were the sole witnesses to her mad scramble for the twelfth-grade building on the other side of campus. The staccato tapping of her flats disturbed the peace in the courtyard. The doors of the main entrance slid shut behind the last stragglers. She sucked in a deep breath.

She quickened her pace but forced herself to stay under a run as she approached the doors. They opened without a sound. The camera mounted above recorded her speed, its red light taunting her. She controlled her expression and ran a hand over her hair as if she had nowhere else to be. As she walked past the open classroom doors on either side of the hall, the startled gazes of teachers and students burned into her back. She didn't acknowledge them. She'd grown proficient in ignoring stares and whispers in the years since her parents' liquidation.

As she came to a stop in front of room 108, her eyes darted to the time stamp on the handprint panel. It changed from 7:59 a.m. to 8:00 a.m. She shot her hand up to the blank screen, and it read her palm-print, temperature, and heart rate. A moment later, it registered her as in attendance, and she slid into the classroom.

Her blood pulsed through her veins as she took her seat, waiting for her name to be called. After all, the computer had logged her tardiness and noted her increased heart rate. Mrs. Rimes frowned at her but began the lecture. Her gaze only darted up toward the camera in the corner for a second.

Olivia shot Maddison a smile, and the air released from her lungs. Maybe a minute's difference wouldn't set off alarms. They wouldn't pull her from the classroom, right? She took another breath, this one much deeper, and looked back at her friend. A large multicolored flower crowned Olivia's light brown hair. Maddison couldn't help but smile back.

Maybe Olivia and Sophie could come over after apprentice hours. It would make their standing ice cream date on Thursday night seem closer. Pulling her v-compad out of her bag, she tried to concentrate on Mrs. Rimes' lecture. No good. The teacher's monotone paired with the endless dates from history couldn't hold her attention.

She pressed the awake button and pulled out the stylus while she waited for the compad to power up. The picture of Olivia, Sophie, and Josh from last summer flashed up as her background, and out of habit, her gaze fell to the left.

She startled. A stranger sat beside her. His light blond hair and steel blue eyes were the exact opposite of Josh's. Not that she'd really expected to see Josh in his old seat, but still. The stranger cut his eyes at her, and his mouth quirked an inch. He typed two words on his compad and tilted it so she could see the screen. "Brandon. You?" Where had he come from?

A set of heavy footsteps echoed in the hallway, and she shot up in her chair. Everyone else did too. Her palms felt slick. Mrs. Rimes continued but spoke with more passion, shooting glances toward the classroom entrance. The footsteps paused outside the door. Maddison's lungs stopped working.

A voice rumbled on the other side. The steps began again, walking further down the hall. Another door chimed open, and then two pairs of feet, one stumbling and one striding. Everyone breathed a sigh of relief—until the sharp four tones sounded.

Her head whipped up to the large vidscreens mounted at the front of the room, awaiting the local announcement. Most of the other students fidgeted, drumming fingers and shifting in their desks, but she kept herself still. The new boy did the same. Local or not, they waited for a government message, which meant one of two things: a Restructuring of Responsibilities or a Liquidation Update.

Considering that stumbling set of feet, she braced herself for the second.

*

"Blood pressure, temperature, heart rate, and respiratory rate." Noah recited the vital signs under his breath as he slammed the door of his vintage gray Mustang. Three weeks of intensive CNA training had tattooed his brain with the information, but repeating it helped him focus his ever-stimulated senses.

Time to go to work. He fought a grin for a millisecond. No need to hold it back. Noah Save-The-World Seforé was a grinner. He crossed the employee parking lot in twenty strides, scanning the area. Forty-five cars sat in the lot. All midrange models. No unique stickers or strange license plates. No one loitered by the entrance. His internal radar remained silent.

The double doors glided open, and the polished voice used in all government facilities welcomed him. A wave of fruity air freshener mixed with bleach assaulted his nose, and he stopped inside the door. A few patients milled around the check-in desk to his left. He surveyed the empty chairs and orphaned snack shop while listening to their conversations. The man at the beginning of the line argued with the nurse behind the desk about his scheduled appendectomy. A mother placated the worried little boy in a cast. The woman behind them in a wheelchair mumbled nonsense while the middle-aged man at the back of the line checked his watch. For the beginning of the week, everything seemed relatively calm. Looked like Sunday wasn't as frantic as he was led to believe.

At the employee terminals on the right, he swiped Seforé's new vidcom and entered his handprint at an open computer. Answering its questions took five minutes. Lying to a computer required only the right pass codes and key words.

His first challenge arrived moments later. She strode

forward, not pleased. Too busy to deal with a new CNA, he assumed.

"Noah Seforé?" Her tone dared him to contradict her.

He didn't even blink. He'd been a Seforé for eighteen years before the Elite changed his name. This was the man he should've been. The man he would've been … if his attempt to throw his Gifting and Aptitude Placement had succeeded.

"Yes, ma'am."

"Manners do you no good here. Keep up." She pivoted and headed back toward the hospital's center.

He caught up in two strides and kept pace. She raised an eyebrow as they turned deeper into the bowels of the hospital. The scent of antiseptic grew stronger, and he breathed through his mouth. Once in the break area, she pointed toward a pile of light blue scrubs.

He killed the smile. Working her would require playing the role of the intimidated employee, so he grabbed a set of scrubs and slipped back into the locker area. The part grated, but if it made Madame Director think she was in control, he'd use it. He changed into the uniform identifying him as a Certified Nursing Assistant, stashed his gear, and returned to her side within minutes. There went the eyebrow again.

"Your paperwork says you served in the ER at a hospital in Coastal South West for the last two years. Med/surg might not be the high intensity environment you're used to, but I think you'll find the diversity of your cases will keep you busy enough. Take the elevator to the second level and report to the nurses' station. They'll handle your orientation." She handed him an ID badge complete with his archived picture before snapping the file closed. "Don't ask me any questions. I don't have time for answers. For your sake, I hope this is our sole interaction. Getting called to my office shouldn't be on your agenda."

Noah nodded, eyes averted, and walked around her toward the elevators. Once her footsteps faded away, he straightened his shoulders. Wonder if her attitude would've been different if he'd used his official last name?

No, she didn't seem the type to relinquish her authority to anybody. Even if her life hung in the balance.

"You don't scare easily, do you?" The voice floated up from his right.

Looking down at his unexpected companion, his smile returned. "I think I'll wait until we're in the elevator to answer."

The blue-eyed sprite in pink scrubs laughed as the elevator opened. "Brave and wise, you must be ER staff."

Noah chuckled, pushing the button for his floor. "You're a bad eavesdropper."

She leaned back against the wall, twisting her long chestnut hair up into a bun with a practiced move. "Not an eavesdropper. Just intuitive."

Interesting. "Well, Miss Intuitive, you're half right. I used to work in the ER, but I'll be in med/surg here." He held out a hand, using the opportunity to study her further. There were hints of green mingling with the blue of her eyes. "I'm Noah."

She took his hand as the elevator dinged. "Nice to meet you."

"And you are?"

As she exited, she shot back, "Miss Intuitive to you."

Heat crawled up Maddison's neck. What had gotten into her? She quickened her pace down the hall and hoped no one would notice her flushed face. Maybe she would be shadowing Dr. Wallace on the other side of the floor today. She could be out of sight before Noah announced himself at the nurses' station. Right?

"Maddison." Nurse Walker's face relaxed at the sight of her. "I'm so glad you're here. We're slammed today. Three new admissions this afternoon alone: a gall-bladder removal, appendectomy, and a Crohn's patient with a case of MRSA. Plus, we have a new CNA, and I don't have time to show him the ropes. I need you to do it."

She pasted on a smile. "No problem."

"Great." Walker looked over Maddison's shoulder. "Maddison, meet Noah Seforé. Noah, this is Maddison James, my best apprentice. She'll be in charge of your orientation today, and you can sign out at six when she does. But I'll expect you first thing tomorrow for the full shift."

Maddison allowed herself one moment to close her eyes and swallow before turning to face him. The corners of his mouth turned up as his gaze met hers. Why, oh why, couldn't there have been two new CNAs today? Couldn't she have flirted with anyone else?

"So, Maddison, is it?" Laugh lines framed the mirth in his ivy green eyes.

He didn't seem eager to embarrass her in front of Nurse

Walker. Maybe this afternoon wouldn't be so bad after all. "That's me." She pulled her ID badge from a pocket and clipped it on. "Why don't we start with a tour so you'll get the lay of the land before someone sends you running for ice chips?"

"Lead the way." He swept a hand in front of himself in a gallant gesture. A single butterfly took up residence in her stomach.

She took her time showing him the optimal routes to and from the various patient rooms and supply closets. By forcing herself to concentrate on the minutiae, she blocked out his confident gait, broad shoulders, and inquisitive face. At least, she tried to.

"Should I be prepared for a quiz on this material?" Despite his question, Noah appeared undaunted by all the information she'd thrown at him in the last thirty minutes. They rounded the last corner, back in view of the nurses' station.

"No. I hate quizzes, so I won't start giving them anytime soon." Although she had more than one question for him—and none of them had to do with hospital procedure. They centered more around the topics of his relocation to Metro Area Four, his age, and if, based on his physique, he'd been a secondary school wrestler or football player.

"You can't hate quizzes because you fail them." His eyes studied her. She hoped he found whatever he looked for. "You wouldn't be an apprentice at a hospital if you hadn't scored well during your gifting placement. So, what is it? I'm intrigued."

Her mental filter malfunctioned. "The whole concept of

our futures being decided by how well we perform on demand makes me sick."

His mouth leveled out, and he grew still. His furrowed brows hinted at a deeper reaction. After a moment, he asked, "Someone close to you?"

"What?"

"Someone you care about is capable of more than their chosen placement?"

"Well, yes, but I've always disliked the premise behind the GAP." She shifted, brushing invisible lint from her scrubs. He was a stranger, and they were standing in a government-run facility. "Then again, I'm just a teenager. What do I know?"

She glanced around the corridors, but no one else was close enough to overhear their conversation. She exhaled and searched Noah's face. What was he thinking? He might be just a CNA, but it didn't mean he could be trusted. Time to change the subject.

"Enough about me. Why would you ever choose to leave sunny Coastal South West for the fickle east coast, especially considering the paperwork involved in requesting re-assignment?" She plopped down in one of the chairs behind the nurses' station.

"So, you did engage in some eavesdropping earlier." He grinned, his teeth gleaming straight and white. "Sunny CSW's not all it's cracked up to be. Besides, I grew up in Coastal South East, so I'm used to the 'fickle east coast,' even if I might describe it as hot and muggy."

"Well, I know you didn't grow up here, so what metro area are you from?"

"MA-16. We lived in a small suburb about twenty minutes from the center. It's one of the few MAs with surviving suburbs. Neighborhoods, small shopping centers, we even had our own baseball park."

"So why move away? Sounds like you loved it."

His voice dropped. "No one left to stay for."

Given his tone, she probably shouldn't push, but … "No family?"

A muscle in his jaw jumped. "An older brother, but our relationship is … complicated."

"My parents are dead too." She slapped a hand over her mouth. What had possessed her to share that? Had his presence short-circuited her filter for good?

His chin dipped. He shoved his hands in his pockets. "I'm sorry, Maddison."

His sympathy made her throat tighten. Only a handful of people offered their condolences after the liquidation. No one knew how to comfort her and Jakob without triggering a visitation. She understood though, really, she did. She swallowed her gratitude and squeezed out a meager "thanks" to Noah.

He opened his mouth to respond when a nurse careened around the corner. "Can I get some help from you two?"

Noah took the lead. She followed with a hand over her stomach. The butterfly had multiplied.

*

Noah shrugged on his jacket, the worn leather conformed to his shoulders. If all went as planned, he could grab something to eat on his way back to the hotel and be under the hot spray of the shower within thirty minutes. Then research. Madame Director, Nurse Walker, Nurse Gardner, and Maddison. No. Apprentice James.

She might intrigue him, he might feel empathy for her, he might even be attracted to her, but her comment about the GAP and the elevated heart rate accompanying it made one thing plain. She had to be a suspect first.

He reached his car and pressed his thumb to the ID pad. The locks clicked open. Sinking into the leather seats, he closed the door behind him.

"Start ignition."

The car roared to life. As the seatbelt clicked behind his shoulder, he sat up to adjust the rearview mirror. Hot pink flashed in the corner, and he turned around. Maddison jogged toward a late model Chrysler. The car fit her somehow. Maybe because the blue-green color matched her eyes. He smiled as her hair swung free from the bun. It fell down her back in rich chestnut waves. Were the strands as soft as they appeared? He shook his head and made himself turn.

He had no business thinking about her like that. He was a dead man walking. Attachment to anyone was a bad idea. More importantly, she fit the recruitment profile he created for the resistance to a T. And if by some chance she wasn't a member, she was clearly no friend of the Elite. She was going to get herself liquidated, soon if she weren't more careful.

Taking one last look in the rearview, he deactivated the autopilot, pulled out, and headed for the beltline. As he wove through traffic, his conscience elbowed its way in between the suspicion and interest.

Any other liquidator would've eliminated her this afternoon. She was exactly the type of person McCray would brand a rebel. Collateral damage had a face, and it was hers. Noah was the only one who would give her the benefit of the doubt. The only one who would bother to find out where her loyalty really lay. He'd have to get close to her, continue building the trust his honesty had fostered.

Still, talking about home and Daniel in the same conversation brought up memories better left buried—memories of Mom's apple crumble, Dad's maps, and Daniel's breakdown. He hadn't been there for the last, but hearing the story from Ryan imprinted its own mental images.

He gripped the steering wheel tighter. If he'd been there …

But he hadn't been, and he couldn't change the past. He shifted to the far left lane and let the car race ahead of the other traffic. All he could do was move forward, and if dealing with those memories won Maddison's trust and gave him an in with the resistance, it was worth it. If it cleared her name, even better.

His nightmares had a large enough cast already.

CHAPTER THREE

MADDISON LEANED BACK in the driver's seat and rested her hands on the steering wheel. Sure, the car drove itself, but that didn't mean a machine had complete power over her. She checked for an open lane to her right as the car sped down the on-ramp of I-440. An eighteen-wheeler barreled past on her left. Her car adjusted its speed and signaled to pull in behind the truck. If only she could feel the rush of hitting the gas pedal and weaving in and out of lanes for herself.

She slumped down in her seat. Not that autonomous cars didn't have benefits. At the end of a long day, paying attention to the road could be dangerous at best. Taylor would no doubt be thankful for the respite between the hospital and home after her last shift. As an ER doctor, Maddison's aunt worked twelve-hour shifts, but a staff shortage this morning meant a mandate to come in four hours earlier than normal. She would be dead on her feet when she walked in the door tonight, which left Maddison in charge of dinner.

Jakob would be home already, but the fifteen-year-old

didn't cook. Grab a bag of Doritos from the pantry? That he'd do. Maddison's stomach rumbled. She would be ravenous by the time she came up with an idea and prepared it.

As the car slowed before a stop sign, the dark blue sticker on the sign's bottom right corner drew Maddison's eye. The flag-shaped sticker waved west—a symbol of a clandestine meeting. Anyone could spot signs of public resistance, if they knew what to look for. Maddison did.

She didn't want to put her family at risk by joining the resistance, but looking the other way from those movements and their activities had become a specialty of hers. One she never would've cultivated before her parents' death….

What had she been thinking about? Oh, right, dinner. Taylor would want to eat and head to bed, so takeout would be a better option. Besides, Maddison's mouth watered at the thought of lasagna and garlic bread. Takeout it was.

After requesting the addition of a stop at La Bella Dioci, she voice commanded the radio's volume up several decibels. She loved this song. The bass pumped, and her head bobbed to the beat. She sang along at the top of her lungs, not caring that Olivia always accused her of being off-key.

The familiar tones broke in, leaving her mouth open mid-chorus. Two beats. A nationwide announcement. She leaned closer to the speakers.

"Attention all citizens, please give attention and adjust your behavior according to the following." Dread filled her. Those words signaled a Restructuring of Responsibilities. When Potentate Marcioni's voice took over the airwaves, she went cold. She rubbed her hands over her arms, now grateful the car didn't need her to continue to its destination.

"My fellow Patrisians, our country has experienced a record year in demand for our goods. Our industries are thriving, and the rest of the world watches in awe at how well we have continued to pull out of the global depression while they remain mired in democratic processes. I celebrate your faithfulness to our ideals, and thank you for doing your part with such steadfastness. Likewise, the Elite want to maintain our responsibility to you, and it has come to my attention that certain members of the population, particularly those gifted in commerce and industry, cannot fulfill the recommended eight hours of sleep due to their specific placements in these thriving times. This should not be so, fellow Patrisians. Therefore, in an effort to give each citizen the freedom to pursue the Ministry of Medicine's recommendations, effective as of tomorrow, Monday, October fourteenth, all non-essential businesses will close by nine in the evening. A curfew of 10:00 p.m. will be mandatory on all days except Friday, when it will take effect at 11:30 p.m. This curfew will be lifted each morning at 6:30 a.m. Any persons traveling outside their homes during those hours should be prepared to present authorization from their employer to any member of the Elite they encounter. Rest, dear citizens, knowing your government is looking out for your best interest."

"Mute radio." Her gaze left the steering wheel now gripped by white-knuckled fingers and shot around for anything else to distract her. "Like he's some benevolent parent." Saying it aloud helped rid her mouth of the alkaline taste his words brought. Her car waited in the turn lane for a break in the oncoming traffic, and her fingers played a rapid beat on the steering wheel. Her brain raced through the possibilities surrounding the real reason for the curfew.

Marcioni was no benevolent leader, caring for his people. The curfew could only mean one thing: trouble brewed somewhere.

*

A frantic pounding snapped Maddison's attention to the sliding glass door. Josh stood on the other side, silhouetted by the flood light. The right side of his face and bare chest were an angry red, and his eye was swollen shut. With a gasp, she sprang to her feet, unlocked the door, and slammed it open. "What happened?"

Josh stepped inside, pain outlined in the arm he held against his chest. Normally he would've made a beeline for the table or the fridge. His stillness made the alarm bells clang louder in her head. He looked past her. "There was an accident. At work. I didn't know where else … I can't see. I mean, out of my right …"

Taylor moved between them. "Out in the field?"

Josh nodded just an inch. He wobbled on his feet. Maddison reached a hand out, but Taylor blocked her.

"Chemicals?"

Another nod.

"Where are your parents?"

He shrugged. Nothing new. As members of the Elite, Brent and Martha Kahl took full advantage of the privileges afforded to Class Two citizens, eating at four-star restaurants, staying out until all hours of the night, and hiring a maid to maintain the house. Too busy to interact with any Class Sixer—even if he was their son.

Taylor turned to Jakob. "Go next door. Get Josh two sets of clothing, everything has to be replaced. And a set of pajamas too." Her eyes speared Maddison. "Lay out several clean towels in the guest bathroom. Then go to my room. Get my medical bag out of the hidden compartment."

Maddison couldn't look away from the burns on Josh's face. Wait, medical bag?

"Maddison, now!" Taylor's voice held an urgency she'd never heard before.

She turned and sprinted toward the bathroom as the front door slammed behind Jakob. Josh couldn't see. The words reverberated inside her as she wrenched the linen closet open and pulled out the fluffy brown towels they saved for guests. He couldn't see. She dropped the towels on the bathroom sink and rushed back around the corner toward the steps.

What had happened? The field. Chemicals. Her heart stuttered, and she grabbed the stair rail to keep her balance. Pesticide. Had he been sprayed with it? *Please, don't let it permanent.*

She fell to her knees on the hardwood floor beside Taylor's bed and dug her fingers into the knot that served as a handle. The board came up in her hands, and she grabbed the heavy black bag hidden in the floor. How had Taylor known about it? Why was she keeping medical supplies at the house?

A muffled cry from downstairs pulled her back into action. The smell of pesticide, heavy and nauseating, grew stronger as she ran back to the kitchen. How had she not noticed it before?

Taylor stood in the doorway of the bathroom. "Strip everything off and get under the shower head. No warm water. No soap. Tilt your head back so only clean water runs onto your face." She took a deep breath. "You're going to have to use your left hand to hold your eye open. No matter how much it hurts. We have to flush your eye out. If you can't promise me you'll do it by yourself, I'll have to come in and do it for you." Another pause. "Okay then. Stay in there until you hear someone knock on the door."

She closed the door and headed for the kitchen. "It's eight twenty. He needs to stay in there for twenty minutes. I need you to help me keep time."

Maddison set the bag on island. "How bad is it?" She set her feet and braced for the blow.

Taylor slumped against the wall, her blue eyes weary. "Bad."

People always joked that she and Maddison could pass themselves off as sisters, but right now Taylor looked a decade older than her age. She opened the medical bag and pulled out gauze, tape, antibiotic cream, eye drops, and an ophthalmoscope. Curses from the bathroom punctuated the air.

"Couldn't we take him to the hospital?"

Taylor sighed. "You know we can't."

"But you said he's bad. He needs an eye doctor. He needs antibiotics. He needs to be in a hospital."

Taylor laid a hand on her arm. "I'm going to do everything I can for Josh. I promise. Call the girls, don't tell them what's going on, but cancel your plans. He doesn't need an audience tonight."

But what if she needed them here? Maddison cut the thought off. Her aunt was right. Josh wouldn't want Sophie seeing him like this. Under any other circumstances, he wouldn't have chanced even her and Jakob seeing his pain. Too much of a tough guy for that.

She grabbed her vidcom and headed upstairs, as far away from Josh's agony as possible. She had to block it out if she had a hope of keeping her friends in the dark. She sucked in one more deep breath. "Call Olivia."

Seconds later, Olivia's face appeared. "Hey, you. What's up?" Her energetic words mirrored the twinkle in her blue eyes.

"Hey, Liv. Listen, I'm sorry but …" What to say now? Why hadn't she thought this through?

Olivia tilted her head to the side, and sandy brown hair cascaded over her shoulder. "Everything okay over there?"

The sympathy in her friend's question almost undid Maddison. "No." The word trembled out. "We've got some … family stuff going on tonight and …"

"This wouldn't be the best time for me and Sophie to show up on your doorstep?"

Maddison shook her head. "I'm sorry."

Olivia smiled softly. "Hey, it's okay. We both know you don't really need the English Lit refresher anyway. Do you want to me to let Sophie know?"

Yes. Yes. Oh, please yes. While Olivia was all sympathy, Sophie would be an inquisitor. "That'd be nice. Thanks, Liv."

"No problem. We're here if you need us, okay?"

Emotion surged up her throat again. She gulped it back down. "Thanks. I'll see you in first period."

Olivia beamed. "Good plan. See you tomorrow."

Maddison disconnected the call just as the bathroom door downstairs creaked open. She headed for the stairs, taking even breaths the whole way. *You're going to listen and keep your mouth shut.* She repeated the resolution with each step down the stairs. When she turned the corner, she had to bite back a gasp. Josh, shirtless, sat on the kitchen table, his red skin screaming at her. How could copper skin be so blood red? She forced herself to keep walking toward the kitchen.

Jakob leaned against the island, hands in his pockets. Taylor dropped three pills in Josh's left hand and waited for him to throw them into his mouth before handing him a glass of water. He gulped it down and handed the glass back to Taylor.

"Before I do an examination, I need details so I'll know what to look for. If you'd rather I send Jakob and Maddison upstairs, I will."

Maddison took a step closer. "I'm not going anywhere." So much for keeping quiet.

"They can stay."

Taylor raised an eyebrow at Maddison. The meaning was clear—no more outbursts or Taylor would remove her anyway. She turned her attention back to Josh. "Okay then. Start from just before the accident and walk me through everything that happened."

"The farm's behind on quota, so the supervisor kept everyone late. Me and the other apprentices were harvesting the last pumpkin field." Josh's chin dipped toward his chest.

"About what time was that?" Taylor's tone was soft and encouraging.

"It was about six thirty." His leg bounced slightly. He'd rather be pacing. "They spray the pumpkins in the evening, around six fifteen, six thirty, once everyone's on their way home. I thought they'd push it back."

They'd kept the schedule with people still in the area? Workers without protective gear?

"The tractor started on the other side of the acreage. A couple of the guys complained. The Super said we'd be long gone before it was a problem. If we were motivated." His leg bounced harder. "We'd been working hard already but tried to pick up the pace even more. About fifteen minutes later, we could smell it." Josh locked eye contact with Taylor. "One of the guys around me got really jumpy, but no one said anything…. The stationary liquidator had joined our supervisor. They both had masks and goggles.

"A couple of minutes later, I got a little dizzy and nauseous. The guy in front of me stumbled. He had a hard time getting back up. The tractor was close now, about six rows away. That's when I felt the wind change." He froze. Not even his chest rose and fell.

Taylor laid a hand on his knee. "The wind kicked up, changed directions?"

"Yeah. I tried to turn away, but the spray still hit me in the face. And then I was on fire." Josh's left hand clenched and pounded his leg. "Everybody was screaming. I'd take a breath and hear the others. Six of us got sprayed. We couldn't even get out of our row. Some of the others had to pull us away. All I could think was, 'Water. Water. Water.'" He pounded his leg again. "The Super stopped the sprayer. We ran, well, dragged each other to the storehouse. That's when I realized something was wrong with my vision."

Rage bubbled through Maddison's veins. She needed a punching bag. That supervisor's face would probably make a good one.

"How long did it take you to get to the spigot, if you had to guess." Taylor's words were even, but her eyes flashed.

"It's a ten-minute walk from the back end to the storehouse. It felt like forever."

"And there was a hose?"

"Yes. I had to share it with the others. A couple of the guys were worse off than me. They'd been facing that direction when the wind changed. We handed it on every minute or so. I trashed my shirt before spraying off. We were still passing it around when the others came back in. The supervisor told us to head home, shower off, and get some rest. The guy to my right asked for a care voucher." A shudder passed through Josh. "The Super said that his injury, our injuries were caused by a lack of initiative, that if we'd been on task the whole day we'd never have put ourselves in the position to be sprayed. And that Arbuckle Farms doesn't give care vouchers to employees that cause their own injuries."

"Seriously?" The words exploded out of Maddison. "Did someone take it over this jerk's head?"

Josh sighed. "Maddison, they don't give care vouchers to anyone. Ever. The rest of us knew better than to ask."

She paced. "Are you telling me something like this has happened before?"

Josh shook his head at her, as though she were a naïve little girl. His dark chocolate eyes held pity. "Class Sixers are expendable. Everyone knows that. There are always more of us to fill whatever positions need to be filled."

"You're not expendable."

A corner of his mouth lifted. "Thanks for thinking so."

Taylor broke in before Maddison's tirade could gain more steam. "She's not the only one. And you came straight here after that?"

Josh gave her a nod. "The burning was worse, and by then I knew it was in my right eye too. I don't know about the other guys. At least I knew I had someone to come to. I didn't want to waste any more time." He ran a hand through his coal black hair, wincing and jerking his hand away half-way through. "Is it … do you think it's gone for good?"

Taylor moved toward the sink and filled Josh's glass with water again. "Do you know what kind of pesticide they were spraying?"

"They don't tell us that kind of stuff."

"Well, then, let me examine you before I answer that question."

Not a good sign.

Taylor went through the pain scale and symptoms list,

took his vital signs, and examined his eye and eyelid for debris. Finally, she asked the question they'd all been dreading. "Cover your left eye. What do you see?"

"Shadows, maybe? There's a blurry circle I think might be your face."

Taylor grabbed her compad off the island. "Find Snellen Eye Chart." A minute later, the top half of the chart appeared on her screen. She held it six feet away from Josh. "Can you see the screen?"

He growled. "No. Even your circle is hard to concentrate on now."

She moved within a foot of his face. "How about now?"

"I see some squiggly black lines on a grey square." He took his hand off his left eye. "What does that mean?"

"The fact that you can see shadows is good. It means your vision isn't completely lost. But I'm going to be straight with you. Your eye was contaminated for over an hour and a half before we could flush it out. Your cornea may be permanently damaged, and without an eye doctor's care, I think we'll be lucky if you escape oncoming glaucoma."

He'd never see again? Because of quotas? Because he was in Class Six?

A strangled sound erupted from Josh's mouth. His jaw snapped shut.

This wasn't okay. This couldn't be okay. Somebody had to do something.

She had to do something.

CHAPTER FOUR

NOAH SHOT UP in bed. His lungs burned. *Breathe. Now. Again, you idiot.* His hands were sticky with blood. He rushed for the sink, twisted the hot water knob on full force, and plunged his hands into the water, scrubbing them raw. The nerves in his fingers screamed at the temperature. Clarity returned. No red stained the water or the skin on his hands.

Just a nightmare. He sank back against the wall and let his eyelids drift shut. Grief-stricken blue eyes appeared. He snapped to attention, finding his own reflection in the mirror before his mind moved to the next snapshot, but it didn't matter. The image of Andrew Brady's lifeless body needed no recall. It always floated on the edge of Noah's consciousness, waiting for a vulnerable moment to accuse him.

He deserved the accusation.

The neon red numbers of the alarm clock read 4:30 a.m. He'd almost made it four hours tonight. Not enough. His body might be conditioned to perform with substantially less sleep, but averaging three to four hours a night degraded anyone. His arms and legs were full of lead, but he wouldn't sleep again tonight, not without more nightmares. At least a run would reduce the churning in his stomach. Slipping on a t-shirt and some socks, he hunted around for his running shoes. There. Under the desk. He swiped his room key and vidcom, complete with its curfew exemption, off the desk.

Minutes later, his feet pounded the pavement. He concentrated on the steps—left, right, left, right, left—and pushed his muscles until they screamed. If he focused on ignoring the pain, he could avoid triggering the images' return.

In the glow of the streetlights, the trees lining the road had begun to turn crimson and ochre. He'd missed fall in the South over the last several years. The vibrant colors and crisp air reminded him of football on Thursday nights, picking apples with his mom, and throwing passes in the backyard with Daniel.

Noah groaned. Evading thoughts of Daniel was like navigating a minefield without a map. Noah quickened his pace until his lungs burned. The door of a house opened. Light spilled out and illuminated the departing man. He compelled himself to pull back. Noah Seforé couldn't run a mile in three and a half minutes—no normal person could. The respectable rhythm felt like a crawl as he crested the next hill on his new route. Under other circumstances, he would have increased his pace to avoid contact with the man. Leaving others in the dust qualified as one of the few perks.

Cursing under his breath, he turned and headed back to the hotel. If he couldn't escape his occupation and the memories connected with it, he should call Kelly. The assistant regional liquidator owed him some answers. Noah didn't have long to separate the guilty from the innocent, and withheld information would slow him down. It was only a matter of time before the Elite sent others in, liquidators who would accuse first and eliminate second. He pumped his legs harder. He wouldn't be the cause of anyone else's death.

Fifteen-year-old Andrew with his shaggy hair hanging in his eyes wasn't the only one etched in Noah's mind. Every night, he relived their last moments, saw their dead bodies at his feet. He'd awaken, like this morning, swearing their blood stained his hands. Though he'd never spilled an actual drop.

Breaking someone's neck didn't require bloodshed, but their panicked eyes and last gasps still embedded like shrapnel inside him.

He sucked down a long breath and willed the thoughts away as he slowed to a walk nearing the hotel entrance. The night clerk looked up to greet Noah but stopped short when he saw him. Breaking eye contact, Noah headed for the stairwell. He must look deranged coming in from a run at a quarter after five.

Taking the steps two at a time, Noah reached the third floor and made the right toward his room. He closed the door behind him as his real vidcom vibrated on the desk. He read the caller ID.

Daniel.

Noah hit ignore and opted for a shower instead.

Nothing good could come from a conversation with his brother at this time of the morning. Daniel would be either drunk and sullen or racing along some twisted stretch of highway on his way home from an activity Noah would not approve of. Daniel had mastered the art of distracting himself from the truth Noah accepted—they were on a quick, downward spiral to hell.

Well, Noah wanted off the track. He'd done what he could in the last year and a half to carry out justice. Maybe one day it would feel like enough. Enough to clear his record. His conscience made it all too plain that God kept score.

After dressing for the day, he grabbed the vidcom and pulled the desk chair out. He had to stay one step ahead. Waking up his compad, he connected it to the vidwall, opting to display the case information on a larger scale. Ignoring the message notification, he initialized a call to ARL Kelly.

"Is there a reason you're calling me before six in the morning, Seforé?" Kelly's disheveled appearance confirmed Noah woke him.

Noah scowled at the use of his real last name by a member of the Elite. "I don't have all the information I need to conduct this investigation. Something tells me McCray and, therefore, you know more than I do about this resistance movement."

Kelly's eyes narrowed, and he stood up, carrying the vidcom with him. "What are you implying?"

"I'm not implying anything. I'm asking. Hacks aside, the stationary liquidators in the area haven't logged any unusual reports. Why do you suspect a group and not an individual?"

Kelly didn't respond, and again, Noah pulled up the reports he had clearance to view. Looking at the average number of liquidations offered no insight. The number matched most of the other regions. The nuclear plants reported no trouble. No evidence of radioactive indicators in the last eighteen months either.

By the sounds in the background, Noah guessed that Kelly had booted up his own compad. "I assume you're aware of the medical inventory discrepancies."

Noah opened the assistant minister of medicine's report about shifting inventories at the hospitals in the area. First aid supplies seemed to be the main items missing. "Why does the Council think the hospital thefts are connected to the hacks? You don't need alcohol and gauze to bypass a computer's mainframe."

Kelly sat up straighter. A sneer marred his face. "Stolen government property of any kind is a serious issue, Mr. Seforé."

"I agree, but you don't need an undercover liquidator stationed in a hospital to solve that problem. McCray could send over a couple mercenary-types to find the thief."

"It's not your job to question your superiors. It's your job to find the resistance responsible for both the hacks and the thefts. They are connected. You don't need to know why."

Why couldn't the man have a conversation without condescension? "I can't complete my assignment unless I know exactly what triggered this threat. You and McCray have told me the potentate wants this situation taken care of without alerting the public. I need to know what has the Council worried."

Kelly quirked an eyebrow. "I see Harrow didn't overstate your attention to detail."

Noah fought a grimace. "Then I'm sure he also mentioned my success rate."

Kelly gave an exaggerated sigh, typing on his compad as he spoke. "Fine, Seforé, you win, but if the information I'm releasing to you gets out, it'll be your head."

Noah didn't need any reminders of that, but he nodded his consent anyway. A moment later, a folder appeared in the corner of his compad, and he tapped it open. The file contained an incident log that included arson and sabotage. "They're violent."

"Within five minutes of every hack, while our attention was diverted, another site was targeted. They're escalating, faster than we like. We've been able to keep everything contained so far, but it's only a matter of time before the public hears. I don't need to remind you how dangerous that could be."

"I understand."

"Good, then if you don't have any more demands to make, I'll be returning to bed." The ARL disconnected the call as soon as he stopped speaking.

Noah took his time looking over the incident log and witness statements. When the first hack took place at a public information booth in MA-6, someone started a fire at the local news office. No one was hurt, but some of the physical archives were destroyed. He opened another file—all of the food transfer trucks in MA-3 had been sabotaged the same afternoon as the grocery store mainframe hack. The hack at the mall in MA-2 coincided with a fire at the regional director of business and technology's house. The family was injured but not fatally. The final hack took place in MA-5 at a computer in the Regional Classification Office. While three programmers worked to override it, a homemade bomb detonated in the office, killing them and injuring fifteen others.

So they'd killed now. The numbers would only climb higher on both sides. Which must be why they needed the first aid supplies. Some of their members must've been injured setting the fires or building bombs. McCray was right. They had to be stopped. He needed to stop them. Without liquidating anyone. That was possible, right? Of course it was. Somehow. He just needed to think on it more.

*

"Have you taken a break yet?" Nurse Walker looked at the clock above their heads.

"Hadn't thought about it." Noah's stomach growled.

"Evidently you should." A hint of a smile crept onto her face. "You've been on duty for six hours already. Take thirty minutes. Everything's quiet here." She consulted a chart, already walking away. "You can take your other break after the apprentices arrive."

Apprentices meant Maddison, and the opportunity to continue earning her trust, which was especially important now that he'd researched her background. Whether he liked it or not, her parents' liquidation in combination with her remark from the other day skyrocketed her up his persons of interest list. She didn't seem the type to start gasoline fires or slash tires, but she might be the key to finding out who was. In the meantime, he headed down to the cafeteria. This would be a prime opportunity to get to know some of the other staff. If the uprising included hospital employees, he'd find out soon enough. The noise of thirty conversations hit him with a shock when he entered the cafeteria, but within a second he adjusted and headed to the line.

He grabbed a tray and then a bowl of chicken potpie, a serving of green beans, and some chocolate cake. As he filled a glass with sweet tea, a man behind him asked, "You new here?"

Noah turned, nodding. "Started Sunday on med/surg."

"That's one of my floors. I janitor two through five. Name's Ben Yancey." The man held out his tray. "Can't shake your hand, but why don't you sit with me?"

"Thanks. I'm Noah, Noah Seforé."

Ben spoke to the cashier, their familiarity obvious. Noah took the opportunity to size up Ben—5'8", middle-aged, black curly hair, green eyes, slim but not muscular. His demeanor fit the textbook definition of non-threatening. Noah paid for his lunch and followed the older man through the maze of tables. Ben dug into his meal, and Noah followed suit. He forked a mouthful of chicken potpie, his mouth twisting as he swallowed. The metallic taste lingered. Sometimes enhanced senses were a real pain. He pulled the chocolate cake closer and ventured conversation. "So, how long have you worked here?"

Ben leaned back in his chair. "About as long as you've been alive, if I figure right."

"Well if it's been twenty years, you're right."

"Near enough." The skin around his eyes crinkled. "I grew up around here, and most of my family's an hour west. No reason to move anywhere else. I don't imagine the same is true for you though."

"Why do you say that?"

"No accent. Which must mean your family is from somewhere west of the Mississippi." Ben's tone held no suspicion or judgment, but Noah reassessed him.

"I don't have much family, just an older brother, and he hasn't settled down yet." Noah let his next words trickle out as slow as honey. "And I am from the South, Metro Area Sixteen to be exact. Guess the accent fades once you've been gone a while."

Ben chuckled. "I reckon so. What brings you here?"

"I missed it, the South, I mean. A CNA position opened here, and I took it."

"So you don't know anyone?"

Noah shrugged. "Not really. Except for Nurse Walker and an apprentice or two, but give me some time. I've only been here four days."

"Fair enough." Ben sipped his sweet tea. "Still, it'd be downright rude of me not to invite you to dinner. I'll check with Ethel, that's my wife, about a night next week. You're on the seven-to-seven Pitman shift, right?"

Noah nodded, acknowledging he had the traditional two days on, two days off, three days on schedule. Every now and then the universe did him small favors—Ben's invitation certainly counted as one. Conversation lulled for several minutes, and Noah glanced down at his watch. He had three minutes to get back upstairs. Shooting to his feet, he grabbed his tray off the table. "I'd better go. Thanks for the company. I'll see you around, I guess."

"I'm sure you will." The unemotional tone of Ben's reply made Noah turn back toward the table. Ben stared at an older, sandy-haired man, sitting in the far right corner of the cafeteria.

The man reminded Noah of a grizzly bear—scruffy, mean, and easy to rile. With the man's unblinking glare fixed on him and Ben, Noah's instinct told him to step in between Ben and the stranger. He couldn't, however, afford to complicate his cover. So, he walked toward the tray return and risked only one look back in Ben's direction. Grizzly had taken Noah's seat, and Ben's body language matched the other man's aggressive stance. Interesting.

As he walked toward the elevator, Noah considered the stranger again. *Now that's the kind of man who builds bombs in his basement.*

CHAPTER FIVE

MADDISON JOGGED TOWARD the hospital entrance as the cold seeped through her clothes. The perils of scrubs. She should've planned to change here instead of at school. Oh well, too late now. She sped to the elevators, her bag swinging in time with her pace. While she waited for the doors to open, she rubbed her hands together. A blast of heat warmed her.

Noah would be on duty today, right? After all, he'd been off yesterday and the day before. Entering the open elevator, she pushed the button for med/surg. Anticipation danced under her skin, leaving her jittery. She'd spent only two shifts, eight hours, in his company. How had he claimed a spot in her head in such a short amount of time? It was just because he was new, right? The doors opened on the second floor. Noah's mussed walnut-colored hair poked out from behind the nurses' station. She didn't even try to fight the stupid grin spreading across her face as she smoothed a hand over her bun. Her other hand flew down to her pocket for her lip gloss. Oh no, definitely intrigued.

"Hey, you." She tried to cover her excitement by giving the most casual greeting she could think of.

His head popped up, and he smiled, one side of his mouth a little more obedient than the other. "Hey, yourself. I hoped I'd see you today."

Warmth spread through her and short-circuited her plan to play it cool. "Me too."

"I'm glad to hear it. How was your morning?"

"Long. This year seems to be dragging by."

"Any particular reason?" He leaned back in the rolling chair he'd commandeered, his eyes twinkling. Stupid green eyes. They made her want to spill all her secrets.

"I guess because I already know what's in my future, and I want to move on to it. There's so much more I want to see." And do. Like support the resistance.

"You sound like my brother."

The clinical words made her want to shrug out of the comparison. "But not you?"

He sighed. "Traveling and new experiences, they're great, but they come up lacking after awhile. I'd rather spend the rest of my life in one place."

"Why don't you then?" Something painful flickered through his face, and she wished she hadn't asked. "Never mind. What's going on here?"

The lines across his forehead began to recede. "It's been busy but not bad. Normal vitals and blood sugar numbers for everyone so far. No major dressing emergencies. And no bed baths today." His nose wrinkled at this. "It's time to chart vitals again. You want to come with me?"

"Sure." She stepped forward to scan her ID at the terminal when four tones sounded from it and every other terminal and vidcom on the floor. Everyone in sight stopped—their attention fixed on the nearest screen.

Assistant Regional Liquidator Watkins' voice echoed through the halls. "At 1:57 p.m. today, Rachel Ann Grady was liquidated due to her actions as an enemy of Patrisia."

Maddison's hand shot out to grasp the solid wood desk to keep herself upright. Rachel's yearbook photo flashed onto the screen. She sat beside Maddison in both English and Calculus.

Watkins continued, "A neighbor reported Grady's proselytizing to a liquidator, and a search of her house revealed a collection of Mormon literature."

Sweet Rachel, who'd never hurt anyone? Beside her, Noah muttered a curse. Maddison closed her eyes to stop the shifting of the walls around them. See, God couldn't exist. Not in a world where governments murdered people like her parents and Rachel, where people like Josh got hurt for no good reason. If he did, Maddison wanted no part of him.

"I do not need to remind MA-4's inhabitants about the intolerant and hate-filled religious philosophy of Mormonism, like Christianity, Islam, and Judaism. These groups would enslave Patrisia's citizens with archaic rules and small-minded tenets, which is why Potentate Marcioni has banned all practice of religion. The Elite will eliminate any, like Grady, who seek to take others in our fair metro area captive with their insipid beliefs. We will never again see violence from their hands as we did thirty years ago. Our society remains free, and even more so today with Grady's liquidation."

A sour taste filled Maddison's mouth as Watkins signed off. The screens returned to their previous settings. The old propaganda turned her stomach. Marcioni had played on the nation's fears during the Religious Uprising and declared a federal state of emergency, giving him the ability to bypass Congress, a power he never relinquished. Students studied and reviewed the written history each spring on the anniversary of the failed coup. Maddison, however, had heard the rumors that claimed the religious were victims, scapegoats in the potentate's grand production. Real Christians, Jews, and Muslims played no part in those bloody months. No, Marcioni had demolished freedom of religion because faith-based groups protested his presidential policies. Even then, the potentate did not tolerate criticism.

Yet another reason she should join those who called for a return to freedom and democracy. And if Taylor was willing to risk her own life to pilfer antibiotics from the hospital pharmacy for Josh, maybe she would understand Maddison's need to act. Maybe. But Jakob?

A hand touched her arm. "You okay?" Noah stood beside her, his eyes shadowed.

"I knew her." She relaxed her grip on the desk and swallowed back the lump in her throat.

"I'm sorry." His quiet apology brought tears to her eyes.

She had to snap out of it, get back to work. Shaking her head to clear the last five minutes from her thoughts, she swiped her card across the scanner and clipped it to her front pocket. "You said something about vital signs?"

He tilted his head and studied her for a moment. "For beds eight through twenty-three."

"Let's not keep them waiting."

*

Her shift had flown by, even with the extra mandated hour. A full floor and Noah's presence helped keep thoughts of Rachel at bay. Slipping back into her jeans, white angora sweater and green ballet flats, Maddison thought back over the last five hours. Noah had been sensitive yet firm with the patients, confident in his tasks, and straightforward and honest with her. Everything she looked for in a friend. She smiled to herself. A very cute friend.

Hearing movement at the front of the room, she stuffed her scrubs into her bag. Maybe he hadn't left yet. She jerked the zipper closed and exited the changing area. Noah spun the combination on his locker and turned to face her, slipping into his jacket.

She pulled down her hair with a tug. "That was nicely timed."

For a moment, he didn't respond. A couple of blinks and a chagrined smile preceded his answer. "Pure coincidence, I assure you."

She stepped closer to the cliff. "I don't mind."

His hands disappeared in his pockets. "I'm glad. Since I don't really know anyone, I was hoping we could be friends."

She gripped the handle of her bag tighter, forced her

smile not to slip. Friends. Sure. She could do that. "Wanna walk out together?"

He shifted his elbow out to her with a smile. She shook her head but took it. "What is this, the 1800s?"

"I've always been a man out of time." Something sharp sliced through his words.

She wanted it gone. "Okay, so, what time period fits you then?"

Seconds ticked by, and silence filled the space between them. Noah's arm stiffened under her hand. She glanced up at him. What changed? He straightened to his full height and squared his shoulders. His face became granite, and though they continued toward her car, he angled his body in front of hers. Tension radiated through him and into her. She bit her bottom lip and swallowed her questions.

Steps away from her car, she peeked around Noah. A bear of a man towered over a trembling teenager on the other side of the lot, hurling choice words and insults. He took a menacing step toward the sandy-haired young man, who couldn't be more than thirteen. Noah laid a hand on her arm.

"Maddison, get in your car and lock the doors."

She nodded and obeyed. He watched her follow his directions before striding toward the pair.

She wanted to throw open the door and tell him to come back. He was no match for the larger man, but she sat still, her heart pounding, and hoped he would be okay.

Within four feet, the pair noticed him, and when the man rounded on Noah, Maddison's hand flew to her mouth. Though she couldn't hear what Noah said, his opponent's crossed arms transmitted how unwelcome Noah's interference was. He stood his ground though, nodding toward the young boy who cowered to his right. The man let out a roar and swung at Noah.

In a flash of movements, Noah dodged the punch and knocked his assailant to the ground. It had happened so fast, she wasn't sure how he did it. Flipping the man over and pinning his arms, Noah held him down with a knee in his back, motioning to the young man to go inside. The teenager shifted on his feet for a moment but obeyed. Noah's gaze fixed on the back of the man's head. He didn't speak long, but the clenched jaw gave away his agitation.

The man gave a begrudging nod, and Noah eased to his feet but didn't move away. Maddison's free hand clenched the door handle. The man moved to his own car and drove away while Noah watched, motionless.

He took several deep breaths before starting toward her. She didn't exhale until he stood in front of her window. Her trembling hand opened the car door. "How did you do that? What possessed you to go over there?"

"He was bullying his son. Someone needed to step in."

She agreed with him, but her pulse still thrummed. "But what if he comes back? Causes trouble for you?"

"He won't." His forehead furrowed again, and he shifted away. "Did I scare you?"

Her hand shot out to stop his retreat. "Of course you didn't scare me. You protected me and that boy. I'm glad you stepped in. You did the right thing. It's just … maybe I was a little afraid for you."

Noah's furrows lessened. "I can promise you I am very aware of my limitations. But I'm sorry I made you nervous." He laid a hand on hers. "Thank you for caring."

"You're welcome."

His gaze fell to the ground a moment before returning to her own. "I'll be off when you come back on Sunday and Monday. So, guess I'll see you on Tuesday?"

"Definitely." She gave his hand a squeeze.

A beautiful smile transformed his face. He stood. "Good. And don't worry, when I see you, I'll be sure to tell you exactly what time period I'm from."

She laughed and shook her head. "I'll hold you to that."

"You do that. Be careful going home."

She nodded and let him close the door. He waited until she gave the car her destination and pulled out of the parking space before waving his goodbye. She sighed. This was the worst possible time to have a crush.

CHAPTER SIX

NOAH THANKED THE barista and carried the steaming Americano to a corner table. So he could keep an eye on the customers in the small shop, he sat with his back against the wall. He pulled his copy of Homer's *Odyssey* out of his messenger bag and took a deep breath, inhaling the scent of cloth, paper, ink, and age. He missed this smell when using his v-compad, and since he'd studied enough background checks this morning to make his eyes cross, he needed a break. He ran a hand along the blue cover, one he'd painstakingly attached to the worn pages when the old one had begun to crack.

The stitches dotted the spine at even, neat intervals, showing how far he'd come since the first awkward attempt a year ago. Restoring that book had been a complete waste. The final product looked like a kindergartener had pasted the pages together, but he hadn't given up because the act of preserving history allowed him a release. And now, he could read one of his favorites without fear it would crumble in his hands.

Cracking the first page, he savored the summary line, "The gods in council agree that the time has come for Odysseus to be brought home to avenge himself on Penelope's suitors and recover his kingdom." Odysseus also lived in a time of war, of deception, of dishonor, but at the center of his story stood a love triumphing over all odds. A love deeper than any circumstances or labels.

What he would never have.

He couldn't afford to forget it. Relationships were off the table. Even though Maddison looked at him like he was a hero. Even though her laugh almost chased the darkness away.

None of that mattered. He wasn't really Noah Seforé, and she was a suspect. Nothing more. He couldn't lead either one of them to believe otherwise.

Taking a sip of coffee, he found the first line of the book again and forced himself to focus on the classic.

"Noah?"

He looked up and couldn't even be surprised. But seeing Maddison, standing several feet away, caused a fissure in his mind. On one side, the Noah who cursed fate for testing his resolve and self-discipline. On the other, the man who wanted to jump up and guide her over to the chair opposite his.

"It is you." Her hands cradled a steaming cup in front of her. "I thought it was just my imagination. How did you find this place? Only the locals know about it."

The locals and her car's GPS. He willed his heart to stop

racing. *You're a trained professional. Act like it.* "I can't reveal my sources."

She nodded her head several times before breaking out into a breathtaking smile. "Well, I wanted to come over and say hello, but I can see you're busy." She took a step back.

"You don't have to go." His gestured to the empty chair.

She gave him a hesitant smile. "You sure?"

"Homer's not going anywhere. I can read him tonight." Warning sirens still blared in his head, but he silenced them so he could focus on her response. Gaining her trust meant spending time with her. He just needed to be smart about it.

"Well, okay then." She set her latte on the table, pulled out the chair across from him, and swung her jacket across the back of it. Her pale green shirt made the green flecks in her eyes more prominent. Beautiful eyes. They complimented her oval face, and the slight blush on her cheekbones? His fingers itched to touch it.

Well, those kind of thoughts had to stop. He curled his hand into a fist. "What are you up to today?"

"I had lunch with some friends up the street and decided to walk down for my first pumpkin spice latte of the season. This place has the best espresso in the MA. Plus, I had no other plans for the afternoon. Everyone else had places to be."

"What if your friends were free?"

"I'd drag them all to the media archives. The main exhibit is a retrospective on the most influential comic artists of the last hundred years. My dad and I would've gone on opening day. It's the kind of thing he loved."

The light in her eyes indicated the answer, but he asked anyway. "And you love anything he did?"

She nodded. "He could talk for hours about art, graphic novels in particular, and he had this way of describing a piece and how it made him feel … you understood it, like the art breathed and spoke to you. He could make anyone love art." She shook her head, her nose crinkling. "My mom didn't share his gift. She introduced me to the great poets, but I never could figure them out, no matter how many ways I looked at a poem. She said I tried too hard to make sense of it. 'Poetry is to be experienced not dissected.'" Maddison took a sip of latte. "Guess I'm too logical to enjoy it."

"I can't give poetry my full appreciation either, much more of a prose man myself." He gestured to the book on the table. In fact, he detested poetry and avoided it at all costs.

"So, what about you? And your parents? I mean, if you don't mind sharing." She drew her hands into her lap, probably attempting to give him space.

Telling her about his family was necessary to further her trust, but unless he picked a story carefully, it also guaranteed an extra set of nightmares tonight. "When my brother Daniel and I started school, we would come home in the afternoon, and my mom would be sitting at the table with a couple glasses of milk and some treat. She loved to bake, and the kitchen always smelled like chocolate and cinnamon." He could still picture her standing by the counter, rolling out piecrusts while she hummed her own melody.

Maddison smiled and nodded, waiting for him to continue.

"My dad was altogether different. His parents raised him to be hard, a man's man. He didn't know how to be anything else." Noah ran a hand through his hair. "His parents emigrated from Italy, and he lectured Daniel and me for hours about our heritage. You can imagine how well that went over with us." Unlike the vivid memories of his mom, time had weathered his view of his dad and softened the impressions somewhat. "But, when I turned twelve, he brought out this huge map of Italy and showed me all the places our ancestors lived. The map made everything more real. So I have him to thank for my love of history."

"Does it get any better?"

His heart clenched at the pain shadowing her eyes. "Being without them, you mean?" She nodded, and he wished he could give her a different answer. "It hasn't for me, but I might not be the best person to ask. Life would be better if they were still alive."

"What happened?" Her tone implied compassion, but she didn't tiptoe around the question.

He respected her more for it. "Car accident. A rich kid sped through a four-way stop. The paramedics told Daniel they died on impact." The callous words still burned. His teeth ground together. "We're supposed to be thankful for that."

"I'm sorry."

He took a deep breath and willed the resentment washing over him to subside. "It's such a waste. I mean, impatience cost my parents their lives."

"You must hate him." The hard inflection sounded foreign coming from the sympathetic girl he'd come to know.

"It's hard hating someone who's dead." He didn't add that he had plenty of other reasons for hating Tristan Worthington, but his reasons paled in comparison to Daniel's.

"What happened to him?"

"He was liquidated. Because of the hit-and-run. He might've found leniency had he not tried to pay that particular liquidator off." Even as he said it, Noah corrected himself. Daniel had vengeance on his mind and a license to kill with the ink still wet. The socialite never stood a chance.

Maddison had gone still. Oh, right.

"What's wrong?" Even though he already knew the answer.

"My parents were liquidated." Her tone and stiff posture spoke of one emotion. Rage. It felt like a slap on the face. A confirmation.

Her body didn't move, but her gaze surveyed the room. "I guess you're grateful to whoever punished your parents' killer, but I can't see it that way. Someone accused my dad of treasonous activities, of promoting democracy in his graphic novels. So a liquidator killed him and my mom. He destroyed our house looking for evidence—after he killed them. He didn't find a thing." Somehow, the hushed tone of her words amplified the anger pouring off her.

Did she really not know about her parents' beliefs? Or was this carefully edited version meant to protect herself and win him over to her side? He'd read Michael and Tamara James' files. He knew the liquidator had proof of hidden pro-freedom messages and symbols in Michael's Elite-approved works. Neither Michael nor Tamara denied it. As members of the Elite working in the Ministry of Media, they should've been more careful. They should've lied. Only liquidation awaited those who defied the potentate from within the Elite.

Still. They shouldn't have died because of some hidden messages. Because of a pro-freedom graphic novel the liquidator couldn't locate at the house. "I'm sorry, Maddison. Lawful or not, what he did was wrong. It's a terrible system."

Her narrowed eyes widened, her mouth forming an O. "Noah, you can't say those things."

Considering anyone might overhear their conversation and report it, she had reason to be concerned. Relief trickled down his spine—being careful about speaking out earned her a tentative mark in his above-suspicion pro/con list. Then again, caution didn't equal innocence. He lowered his voice. "You're right, but it's still true."

She deflated in front of him and tore tiny pieces off the sleeve on her cup. "I'm so mad about it, and not being able to be honest about how I feel just makes me angrier. I keep myself in check for Jakob's sake, but I won't ever forgive that man. I hope he rots in hell. I hope all of them do."

One more mark for innocent. Another mark for guilty. She was a mess of contradictions, but one reality was clear: she could never know the truth about him.

"For what it's worth, it's safe to be honest with me." Regardless of her loyalties, he'd be fair with her. Always fair.

She gave him a watery smile. "How do you always come up with the perfect response?"

"Luck?" He cupped the cooling mug in front of him.

Shaking her head, she leaned forward. "No, I think it's more. I think it's because you listen when people talk instead of hijacking the conversation for yourself. You're kinda like my dad in that way."

He didn't deserve compliments or comparisons to people she loved. Time to refocus the conversation. "I'm pretty sure it's luck. But enough about me. Besides hanging out at the media archives, what else do you like to do?"

"Well, I like to try new restaurants, find interesting places in the MA I've never been to before. I like to explore, I guess, and spend time with friends. Between school and the apprenticeship, I don't have time for much more."

He chuckled. "Sounds like enough. What are some of your favorite places you've stumbled into?"

She sat up straight with a light in her eyes and told him, beginning in the present city block and moving outward. She knew every piece of the metro area and had stories about each section. As she began to wind down, he drew her into new topics to keep her talking. She was appalled he didn't watch TV or movies. He built a mental list of books to introduce her to.

The conversation shifted to his hobbies, and though she didn't like to read, her questions showed she appreciated the skill and technique required for bookbinding. She had just asked to join him for a run sometime when her vidcom rang.

Pulling it out of her pocket, she cringed when she saw the time and the caller ID.

She touched the screen, accepting the call. "Sorry I'm late, but I'm on my way, and I'll explain when I get there. Ten minutes, I promise." She disconnected and stood, grabbing her coat. "I was supposed to be home for dinner twenty minutes ago. Who knew two hours could pass so quickly, huh?"

"I had no idea."

She smiled. "See you later?"

He nodded. "Later." As she walked away, he sighed, grateful he didn't have to dodge her invitation for company on his morning runs.

That would be a little too personal for him. From now on, he needed to plan out his interactions with her, so he could elicit information without crossing any more emotional lines. He couldn't distance himself while her safety depended on him. He needed to clear her. Then he could build as much distance as needed.

It was time to go back to work. Tucking the unread book back into his bag, he headed for the door. He turned to grab his mug and collided with someone.

"Oh, good. You haven't left." Maddison pulled back, face flushed. "I got to thinking, you should come over for dinner one night. Not tonight of course, but maybe next Friday? You could meet Aunt Taylor and Jakob. Enjoy some real conversation and a home-cooked meal?"

He froze. "Um, I'm not sure, that's ..."

"I think you should come. It'll be good for you. Come next Friday."

"Let me think about it."

"You can think about it, but I'm going to keep asking until you say yes." With that, she swung around and headed for the door.

He was sure she meant it. And that he would regret it.

Bring on the pain.

CHAPTER SEVEN

MADDISON PULLED THE pan of chocolate chip pumpkin muffins out of the oven as the doorbell rang. After setting the pan down, she ran toward the front of the house. The vidscreen in the entrance displayed Sophie and Olivia's faces. "Disengage lock," she whispered, waiting for the audible click before swinging the door open.

"Hey, you." Olivia bounced into the house, her energetic words mirroring her appearance. "What's up?"

Maddison opened the door wider but held a finger to her lips, her head nodding to the bedroom at the top of the stairs where Taylor slept.

"Oops. Sorry." The twinkle in Olivia's blue eyes contrasted with her chagrined smile as she skipped toward the kitchen. Sophie followed, an indulgent smile planted in its normal spot. She had always been the most mature of the three of them. Add to that her dark chocolate hair and latte-colored skin, and Sophie had an air of sophistication neither Maddison nor girl-next-door Olivia had. It rather awed Maddison sometimes.

As Maddison re-entered the kitchen, the sliding glass door glided open.

Josh stuck his head inside. "Something smells incredible." He made a beeline for the baked goods, his aim off by a few degrees. It was one of the only tells that he couldn't see out of his right eye since he refused to wear the eye patch Taylor acquired for him. "I wandered over to throw a little with Jakob and Ethan, but I'm being drawn inside." His ebony hair glistened from the shower he took every evening. She'd never understood why he cleaned up before volunteering for any athletic endeavor he could find. But at least that was still the same. He seemed determined that nothing change.

"Are these for me?" He didn't wait for permission before reaching for a muffin.

Maddison swatted at his hand. "They're hot. Let me at least get them out of the pan."

He grabbed one anyway and jumped up to sit on the counter.

"You do know this isn't your house, right?" Sophie's mouth quirked, softening her tone of disapproval.

"Might as well be." Josh shrugged, but a faint pink hue surged up his neckline. Maddison smiled, her suspicions confirmed. Her baking hadn't snagged Josh's attention—Sophie had.

Josh swallowed half of the muffin in one bite. "Hey, these aren't too bad."

Maddison brushed past him with a light shove and offered napkins and glasses to the girls. Olivia flitted over to the refrigerator and pulled out the milk. Sophie drew a familiar container from her bag. "May I?"

"Sure. None for me though." Maddison set the pan in the sink with its twin to soak and waited for the bubbles to flow over them. She smiled at the choreography they'd developed: Sophie making her signature up-all-night coffee, Liv waltzing around the kitchen to hand out mugs, and Josh wandering in from next door on cue. Despite her desire to experience all that life had to offer, she craved predictable nights like this one. A truth Josh pointed out on more than one occasion.

Olivia handed him a glass. The careful way he held it triggered an alarm bell in Maddison's head. "What's wrong with your hand?"

Everyone grew still. Josh shot her a glare. "It's fine."

The girls took a couple of steps back. Her intuition hardened into knowledge. "Let me take a look." Anyone else would have complied within a second. Then again, Josh had heard this tone often over the years. He didn't move. She stepped in front of him, laying a hand on his knee.

"Maddie." A warning from him, but it had the opposite effect.

"Maddison, maybe you should—" Sophie began.

"Joshua Kahl, let me see your hand."

He held his arm out. The skin on the back of his hand was tight and inflamed. She gently pushed his long sleeve up and inhaled a short quick breath. More of the same. She forced an exhale and turned to Olivia. "Go wake Taylor up, please."

Feet scurried away behind her, but she didn't move,

answering Josh's angry stare with one of her own. Moments later, Olivia returned alone. "She'll be down in a few."

"It wasn't going to heal overnight," he said.

"Shut up. It's been two weeks. How much mobility have you lost?" Her voice trembled a little on the last word.

"Not much."

"How much is that? And while we're on the topic, how much pain are you in? What exactly are you hiding from me?"

"Maddison." Sophie stood beside her, her hand reaching out for Maddison's arm. "This isn't his fault."

She twisted away from Sophie's reach. "He's already lost half his sight. Now his hand might not be healing the way it's supposed to either." She gestured in Josh's direction. "I can't stand by without a word and let this happen. Sorry, I'm not quite as in control as you."

Sophie flinched.

"Enough." A muscle in Josh's clenched jaw twitched. His posture straightened, towering over her now. "You think you're the only one upset about this? It's my sight. It's my hand. I'm the one who has to live with it. I'm the one who can't let it affect my quota. I'm the one whose parents can't look at him anymore. Me. If somebody's going to get angry and do something about it, it's me. Got it?"

Maddison hung her head, heat warming her cheeks. What had come over her? She forced her eyes back up to Sophie. "I'm sorry, Soph, I don't know why I said that."

Sophie gave her a little nod. "It's okay."

Josh's shoulders relaxed. "Better. Let's talk about

something else, okay?" The tension rolling through the room began to dissipate.

"Are you going to do something about it?" Her words were a whisper.

Olivia gasped her name. Sophie didn't even flinch.

Josh pinched the bridge of his nose. "How about you and I talk about that some other time?"

"I would recommend that time be never." Taylor stood at the threshold of the kitchen, hand on her hip, eyes blazing.

"Tay—"

"Sophie, Olivia, why don't you go into living room and find a movie for all of us to watch. I need a moment with these two." Both girls skirted around her without a word. Taylor put the medical bag in her left hand on the table and pointed to a chair. "Sit, Josh."

He complied with slumped shoulders.

Taylor radiated enough anger to dissipate all of Maddison's. "You two are old enough to make your own decisions, but you'd better weigh each and every word out of your mouths or someone's going to get hurt. And it probably won't be you. It'll be someone you know, Olivia or Sophie or Jakob."

She cursed under her breath, inhaled shakily. "You've got to be careful. I know that better than … You just have to be more careful."

*

Couldn't this woman talk about something else? Noah rolled his shoulders and cracked his neck. Hours of watching

Madame Director and her husband in their home had garnered him nothing but a headache. All she talked about was the incompetence of every other hospital employee. Her husband bowed and scraped and made sympathetic noises without expressing a single opinion of his own.

Noah wanted to shake him. Considered driving over to their house for that very purpose, just for something to do. This was the one problem with surveillance—the sheer monotony of it. His fingers itched for the other compad, the one belonging to Noah Seforé. If he could view video with one and research financials with the other, this would go faster. But Noah Seforé didn't have access to the Elite's secure sites.

Good thing he had a photographic memory. Leaning his head back against the headboard, he closed his eyes and recalled the couple's financials. The audio from their home faded into the background. Mortgage payment, car payment, incidentals, everything looked normal. There were no payments or deposits which couldn't be accounted for. With nothing unusual there, he mentally shifted to their general backgrounds. If nothing popped soon, he'd have to comb through their vidcom and compad histories again. Which was possibly more boring than watching the couple interact with each other.

"If I could move up into regional administration, things would be different."

His eyes shot open. *Here we go.*

Madame Director stood in the doorway between the kitchen and living room, wielding a wooden spoon in her hand. "Hospital administrators should have the power to investigate their employees. I know Matt Dooley can't have been the only idiotic troublemaker on staff. But all I can do is pass the suspicious names on to one of the stationary liquidators. Think about if I could discreetly interview the 'off' ones myself. If the other administrators could do the same. We'd rid the health care system of any malcontents within a month's time."

"I'm sure you could, dear."

Enough. Noah clicked off the surveillance feed and opened the *Innocent and Uninvolved Parties* file. Madame Director's name would be the first. Just as he suspected. He stood and paced the room. Opened the window. Couldn't force himself to start over with the next person in question. His stomach grumbled.

The perfect reason to take a break. He'd walk next door and get dinner. Then he'd start surveilling John Henderson. Noah had about thirty-six hours before his next shift at the hospital. Maybe he could sort Henderson before then. Too many others waited in his *Undetermined* file.

His real vidcom vibrated on the bed. Callista. Again. He rolled his eyes, hit ignore, and shoved it and the Elite-enabled compad back into the hidden pocket in his messenger bag. Across the room, his cover vidcom played "Hungarian Rhapsody No. 2."

He grabbed his keycard with one hand and the blaring vidcom with the other. The caller ID read Liquidator Callista State. Seriously?

Might as well get it over with. He hit accept. Callista's

face appeared on the vidcom. "I'm beginning to think you're dodging my calls. But that can't be right, can it?" She smiled, but the tightness around her eyes told him it was just an act.

"How did you get this number?"

She pouted. "Why can't you be nice to me? No, 'Hi, Callista. Sorry I've missed your calls. How are you?' I mean, aren't we friends, Noah?"

If you'd be happy with that, sure. The pain in his head pulsed faster, but he resisted the urge to massage his temples. "How, Callista?"

The smile dropped off her face, and her eyes narrowed. "You haven't been answering your vidcom. So I asked for a status report on you. ARL Kelly contacted me personally to let me know you were fine, just undercover. It wasn't hard to find Noah Seforé's number after that."

She'd asked for a status report? He counted to ten. Twice. "If you know I'm undercover, why are you calling this vidcom? Anyone could've seen the caller ID."

"But no one did. Am I right?"

He unclenched his jaw. "I can't have you calling this number. It's too much of a risk."

"So you'll answer your real vidcom when I call?" A tentative smile matched her tone of voice, but her eyes still pierced. Steel underneath silk. Vulnerable question and direct threat in one.

"I will." Would that be enough to placate her? Her smile grew. Good. "Listen, I'm sorry for being short. I've been doing surveillance for the last eight hours. My head hurts.

And I'm starving. Can we postpone catching up until next time?"

A sigh. "I guess. Go get something to eat, Noah."

"That's the plan. Talk to you later."

"Definitely."

He disconnected the call and sank down on the bed, the vidcom dropping beside him. Four years of conversations, and he still didn't know how to read her. One part potentate disciple, one part calculated assassin, and one part flirt with a dash of stalker. Talking with her was like playing hot potato with a stick of dynamite. He scrubbed a hand over his face. Oh well, it was over now. Time for food.

Twenty minutes later, Noah set his large cola and dinner on the desk and pulled it closer to the bed. Steam wafted from the takeout container when he opened it, and he sucked in a deep breath. Nothing smelled better than a greasy cheeseburger. He grabbed a handful of fries and shoved them in his mouth then headed to his messenger bag to retrieve the other vidcom and compad.

He navigated past the home screen, opening the remote spy program that allowed him to view audio and video from any vidcom, compad, and vidwall on the network. He entered his password and typed in "John Henderson, MA-4, Coastal South East." A list of devices came up, and he double-clicked on the living room vidwall. Sound and motion filled his screen. Sandra Henderson browsed on her compad while the Henderson boy—Steven?—channel-surfed.

Noah sent the images to the vidwall in his hotel room. Vidwall. He stared at the top left corner where he knew a camera and microphone were embedded. How did Callista know he was dodging her calls? She'd disconnected the call to his real vidcom as soon as he hit ignore instead of leaving a message. And she'd sounded certain that he was alone during their conversation. Could she have been watching him? She wouldn't have the access to view another liquidator ... unless the higher-ups approved it.

Ice water flowed through his veins. They'd tapped his compad before he was a liquidator; why wouldn't they now? He forced a bite of hamburger while concentrating on the footage in front of him. He had to find out without tipping his hand. If they were watching, he didn't want them to know he knew. He glanced at the battery level of the vidcom on the bed. Eighty-seven percent. Not conclusive.

As he stared at the Hendersons' Tuesday night routine, he picked up the compad. He left the surveillance program up but gave the command to open the user interface. The instructors at the Academy had spent a scant hour discussing surveillance techniques, and only one sentence to name the spyware that could nest in anyone's electronics. But he had been paying attention, and an afternoon later he'd found the program hidden deep in the lab computer's operating system.

It took him a minute and a half to navigate within his compad's operating system now. He scanned the code. Optimization.679355.779. There it was. He closed the interface window and left the Hendersons' feed open. So they were watching.

ARL Kelly and Callista and who knows who else were watching ... and listening. As he investigated people and worked shifts at the hospital. As he chatted with Maddison over coffee. Maddison. He closed his eyes and swallowed a groan. Was she already on their list? Was she on Callista's? His shirt collar seemed to shrink. How was he supposed to minimize collateral damage while hunting a violent resistance with Big Brother looking over his shoulder? He needed a new plan. One that kept persons of interest off the Elite's radar until he was certain of where they stood. Even better, one that guaranteed those with anti-regime feelings but no resistance ties would be safe from any cleansing McCray planned. And he needed to come up with this new plan fast.

CHAPTER EIGHT

MADDISON SLIPPED THE apple pie in the oven and checked her reflection in the glass door. She tucked a lock of hair behind her ear and reapplied her lip gloss. She glanced up at the clock. It would have to do. He would be here any minute.

She turned and jumped. Taylor laughed, leaning against the kitchen counter. "Sorry to scare you, but you seemed so involved. I didn't want to tear you away from your primping."

Maddison growled and threw a towel at her aunt. "I wasn't primping."

"No, of course not. So, to clarify, you aren't interested in Noah?"

"I've known him less than three weeks. How could I be interested in him? We're friends, and he's living out of a hotel for heaven's sake. Can you imagine never getting home-cooked food?"

"I just asked a question." Taylor smirked, laugh lines

framing her blue eyes. In that moment, she looked much younger than thirty-four.

"Well, I'm not interested." Joining the resistance ruled out any possibility of a relationship with Noah. At least, that's what she kept telling herself.

"Not interested in what?" Jakob strolled into the kitchen with his hands covered in chalk. He snagged a piece of bread from the waiting basket on the way to the sink, earning him a smack from Maddison.

"Interested in our guest." Taylor ducked her head, still smirking, and folded the towel in her hands.

He let out a barking laugh. "Come on, who do you think you're fooling, Maddie?" She glared at him, but he'd built up an immunity after all these years. He dried his hands on a dishtowel and swallowed the bread whole before responding. "You babbled about him to Olivia and Sophie for like an hour the other night, and you made an apple pie for crying out loud." He paused, eyes narrowing. "Besides, what's so wrong with being interested in somebody?"

"I'm being careful. That's all."

"I get that." He cocked his head, and his sandy brown hair fell into his eyes. "But you should trust your gut, sis. Don't over think it."

What if her gut said maybe she could have it all? The ability to make a difference and the boy who turned her insides to mush? After all, he hadn't turned her in for speaking so freely. He'd even said it was safe for her to be herself. It could work, right?

The doorbell rang, and Jakob shot off for the door. "It'll

be more fun if you're interested anyway. At least it will be for me."

She rushed after him. "Jakob, don't you dare—"

He swung the door open wide.

Noah looked incredible. His leather jacket, khaki dress shirt, jeans, and boots made her toes curl. She stared and smoothed a shaky hand over her skirt. His hesitant smile took her breath away.

It could work. It had to.

"Hi," she managed to choke out.

"Hi to you too." He faced her brother. "You must be Jakob. I'm Noah."

Jakob shot her a mischievous look but behaved. "That's me. Come on in."

"Thanks. It smells wonderful in here by the way."

"I made Italian, caprese ravioli and garlic bread. It seemed like a safe bet." Warmth flooded her cheeks.

"And apple pie." Jakob chimed in, ever the helpful little brother. She could kill him. "My sister's a whiz in the kitchen."

Noah grinned, his eyes lit with a new emotion. "Sounds perfect. Those are some of my favorites."

"Well, why don't I go help Aunt Taylor in the kitchen while you give Noah a tour of the house?" Her brother winked at her before disappearing.

Dropping her head into her hands, she let out a small groan.

Noah chuckled. "He's about as subtle as you are."

Her head shot up to interpret his words. The tender

way he looked at her softened the sarcasm. "Subtlety is not a trademark either the Kings or the Jameses are known for." She took a step toward him. "How are you?"

For a moment, he didn't respond. Something had shifted between them somehow. Here in her home, with its soft lighting and comforting smells, something pulled her closer to him. She took a step forward. He searched her face. For what? Then the spell broke, and he stepped back. "The hotel's getting old, but other than that, I'm good. Work kept me busy today. Jakob said something about a tour?"

She took another step back herself, feeling disappointment rush in to take attraction's place. What made him keep his distance? Since last Saturday, he hadn't been as free with her. She'd caught him staring at her a couple of times, and once or twice, he teased her with a wink. But those moments diminished with each day. What made him fight the attraction she was sure he felt?

"Oh, we can tour the house later. Come in to the kitchen and meet my Aunt Taylor. Then we'll eat."

"Lead the way."

Taylor set the last dish on the table as they entered. She turned, brushed her palms across her jeans, and held out a hand. "Noah, I presume? I'm Maddison and Jakob's aunt, Taylor. And please, don't make me feel any older by calling me anything but Taylor."

Noah dipped his head, almost bowing. "Yes, ma'am. I mean, Taylor."

She laughed. "I can see this is going to be a learning

experience for you." She motioned to the table. "Are you hungry?"

"Starving. I downloaded a new biography this morning and ended up reading instead of eating on my lunch break."

"You sound like this one over here." Taylor inclined her head to Jakob and moved around the table so they could all take their places.

"You read, Jakob?" Noah sat down as Maddison handed him a plate full of food. "This looks great. Thanks, Maddison."

"Yeah, but I think Aunt Tay's referring to the fact that once I sit down with my pad and chalk, I become a zombie." Jakob shoveled a mound of food in his mouth.

"So you inherited your dad's love of art?" Noah asked.

Taylor's eyebrows shot up. Great. Now she'd have even more questions.

"Yep. What about you? Are you creative?"

Noah shook his head "I'm afraid not. The closest I come is some book binding, but it's just about being precise. Not much creativity required."

"What made you pick it up?" Taylor leaned forward, resting her fork on her plate. Maddison sat back, letting her family monopolize the conversation with Noah. Wow, that smile of his did not grow less devastating with time.

"I kinda stumbled into it. I prefer holding a paper book to a digital screen, but most of those are in such bad shape that I decided to rescue a few. It seemed like the logical choice." He glanced over at Maddison. "Guess I'm like Maddison in that way."

She smiled back at him. "Guess so."

Conversation continued to flow across the table as Noah asked Taylor about her role as an ER doctor, and Jakob and Taylor continued to pepper him with questions of their own. Every time Noah got the chance, he brought the conversation back around to Maddison. They passed the serving dishes again and heaped extra portions on their plates. Maddison relished the dance of tomato, basil, garlic, and mozzarella in her mouth, and the enthusiastic back-and-forth at the table.

Taylor began to stack the serving plates, but Noah stood. "No, please, let me. In our home, my brother and I cleaned up since my mom cooked. I don't get to do it much anymore."

Taylor's eyes twinkled, darting over to Maddison and back to Noah. "Well, okay then." She relinquished the stack of dishes to Noah and stepped away from the table.

Jakob jumped up. "I'll help you."

Both women laughed, and Maddison relaxed in her chair, crossing one foot over the other. "If you can get Jakob to help with the dishes, you can come to dinner anytime."

"Sounds fair to me." He winked and spun toward the sink with his arms full of plates, bowls, and dishes. It didn't look even a little precarious. Nothing clinked against anything else. The forks and spoons didn't even slide around. What taught him to move like that?

"Psst." Taylor nudged her.

Maddison shot her a look. "What?"

"Come to the living room with me."

She rolled her eyes but complied. Behind her, Jakob let out a "no way, man!" in response to something Noah had said, and she smiled.

She and Taylor sat down on the other end of the living room, out of earshot. Still, Taylor leaned toward her on the couch. "Don't let him get away."

"Huh?"

"Noah's worth hanging onto." Maddison made a sound of protest, but Taylor waved it away and pointed toward the kitchen. "I know what you said earlier, but you like him and he likes you. It's clear in the way he looks at you, in the way he talks about you. It's clear in the way he made such an effort to get to know me and Jakob. He's a good guy."

"You've spent less than two hours with him."

An indulgent smile blossomed on Taylor's face. "As your aunt, give me the benefit of the doubt when I tell you, sometimes you just know."

Well then, commence Operation Get Noah To Date Me.

*

It had been a long time since Noah felt at home somewhere. Here, in Maddison's house, the feeling came close. He took another glance around at the bold colors on the walls, the well-loved furniture pieces, and the items strewn about.

He wanted it too much.

Grabbing the final bowls from the table, he turned back to Jakob, who loaded the dishwasher. "So, other than drawing, what do you like to do?"

"Play baseball. Or read. Things by Brody McAllen, James Stevens, Mark Brestin."

The names sounded familiar to Noah, and he wracked his brain for the connection. "They write historical fiction, right?"

"Yeah. It's no fun to read about life now. I'm living it. I don't want to read it too."

"That I understand. Do you have a favorite period?" Noah rinsed off the last plate and handed it to Jakob.

"McAllen writes a lot of World War II stuff. But I like the Old West stories too." He air quoted 'Old West' as he said it. "Sometimes I wish I lived back then. Everything seemed so black and white. Identifying the good guys, or the bad ones, was easy. And men were men."

"How do you mean?" Noah folded the drying towel and set it by the sink before leaning a hip against the counter.

"Men built their own houses, shot their own food, protected their loved ones. They lived by codes. They put the needs of the group or their family ahead of their own. Surviving put things into perspective for them, I guess."

Hmm, the puzzle that was Jakob became a little clearer. Throughout dinner, Jakob had been easy going, quick to tease Maddison, yet hard to ruffle. Not at all like someone who'd lost their parents, but the mature perspective peeking through now—that's what Noah had expected. He sensed a fierce protector lay beneath Jakob's teasing little brother persona. "Maybe manhood meant something different then. But, that doesn't mean we can't strive for those things now."

Jakob stared him down, maybe looking for a hint of patronization, but the teen was right. Becoming a man used to mean something, something good.

After a moment, Jakob seemed satisfied Noah was being honest with him, but he didn't break his gaze. "I like you, Noah. I think my sister likes you too. Don't mess it up, okay?"

"I'm doing everything I can not to." He couldn't offer more.

For the last three days, he'd been at war with himself. He was drawn to her, but showing her attention made her look more suspicious to the Elite—and Callista. So he had to keep his distance, even though he wanted her, even if it hurt her. First and foremost, he had to keep her safe. It was why her name now rested beneath Madame Director's on the *Innocent and Uninvolved Parties* list.

Maddison stuck her head in. "Hey, sounds like you guys are done?"

Noah looked to Jakob for confirmation. The young man gave a satisfied nod, and he returned it before facing Maddison again. "What's next on the agenda?"

*

The tour of the house ended with Maddison's room. A white comforter covered the four-poster maple bed in the center. Dozens of white and lavender pillows rested on it. Pictures of her family and friends dotted the walls and her dresser. Travel books lay on the nightstand by the bed. If someone had asked him to identify her room in a line up, without a doubt, he would've chosen this one.

She sat down on her bed, and he opted for the window seat. Jakob's words echoed in his head. He had to warn her. Before she shared anything else. Leaving his vidcom in the car had definitely been the right decision. *Tell her, now, before you get distracted again.* He sucked in a deep breath.

"Hey, um, I want to apologize for what I said the other day at the coffee shop. About the Elite, I mean. It's not safe to … criticize them, and I don't want you to get in trouble because of me. So, I'm sorry."

"It's okay." She grimaced. "It's not like I haven't done the same."

"But we'll be more careful now, right?"

She gazed over his shoulder. "Right."

Seconds ticked by. The silence grew uncomfortable. *It had to be done.* He surveyed her room again. To his right sat a small bookshelf. Digital frames and a couple of candles filled the top shelves, but a small stack of paperbound books claimed space on the bottom shelf. "Your parents'?"

"A couple of their favorites. They liked to own those in both digital and ink form." She walked over, sank down in front of the shelf, and pulled a book out. Her hand traced the title before holding it out to him. "This was my mom's favorite."

"Rowing Against the Current." He cradled the book and used the pad of his thumb to turn the pages. Blue ink bled under passages throughout. Slanted scribbling danced in

the margins. He smiled at Maddison. "She dialogued with it."

Maddison nodded. "She'd read her favorite passages to me before bed when I was little. I think she hoped I would be a little more like Amelia Moss."

"Not quite the rebel growing up, huh?"

"My parents didn't know what to do with a little rule follower like me." A smile and small headshake accompanied her answer, but the way her eyes darted to the ground and around the room told him the words hurt. "Add to that the fact that my world's pretty black and white, and you can see how I drove my very creative and free-thinking parents crazy."

"Well, I think you've struck a good balance between the two. You have more sense than Amelia ever did, and just as much heart."

Her eyes filled with tears. "Thanks. No one else's ever said that."

Did no one see her? When it came to the people she loved, compassion ruled. He admired her most for this.

He slid down to sit in front of her and brushed a renegade tear away. "Well, I have better eyesight than most."

A giggle escaped her. "Noah, I ..."

"Hey guys, if you want any apple pie, you'd better get down here. Jakob's acting shifty. I think he might be planning to carry the whole thing off to Josh's house," Taylor yelled up the stairs.

Disappointment, mirroring his own, flashed in

Maddison's eyes. He pulled her to her feet but didn't release her hand.

Her gaze flitted down to their entwined hands for a moment. The disappointment faded. She tugged him forward. "Come on, she's probably not kidding about Jakob and the pie."

Noah laughed and followed her down the stairs.

You're supposed to be distancing yourself. But he couldn't. She had worked her way deep inside him, and he didn't want to extricate her now.

CHAPTER NINE

MADDISON WOVE THROUGH the packed cafeteria, picking the route furthest away from Debbie and her cheerleader clones. She'd managed to stay under their radar for ten years—until her parents' liquidation landed her on their Top Five Social Offenders list. Avoiding Debbie's group proved easier than engaging. Turned out, some stereotypes existed for a reason.

Olivia and Sophie waved from the corner table they'd adopted, and Maddison nodded back before stepping over a backpack strewn on the floor. When she reached their table, she plopped the tray down and sank into the chair across from Olivia. "Is the year half over yet?"

Sophie quirked an eyebrow. "Aren't we a little old to be whining?"

"But, Mom." Maddison drew the syllables out in an exaggerated moan.

Sophie rolled her eyes, but a smile crept onto her face. "Speaking of how slow time's moving ..." Her hand froze halfway between her plate and her mouth.

"Hi guys, can we join you?"

If there was ever someone Maddison wanted to say no to but couldn't, it was Grace Richards. She stood to Maddison's left, her heart-shaped face lit with an eager smile. She looked like an animated bunny, all wide eyes and twitchy nose. The new kid standing beside her gave them all a chagrined smile. Maddison stifled a groan.

"Of course." Olivia pulled out the chair beside her.

"Thanks. You know Brandon, right?" They all nodded. "Great. I spotted him in the corner all by his lonesome and couldn't let that stand. I knew you guys would be cool." An exclamation point punctuated every phrase. Way too perky. "So, what are we talking about?"

Sophie shifted back and forth in her chair. "We were talking about how the school year seems to be creeping by."

Grace's head bobbed up and down. "I feel the same way, but maybe that's because I have a whole year left before I'm full-time at the shop. I just can't believe I get to sell clothes for the rest of my life. It's a dream. Don't you feel the same way, Olivia?"

To meet quotas and stand behind a cash register for eight hours a day only to scrape out a living? Maddison fought off an eye roll.

Olivia's smile faltered for a split second. "I'm glad I'll be surrounded by colors every day." Grace didn't notice her lacking enthusiasm, but Maddison's gut tightened.

"Exactly. I mean, what teen girl wouldn't kill for our job?" More exclamation points. "We aren't stuck in a dreary office or factory all day. We get first crack at the latest fashions, and we can apply to work in a different store or MA if we want, so we'll never get bored. The GAP could not have placed us better, don't you think?" Her gaze fell on Sophie and Maddison, and she blushed. "Not that you aren't totally lucky to be Class Four. You guys are so smart."

Okay, bunny, let me tell you a thing or two about the GAP and what your life is going to be like in Class Five.

"Thanks, Grace." Sophie elbowed Maddison before switching her focus to Brandon. "Have you started your apprenticeship yet?"

"Yeah." His fingers traced the lines in the table. "I have no clue what I'm doing."

The vulnerability in his tone pricked something inside her. Given his blond hair and baby face, she'd pegged him as the guy most likely to be swarmed by the junior girls. But there was something fragile about him. He'd been sitting alone?

"It always feels overwhelming in the beginning. What's your position?"

He tensed. "Classification apprentice."

The girls froze.

"Do you want me to leave?"

Olivia recovered first. "No, it's okay. Stay."

Words poured out of him. "This is the first time I've eaten lunch with people since my first day. Everyone thinks I'm Mr. High and Mighty, but I didn't ask for Class Two, you know? My parents are Class Six. My friends in my old MA all were too. I know that life. But I mean, what do I know about classification?"

Their conversation had drawn the attention of those sitting at the tables near them. A chill swept through Maddison. *Fix it. Change the subject. Do something.* She braved a sideways glance at the other students. The cafeteria was eerily quiet. She forced a smile. "Well, since you're Class Two, you're definitely smart. It'll get easier, Brandon, I promise."

Beside her, Sophie let out a slow sigh. Olivia agreed and launched into telling them about the collection of dresses she and Grace had unpacked yesterday, but the story, and Grace's interjections, sounded faint and tinny. Brandon caught her gaze, relief shining in his blue eyes.

They'd come too close. They both knew it. She gave him a nod then made herself lean forward and engage with her friends. There'd been too many narrow escapes in the last month, and she could only thank her lucky stars that none of them had been around a liquidator. Rubbing her hands over her arms, she tried to get her blood moving again. Taylor was right; if she was going to talk to Ritchie about joining the resistance, she had to be more careful. For everyone's sake.

*

Noah stuffed his arms into his leather jacket, jerked the collar up, and slammed the locker door. He'd built rapport with everyone he met, frequented places troublemakers gathered, and looked for signs. What did he have to show for his effort? Nothing. Not a single lead.

With three months until his deadline, he should've initiated damage control already, but coming up empty allowed Noah Seforé more time to exist, more time with Maddison.

He straightened, his tense muscles unfurling. He'd been weighed down for so long he almost didn't recognize the feeling. A smile filled his face at the thought of her. He started for the door, powering up his vidcom.

"Noah." A whisper from behind him. He turned to see Nurse Walker waving him back. Were her pupils dilated? She waited until the doors swung shut behind him. "Since you're new, I thought I should warn you."

He stilled. "About what?"

Her gaze locked on his face before returning to the doors. One hand clutched the strap of her purse, elbow locked close to her body. A slight musk drifted away from her, and her heart rate was much faster than normal. What was going on? As head nurse on their floor, she had always appeared in control. The frightened woman standing across from him looked smaller than her 5'6" frame.

"About what?" he repeated.

She took a deep breath and lowered her voice even more. "It's the fifteenth."

"What has you so spooked?"

She stepped closer. "Inspection day. There'll be liquidators waiting at every entrance and exit, to screen employees and visitors." She shuddered. "The floor sweeps will happen during night shift."

His short CNA training hadn't included anything about an inspection day. The procedure must be specific to CSE or to MA-4 in particular. He'd have to ask ARL Kelly at his next check-in. "This happens every month?"

She nodded and forced a smile. She ran a hand through

her strawberry blonde hair. "It's not that bad. I mean, it's not like you or I have anything to hide. It's standard identification and activity questioning, but the ... well, there's this one liquidator." Her voice tripped over the words and stalled for a moment. Her face paled. If fear had a color, it was definitely the color of her skin right now. "He's especially ... demanding."

Noah fought the tightening of his jaw. He could imagine the type of man who would gain too much enjoyment from scaring the female employees. "And you think we should avoid him?"

She gave a quick, tight nod, looking very much like a small mouse terrified to encounter the house cat. "He likes to wait at the entrance of the main elevators, so I thought I'd take the back stairs today. I didn't want you to be unprepared. You know, since you were off duty during the last inspection."

She didn't have to speak the request. "Why don't we go down together? That door's closer to the employee parking lot anyway."

The air whooshed out of her, and a tremulous smile appeared. He opened the door for her, letting her take the lead toward the stairwell. He'd get her to her car and then go around to the front. To see a confident woman like Nurse Walker hiding in fear stoked a fire in him to do a little intimidating of his own. He couldn't confront the sadist without blowing his cover, but he would get his name and lodge a complaint with Kelly, making sure the ARL kept the man far away from him, Nurse Walker, and the hospital.

As they pushed into the stairwell, Noah nodded to several other nurses scurrying down from higher floors. He sucked in a deep breath. The shadow of a man stood outlined in the exit.

They stopped at the bottom of the stairs, pooling in the entrance, waiting their turn. He stayed close to Nurse Walker, sizing up the liquidator standing eight feet away. The man's voice rumbled out in short, gruff barks, but the slouch in his stature screamed boredom. His hair glinted with strands of silver in the sunlight. He waved each woman and the occasional man through with a half-hearted motion.

He gave no one problems, and Noah positioned himself in line behind Nurse Walker as she shuffled forward.

"Vidcom." McGruff demanded, hand outstretched for the device. Nurse Walker's hand trembled as she dropped it into his palm. He scrolled through several pages before glancing up to match her face with the information on the screen. "Med/surg, Nurse Walker?"

"Yes, sir."

He checked this information against his own compad, making a note. "And where are you headed?"

"Home." It sounded more like a question than a statement.

The liquidator didn't even blink, releasing her vidcom into her hands. "On your way, then. Next."

Noah handed his vidcom over, eyes fixed on Nurse Walker's trembling form. She moved a step closer to him although her car sat yards away.

"Seforé, is it?" Interest filled the old man's voice. "You're new to the area."

Noah pulled his eyes over to meet the other man's. "Yes, I am."

McGruff's face held recognition as he read Noah's cover information. Noah tensed. McCray and Kelly had passed his cover ID through the channels, allowing Noah a measure of safety and, of course, additional accountability. This old man could blow it all with one wrong remark.

His gaze held Noah's for a moment longer than necessary before the disinterested look fell back over his face. "You're on med/surg as well?"

"Yes, sir."

"Very well." He dropped the encoded vidcom back into Noah's hand and waved him on with the slightest of nods.

Noah's vidcom buzzed a message alert as he slipped it into his back pocket. He ignored it and rejoined Nurse Walker, her eyes even larger now. He couldn't leave her alone. Taking her arm, he led her away from the door and toward the corner. "Why don't we grab a cup of coffee?"

"Okay." The word stuttered out, and again his mind concocted reasons for her behavior. None of them relieved him. He didn't push conversation as they rounded the corner and headed for the twenty-four hour restaurant that catered to the sleep-deprived hospital staff.

Once they sat in a booth under the too bright lights, her shoulders slumped. She sank into the cushion. He pushed a mug of hot coffee closer to her limp hands. She grasped it, lifted the steaming cup to her lips, and took a huge gulp. The scalding liquid unleashed a torrent of words. "I'm sorry. I was pitiful back there. I don't know why I let them get to me. You must think I'm such a baby. Worse, I've undermined every ounce of authority I might've had with you, haven't I?"

"Impossible. You deserve a medal for the way you handled last Wednesday." He leaned back against the seat and rested one arm on the top of the booth.

A faint smile crept onto her face, and she sat up a little straighter. "Give me more patients than I have beds for, interns fresh out of med school, and staph any day. I know how to deal with those problems. I can handle them with my arms tied behind my back." She smirked. "Even without the help of a practiced secondary school apprentice and an enamored CNA."

Heat crept up his neck and toward his face. "Nurse Walker, I ..."

She waved his apology away. "I'm teasing. You're so serious all the time. And please, call me Lynn. We're not on duty, and you've earned it, putting up with me today."

He studied her again now that the panic had drained from her face. Dressed in a light blue sweater complimenting her strawberry blond curls, she looked like a Lynn and not the stern, early-forties Nurse Walker he was familiar with.

"Lynn, I've worked with you long enough to know you're hard to ruffle. You obviously had reason to be afraid."

Her eyes dropped to the table. "I'm a grown woman. But just a glimpse of them, and I become a quivering, powerless—"

He laid a hand over her fist, stopping her mid-sentence

before she garnered more attention from their fellow diners. He couldn't protect her if she misspoke.

When she spotted the glances in their direction, she dropped her head into her arms on the table. He stared down the other patrons, one by one, until no one dared look in their direction.

"It's okay."

Her eyes darted out of their hiding place to assess the room before catching his gaze.

He nodded. "It's all right."

"I'm so sorry. I … I'm an idiot. Such an idiot."

He leaned closer, set his coffee to the side, and steepled his hands in front of him. "Lynn, stop. I'm on your side. I understand. Okay?"

A tear spilled down her face, and she dashed it away with her hand. "Okay. Thank you. I knew I could trust you." She sighed in relief.

He schooled his expression. Trust him? No one should do that. Unable to make eye contact, he glanced around for the waitress and noticed the lingering attention of two patrons in the back.

He stood and motioned to the register. "Let me walk you to your car."

She startled at his abrupt change of topic but complied, keeping silent as he tracked down the waitress and signaled toward the door. It took eighty-five seconds for the woman to make her way to them and enter the total in the machine, and the men's eyes stayed on them during each one. Pulling the vidcom from his back pocket and swiping it across the scanner, he listened in on their conversation. It seemed innocent despite their frequent glances in his direction. Once the scanner confirmed the withdrawal of funds from his account, he ushered Nurse Walker out the door and back across the parking lot.

"I am sorry, Noah. I apologize for putting you in that situation." Her words weren't frantic like before but measured and sincere. "I have to get a handle on my fear."

He braved eye contact. "It's okay. Really."

She pulled the car remote from her bag. "Thank you for the coffee, for everything."

"You're welcome. See you tomorrow, Nurse Walker."

"See you tomorrow, CNA Seforé." Slipping into her car, she waved as he stepped away.

As the car door shut, he heard her whisper, "I was right about him. I knew it."

Forcing himself to keep walking, he pulled out his vidcom and headed for his car. Without his enhanced senses, he never would've deciphered her words, so he had no way to question her without tipping his hand. What was she right about?

She couldn't have been referring to his sympathies, could she? He shook his head, thumbing the car locks to disengage. No, fearing liquidators didn't equal involvement in the resistance. If it did, then he and Maddison would be members as well. There had to be some other meaning behind Nurse Walker's words, but to be thorough, he should find a way to discreetly run her background in the system anyway.

He activated the vidcom and saw a waiting message. He

opened the three-word text. "We'll be watching." He didn't need a signature to know who'd sent it, which reminded him he had a report to file. Relocking the car, he marched toward the hospital entrance. He and Kelly needed to talk soon. The ARL and his stationary liquidators needed to give him some space, or he'd never infiltrate the anti-regime group. But first, he'd make sure Kelly transferred the tyrant guarding the main elevators.

CHAPTER TEN

NOAH PAUSED, PEN hovering over the page. He couldn't avoid it. Sighing, he added Nurse Walker's name to his suspicious persons list. He hadn't surveilled her officially, but the interaction he'd overheard today couldn't be denied. It was a coded message, one he hadn't been able to crack yet. One John Henderson had also received. He might've burned all the bridges with Henderson, but he'd have to exploit his relationship with Lynn. They were running out of time.

He added Ben Yancey's name to the list as well. By himself, Ben wasn't all that problematic, but his brother was an outspoken hothead, and Ben seemed to be the only connection between John Henderson and Lynn Walker, two very different people. The connection meant something. But what?

He slipped the paper notebook and pen back into the plastic baggie. He'd been able to hide his strategy once before with a hidden notebook. This time the stakes were much higher. The new notebook held names he didn't want to record electronically, his theories, and his plan to keep Maddison off the Elite's list.

Maddison. He had to orchestrate one interaction with her, one interaction that made her seem vehemently pro-Elite, without her being aware of why.

He huffed. Yeah, no problem there.

But he wasn't giving up. So he had pages full of not quite right ideas. He only needed inspiration to strike once. It would come sooner or later.

He leaned over and pried out the small piece of drywall he'd slit away from the rest. He pushed the baggie into the wall then replaced the sheetrock. Even to his eyes, the small crack near the floor behind the toilet looked like exactly that. Just a crack and not a hiding place. The alarm on his vidcom beeped. Almost time to go. He brushed his hands off on his jeans and headed for the bedroom. Picking up the vibrating device, he silenced it and slipped it into his back pocket. He'd have to keep it on tonight. No more leaving it in the car when he saw her.

If only there was a way to mute or censor what the microphone picked up. Then maybe he wouldn't have to be on edge twenty-four hours a day. Functioning in a state of high alert was taking its toll.

Tonight should help. If he couldn't catch a break with the coded message, he'd give himself one. Fresh eyes always triggered insight. For now, he'd put it out of his mind. Grabbing his keys and leather jacket, he headed for the car and for her.

As he exited the hotel, his breath floated out before him, and he quickened his pace. If the temperature continued to drop, his plan for the evening would have to be trashed, but maybe the weather would cooperate for a couple of hours.

In the last three weeks, all efforts to keep his distance from Maddison had failed. Ignoring his attraction had become a lost cause, and he didn't want to fight it anymore. After the first dinner at her house, something had shifted between them. They texted back and forth in the morning. They went out to eat after work. He'd come over for dinner with Jakob and Taylor several times, comforted by the home-cooked meals, teasing banter, and after-dessert card games. Last week, he joined her and her friends for a movie. Josh kept his distance, but Sophie and Olivia welcomed him with open arms.

Noah Seforé became more fleshed out every day. He had a stressful but respectable job, people to hang out with, and someone to come home to. Everything fifteen-year-old Noah wanted and planned for, he had a taste of now.

But it was all a mirage. Noah Seforé didn't exist. Not anymore. And in three months, Noah State would be dead also. *What will happen to her then?*

She deserved to know the truth, but he wanted to be selfish ... just one more night. He downshifted into her neighborhood.

More lying, Noah? The questions sounded more like his nonna's than his own. He and Daniel would've broken her heart countless times by now, if she hadn't died with their parents four years ago. A nonna's love stretched wide, but murder wouldn't have been covered. If she wouldn't have been able to forgive him, her God definitely wouldn't.

Nonna's voice told him to come clean, but he shrugged it off and rang Maddison's doorbell. She opened the door, wearing a white sweater dress, gray leggings, and a long burgundy coat. A filmy green fabric wove through her hair. The voice in his head shut up.

"You look amazing."

She blushed. "Thanks. You don't look so bad yourself."

"Shall we?" He held out an arm and bowed.

"Of course, dear sir." She giggled and closed the door behind her. She shook her head as he led her around to the passenger side. "You really should've been born earlier."

"Yes, but then I wouldn't have met you." The thought sent a sharp pain through him.

"That would've been a crime." No teasing in her soft voice this time.

"You're right." His hand tucked an errant strand of hair behind her ear. The glow in her eyes brightened. He resisted the urge to kiss her by stepping back so she could slide into the passenger seat. He closed the door behind her and sprinted around the back.

Maddison leaned back into the warm leather seat and angled her body toward Noah's. She batted her eyes. "Can I ask where we're going?"

He grinned that fabulous lopsided grin of his. "I think I'll keep it a secret for just a little longer."

"But I'll like it?" Silly question. Of course she would.

"I think so."

"Well, then step on it, mister."

He chuckled. "Yes, ma'am."

Life had been dimmer before him. How had she not seen it? He evoked something in her no one else had. She fell harder for him every day, and it should scare her.

But he didn't. So it didn't.

If only he'd get on board and make it official.

"How warm is your coat?"

She shot him a questioning look. "Pretty warm. I have some gloves in the pockets I think. Am I going to need them?"

His only response was a smile.

"Should I be nervous? We don't have long before curfew, you know."

"I'll have you home before eleven-thirty, I promise."

She brainstormed, knowing she couldn't use the car's GPS as a guide. The car allowed for manual control, and Noah took advantage of the feature.

"Hey, how come you can disengage autopilot? My car doesn't even give me the option."

His head whipped toward her in surprise before he pulled his eyes back to the road. "All older models have the function." His words leaked out through tight lips.

She didn't press. His demeanor made clear the answer to her next question as well—the reason he could afford one had to be connected to his parents' deaths—so she changed the subject. "Are you sure you don't want to tell me where we're headed?"

The tension around his eyes faded, and he smiled but shook his head. She went back to wracking her brain for options. They wouldn't need warm clothes inside the archives, coffee shops, or movie theaters. Could he be taking her to the Plaza? The observation gallery with its wine and coffee bar offered an exclusive way for couples who could afford it to end their evening. She'd heard the view of the metro area's skyline took your breath away, but to mingle with all the people in Class One and Two? *Please don't let that be what he has planned.*

Several minutes later, he turned away from downtown. She breathed a sigh of relief, but that left her out of options. She leaned over to lay her head on his shoulder. "Can I have a hint?"

His gaze warmed her. "Be patient for three more minutes."

She sat up and crossed her arms. "You're being stubborn."

He laughed. "And you're being difficult."

Well, yeah, maybe. "Sorry."

"You're forgiven. Anything look familiar to you?"

She couldn't make out much in the darkness. "It looks like a place I went hiking with the girls once, but I couldn't be sure."

"Hiking at the nature park?" He turned into an almost empty parking lot.

"Yes, but this can't be it because they close at sundown."

"For us, they close after the meteor shower tonight." He looked down at her, waiting for a response. One lone finger tapped against the steering wheel. Oh. Her confident Noah was nervous.

"Are you telling me you talked the rangers into

postponing their closing duties so you and I could watch the meteor shower?"

He nodded. "My trunk is stocked with blankets, hot chocolate, and flashlights. The junior ranger will meet us at the visitors' center and guide us to an open field with a perfect view of the show. But if it's too cold, or you don't feel comfortable being out here alone, or it doesn't sound like your kind of thing, say the word and we can go. "

She covered his hand with her own. "I think it's incredible."

"Seriously?"

"I never get to see stars. Never. I love the idea." She kissed his cheek. "Thank you."

"You're welcome." His fingers brushed her cheek, trapping the breath in her lungs. "We'd better get going, or we'll miss the beginning."

Did he not know what his nearness started in her? If he didn't follow through on those promises his touch made soon, she would be forced to take matters into her own hands. She pulled on her gloves and came around to join him at the trunk. He handed her a temperature-sensitive thermos and picked up a huge pile of blankets.

She smirked. "Do you think you have enough?"

"You'll thank me once we're sitting on the cold ground. Come on, I see John waiting for us."

They made their way forward on the asphalt path. "Is he a friend of yours?" she asked, although she had no idea how he could've known the bearded man waiting on them.

"Nope."

His planning meant even more.

"Hey guys, you made it right on time." The ranger smiled. "Looks like you'll be outfitted once we get there, but can you walk the trails?"

Noah looked over at Maddison to make the call. She shrugged. "My ballet flats have traversed worse. Thanks for doing this by the way."

"I thought Noah had a great idea, might use it myself sometime. Don't be fooled though. He made it more than worth my time. Ready, then?"

Maddison looped her arm through Noah's. "Lead on."

John turned on a high-powered lantern and started down a path to the left. They followed several steps behind. She squeezed Noah's arm. "I still can't believe you thought to do this."

"I like to get away from the hectic noise of the city, and I know you're always looking for a new adventure. Good idea?"

"A very good one."

They set out their blankets, three deep, in the middle of the field while the ranger slipped away. Noah settled another blanket around her shoulders before he sat. "Would you like some cocoa?"

"Yes, please." She grinned and held out her hand for the steaming cup he poured. Holding the cup to her face, she took a deep whiff, enjoying the rich chocolate smell. Noah poured his own cup and shifted closer to her.

Once the initial wonder subsided, Noah pointed out several stars and constellations as he found them. After a while, his hand dropped to his side, and his voice faded into the background. She leaned into his side and focused on the streaming lights in the sky. Tomorrow, her neck would be stiff from being tilted back so long, but tonight, she didn't care. For the first time in her life, she wished she were creative enough to paint or sketch. The inability to capture this night in her mind seemed tragic somehow. She never wanted the memory to dull.

CHAPTER ELEVEN

NOAH SLID INTO the booth, balancing a tray piled high with two steaming plates of chicken *tikka masala*, *palak paneer*, and *naan*, and two short mugs of hot tea. Inhaling the steam drifting upward, he set the tray down and broke off a piece of *naan* to drag through the *tikka masala*. "I can't believe you've never had Indian food before. Why didn't you drag Sophie or Olivia out here with you one time? Aren't you the girl who's introduced me to every cultural center in the metro area over the last four weeks?"

Maddison laughed, shaking her head. "Olivia's allergic to anything that looks spicy, and Sophie's not adventurous." She cleared the tray of silverware and drinks as Noah arranged the dishes between them.

"Well, it's their loss. Now, if you want to be …" He froze. He was hallucinating. Right? Blinking twice didn't clear his vision. Not fifteen feet away, by the door, stood his older brother in full liquidator mode. Daniel was intimidating enough dressed in black from head to toe, but his predatory gaze and confident posture made plain that he was a man who got his way.

"Noah? If I want to be what?"

Maddison's words sounded far away. Had his cover been blown? If not, what was Daniel up to? Noah's gaze shot back to her face. He should've told her. He couldn't have hidden it forever anyway. This moment was inevitable—but why did she have to find out like this?

She didn't. Not if he held Daniel off. Noah only had to buy them some time. Squaring his shoulders, he looked back at the entrance only to find Daniel striding toward them. He leveled a threatening glare at his brother.

Daniel's mouth lifted in a smirk, and mischief played in his blue-gray eyes. Noah maintained eye contact. Inside, every alarm blared.

Maddison reached over to squeeze his hand, her eyes locked on Daniel's signet ring.

"Well, I was going for surprised, but I'll take shocked." Daniel slid into the booth beside Noah. "Given how hard I had to search to find you, that's to be expected. Your com-pad, however, proved very helpful. You might want to change the security measures on it by the way. Anyone with a little knowledge could hack into all your private data." He turned his attention to Maddison, her face emotionless and still. "Oh, how rude of me." He smiled and leaned forward, holding out a hand. "I didn't introduce myself. I'm Noah's big brother, Daniel."

Her fingers flew off Noah's like a startled bird.

Noah laid a hand on Daniel's arm, his right hand to be

exact, the one missing his signet ring. Daniel's eyes flickered over it, and though it seemed impossible, his smile grew wider.

"Daniel." A low growl escaped with the warning.

"Listen to him." Daniel leaned back in the booth, kicking his feet up on the opposite booth seat, blocking Maddison in. "You would think he's a liquidator, the way he acts."

Noah fought back the red flooding his vision and worked to keep his voice flat. "You should have called."

"I did. Several times, and well, you haven't been taking many of Callista's calls either—you really should keep that girl happy, you know—so I decided to cut the vidcom out of it and pay my little brother a visit. Tomorrow's Thanksgiving after all, and you should spend it with family." Daniel's eyes glided over to Maddison. "But I'm not making much of a first impression, am I? Let's start over." He switched sides of the booth before Noah could protest and faced Maddison. "Daniel State, the good-looking and fun brother. And you are?"

Maddison's spine straightened like a rod, and the look she gave Daniel would've wilted a lesser man. "Maddison James."

Would this have been her reaction to Noah if she'd known his real last name from the beginning? Or did Daniel's behavior produce this particular attitude? Noah placed his bet on the latter. Daniel excelled in the art of provocation.

"Well, I'd love to say I've heard all about you, but my little brother doesn't write often." He threw a smile to Noah. "So you'll have to tell me all about how you two met."

She shot Noah a sideways glance, and he hoped his face

had an apology engraved across it. Hers softened, a little. "I think I understand 'complicated' better now."

"The tip of the iceberg." Noah nodded his head in time with the words.

"Look at you two, with your clever insider-only conversation." Daniel waved a hand in the couple's direction and gave them a saccharine smile. "So cute."

Maddison took Noah's hand before turning back to his brother, defiant once again. "Oh, I can decode it for you. Noah mentioned your relationship was complicated. I couldn't imagine how, considering that he gets along with everyone, but it's becoming clearer."

Daniel leaned closer. To her credit, Maddison didn't flinch. "Spunky. I like it. Wherever did you find her, brother?"

"At the hospital. I'm sure I told you I transferred CNA positions."

"I'm sure you did, but you know me, moving from MA to MA." He shook his head and dropped his eyes. "It's hard to keep track. A liquidator's work is never done."

The remark sliced through muscle and hit bone. "Enough."

Daniel sat back with a hand over his heart. "I'm sorry. Sometimes I'm too blasé. It's a way of coping, I've been told. I apologize."

Noah gritted his teeth to keep from grabbing Daniel and ripping him out of the booth. His brother's tactic mirrored the way cats tease their prey before devouring it, and Daniel knew he hated it.

He focused on Maddison. "Dinner doesn't seem like such a good idea anymore. Why don't I take you home?"

She nodded.

Noah pinned Daniel with a glare. "I'll see you at my hotel."

Daniel stood and saluted. "I'll get right to work on that turkey." He pivoted. "Until next time, Miss James."

Noah didn't shift his gaze, holding out a hand for Maddison to go ahead. She shuffled to the door as he dumped the trays full of food in the trash. They walked in silence to his car, and for once, he didn't deactivate the autopilot, mumbling out her address when prompted. His hand gripped the gearshift out of habit. Several times during their drive, he opened his mouth to apologize, to explain, but nothing came out.

Once they'd pulled into her driveway, he shut off the car and faced her. "I'm sorry. I had no idea—"

"Is he always like that?" Anger flashed in her eyes.

"Like what?"

"Arrogant, insulting, demeaning. Smirky."

Noah clamped down an inappropriate laugh. "You got it in one."

"How do you stand him? I wanted to slap that stupid smile off his face. I don't know how you do it. I mean, I know he's your brother, but …"

"He gets under your skin?" The phrase didn't even come close to doing Daniel justice. "You handled him well. It's been a long time since I've seen Daniel unable to make someone shrink back."

"I hid my fear well then." Her eyes dropped to her lap.

Noah clenched his jaw and tipped her chin up to meet his gaze. "You don't need to be scared. Let me handle Daniel."

"That's what I'm afraid of, you stepping in between us and taking the brunt of his wrath," she whispered.

"He won't hurt me, even if it would be government sanctioned. Besides, I know how to pick my battles."

"So you've said." A half-smile snuck onto her face before disappearing again as she fixed him with a serious look. "Help me understand. It's obvious you don't like who he is, but the way you've talked about him, like you idolized him, I don't get it."

Noah shifted in his seat. His fingers traced the Mustang symbol on the steering wheel. "Daniel wasn't always this man. I guess I remember who's buried beneath the bravado. At least I hope he's still underneath it. Some days I'm not so sure."

"What could've happened to turn a decent human into him?"

The images he conjured made him shudder. Anyone who'd been through what Daniel had would be scarred for life. Knowing the truth might give Maddison some sympathy, but Daniel would rather be hated than let anyone see the internal damage. Noah had to respect that.

"It's not my story to tell."

But Noah could tell her his ... and he should. To protect her from Daniel and the way he would delight in crushing her with his words. Noah had been granted a reprieve here at least, and he needed to take full advantage of that. Once she was calm. Soon.

He sighed. "I'm sorry, Maddison. If I'd thought for a second Daniel would show up, I'd have told you."

"You could've at least told me he's a liquidator. When I saw him walk in and zero in on you …" She crossed her arms and rubbed her hands against them.

He wanted to tell her, erase the fear paling her face, but the words lodged in his throat. He had his own battle. "You're right. But I know how you feel about liquidators, and I didn't want to put distance between us. I kinda hoped you'd never meet him." He rolled his eyes. "Unrealistic, I know…. It's hard to know how to tell people about him."

"Did you think I would push you away because of something you couldn't control? You have no say over Daniel's occupation or how he chooses to live his life."

Noah let out a shaky breath. "I needed to hear you say that."

Her fingers grazed his cheek. "We are okay. I promise, but … I won't spend time with him. I can't."

He took her hand in his. "Believe me, I don't want to spend time with him either."

"How long do you think he'll stay in town?"

"With Daniel, you never know. He could be gone tomorrow morning, or he could decide to stay and torment me indefinitely." Noah cringed, hearing the self-pity creeping into his voice. He pushed it away with his next words. "But I'll set some boundaries if he chooses to stay."

"Can you do that?" The words were soft and incredulous.

Noah locked eyes with her. "I can, and I will."

CHAPTER TWELVE

PUSHING THE DOOR open, Noah frowned. No lights meant no Daniel. He did not want to hunt down his brother. He let the door slide shut behind him and shuffled toward the bed. Shrugging out of his leather coat, he sank down on the bed and pulled out his vidcom.

"You do know you can't create a new life for yourself, right? It doesn't work that way." The voice came from the darkest corner of the room.

"Light on." He looked over his shoulder. Daniel lounged in the armchair. He spiraled a book in his hands. Noah grimaced. "Well, aren't you going for dark and sinister."

Daniel quirked an eyebrow. "Did I achieve it? I've been practicing. I did have hours on my hands while I waited after all."

"Cut it out."

"You first." He sat up, elbows on his knees.

Noah stood and leaned against the wall on the opposite side of the room. "What kind of act do you think I'm pulling?"

"Oh, you know, innocent Southern boy working a regular job while wooing the equivalent of his secondary school sweetheart. She will find out what you are. Pretending you aren't a liquidator doesn't change anything."

"Why are you here, Daniel?"

"I hadn't seen you in a couple months. I was curious what kept you away. I'm guessing I know now."

Noah crossed his arms and rolled his eyes. "Not as much fun to cause trouble when I'm not there to lecture you about it?"

Daniel sat back, relaxed. "No one ever declared you my chaperone, least of all me. You're the one who feels duty bound to hold me to your moral code."

"You kill people for looking at you the wrong way when I'm not around. What else do you expect me to do? If I don't follow you around, people die."

"That's a given."

"It doesn't have to be."

Daniel threw his hands into the air. "Yes, it does. I'm a liquidator. Like it or not, you are too. And no amount of whitewashing or guilt tripping is going to change it. We kill people. It's who we are. And if you don't accept that, you'll have to clean up more messes."

"No, I won't."

"Right, because giving people second chances has worked out so well for you in the last year."

Blonde cherubic faces flashed before Noah's eyes again. Then the face of the offender, still defiant, when Noah apprehended and liquidated him later.

Daniel stood and strode toward Noah. "But when you do your job right, the rest of the world is a safer place. CNW and CSW were definitely safer."

More faces. Rapist. Murderer. Drunk driver. All but one faded away when he blinked. The fifteen-year-old's blue eyes were hard to shake.

"And where has this moral code gotten you? You torture yourself for actions that had to be taken. You put yourself in unnecessary danger to give everyone else the benefit of the doubt. You're scraping by on what's left of Mom and Dad's insurance settlement because you hand over your salary to the families of your," he inserted air quotes around the next word, "victims to assuage your guilt. Do you feel better? No." He jabbed a finger in Noah's chest. "You have got to accept it—the Elite have deemed you worthy for this responsibility. Do your job."

Noah pushed Daniel's hand away. "The whole system is flawed. Justice without accountability is flippant retribution."

"Thinking like that is going to get you executed. Do you want to die?" Daniel sank back onto the bed. "Don't answer that question."

"I'm never going to be like you."

"So you've decided to be someone else altogether? It won't work. Sooner or later, you'll run into someone who knows who you are. And that's best-case scenario. You can't go off grid. Harrow and McCray will be looking for you."

"No, they won't. I'm here under orders."

"How so?"

Noah sat in the desk chair. "You can't play around with

what I'm going to tell you." He waited for Daniel's response. The mocking nod would have to be good enough. "I'm undercover by Harrow's recommendation. There are rumblings about a rebellion, but no one wanted to be rash." Another pause to shoot Daniel a pointed look. "So for now, I'm Noah Seforé, CNA at MA-4D. And that's all anyone can know if I'm going to be able to make contact with this resistance."

"Go on."

"Our history is the same, except I didn't go to the Academy, of course. I lived in Coastal South West MA-6 for the last two years and worked at a hospital there."

"And Maddison is part of your cover?"

He shook his head. "No. I don't want her involved."

"Don't be an idiot. Of course, she's involved." He held up a hand to stop Noah's interruption. "I talked to Callista earlier. I mention it for the second time today because the crazy stalker had some interesting info to share. Tell me you aren't completely stupid and you know they were watching you?"

"I know." *But thanks for letting them know that, brother.*

"They aren't listening now. Since I'm here. Respecting my privacy and all, so you know, you're welcome."

Noah almost rolled his eyes but didn't want to give Daniel the pleasure of a reaction. Instead, he leaned back in his chair, waiting for Daniel to meander around to wherever he was going with this topic.

Daniel kicked Noah's chair and cursed. "Would you show half as much concern for your own life as you do everyone else's? They gave you this mission, which probably came with a very specific incentive."

No way was he sharing the deadline with Daniel. Things would go sideways if he knew.

"Fine, don't tell me. Callista didn't know what it was either. But they gave you this mission, and they had a team of people watching your every move. You'd better stop playing house and find that resistance."

"I'm working on it."

"Well, work faster. You have the Regional Liquidator's Office breathing down your neck. You'd better not be getting any ideas. This martyr complex of yours makes me want to kill you."

Noah smirked. "That would be a little counterproductive, don't you think?"

Daniel growled. His eyes narrowed. "Callista knows about her, which means McCray does as well. I put in a good word for you with Callista, but when she calls next, you'd better take that call and you'd better lie about Maddison being a part of your cover. If things go wrong—"

Noah's muscles tightened from his shoulders to his toes, ready to attack. "They won't."

"If things go wrong, people will target her to get to you. I should know—it's what I would do."

"No one is going to hurt her. Not you. Not Callista. Not anybody." Still, he ran through protection details in his head. "Are you staying?"

"You clearly need me to." Daniel walked over to look out

the dark window. "McCray seems to think I could be useful as well."

"Care to explain why, if you knew about me being under-cover, you needed to give me the 'You can't start a new life' speech?"

"It's clear you're involved with this girl, Noah, and I know you. I needed to make sure you plan to follow through with your objective." He faced Noah, deadly serious. "Don't forget—they won't let you go."

"Believe me, I know. It's burned into my brain ... and my shoulder."

"Good. You hungry? I'm in the mood for Chinese."

Noah blocked the exit. "We need to go over some ground rules."

Daniel sighed and fell back onto the bed. "Here we go."

"I'm serious."

"Noted."

"First off, you will not seek out Maddison, her family, or her friends. I assume you already know who those people are, since you've been so busy this afternoon. You will not involve them in any games you intend to play. They are off limits. Understood?"

"Fine." Daniel stood. "Can we go eat?"

"I'm not done." Noah crossed his arms.

Daniel groaned. "Of course you're not."

"I won't tolerate unnecessary trouble here. I already have my hands full looking for this resistance without keeping you on the straight and narrow. If you expect to spend any time with me, you will not terrorize people, guilt them into being extra nice to you, or punish someone beyond their offense. Got it?"

"I understand your position. Now, dinner?"

Noah shook his head, his hands falling to his sides. He leaned over and grabbed his jacket. "We can do dinner a couple of blocks over, if you're on your best behavior."

Daniel brushed by him with a smile. "Well, of course, I would never cast a poor reflection on my sainted younger brother. Besides, I'm very good at following orders."

"Since when?"

"You're not the only one giving them." He strutted into the hallway.

Noah froze. "Why did McCray think you'd be useful here?"

Daniel leaned back into the doorway. "Well, for one, he could pull the surveillance team off you, since I would be here to keep tabs and check in with them. You're welcome again for that by the way. Except I make no promises about Psycho Stalker. She may continue on her own time. As for the other reasons?" His eyes lit up. "I'm not authorized to read you in."

Noah swallowed the acid in his throat.

"Come on, Mr. Furrowed Brow, what's the worst I could do?" Daniel winked.

CHAPTER THIRTEEN

MADDISON TWIRLED FROM the oven to the island, making room for the pan of cookies on an already overcrowded counter. After setting them down, she closed the oven door and adjusted the temperature to 325 degrees. Pies would be next. Apple or cherry?

Olivia walked into the kitchen and skidded to a stop. She held her hands up as though she approached a skittish animal. "Put down the oven mitts and step away from the pie crust."

Sophie barreled in behind her. "I came as soon as I got Jakob's text. What's wrong?" She surveyed the damage and let out a long "oh."

"What are you guys doing here?" Maddison cocked her head. "Wait, did you say Jakob texted you? I haven't seen him all day."

Sophie nodded. "He was worried. I can see why."

Olivia spread her arms wide over the counters. "You have enough food here to feed the whole school. Cookies, cupcakes, wait, is that a chocolate torte?"

"The bake sale is Sunday. I promised to help out." Maddison scrubbed a spot of melted chocolate off the counter.

"You promised them five dozen cookies. This is enough food for the entire sale." Sophie took a step closer. "What happened?"

"Do you guys want some scones?" She turned to grab plates out of the cabinet.

Sophie laid a hand on her shoulder. "Maddie, talk to us. What's going on?" She led Maddison to the kitchen table. Olivia put a kettle on to boil, pulling mugs and tea bags out of the pantry and laying them beside the stove before joining the other two.

"Noah's brother is in town." The spidery feeling crept up and down her spine again. Daniel State was a dangerous man. A dangerous man like the one who'd killed her parents and taunted her with the news.

"And ..." Sophie prompted.

"He's very different than Noah." She couldn't seem to force the words past her throat.

Olivia lunged forward, conducting her words with an outstretched finger. "In looks? In personality? Wait, is he cute?"

Maddison chuckled despite herself. The tension in her shoulders eased. "He's all shaggy midnight black hair, light blue eyes, and cocky smirk. He moves like a predator. Not like Noah at all." Noah controlled his power, every shift of his body deliberate.

"Sounds hot." Olivia stood and made her way over to the

whistling teapot, turning the stove off and pouring the water over the peppermint tea bags.

Sophie shot her a look.

Olivia shrugged. "What? Aren't you curious after meeting Noah? I mean, he's an unreal kind of hot. You don't think those people exist outside of an airbrushed magazine. Be honest, didn't you lose your breath a little when she introduced him to us?"

Sophie's glare grew deeper. "Would you be serious—"

"Anyway, it's logical I'd be interested in whether or not his hotness is a family trait." Turning the mug handles in on each other, Olivia carried them over and sat one down in front of each girl.

"He's not your type, Liv." Maddison wrapped her hands around the steaming mug, willing the warmth to seep into her as well. "He's a liquidator."

The other girls froze. "Oh, Maddie." Sophie sighed.

"Daniel, that's his name, came striding into the restaurant in all black, looking for his next victim. When he fixed his gaze on Noah, for a second, I thought …" Her voice broke. Sophie's hand settled on her own. Maddison raised her eyes. "He's my worst nightmare come to life." A sob escaped her.

Olivia pushed a napkin into her hands and put an arm around her. "I'm sorry."

Daniel's narrowing gaze from Wednesday flashed before her again. What if Noah couldn't contain him? What if trying made Daniel angry? He wouldn't liquidate his own brother, right? Anxiety, like a pair of steel hands, pressed against her throat. She couldn't breathe.

Stop panicking! Noah said he could handle it. He told you Daniel wouldn't hurt him. You have to trust him. The hands released her. Oxygen flooded into her lungs. Trust Noah. Okay, she could do that. She took one more shaky breath. *It's going to be okay. It is.* She wiped her eyes and gave the girls a small smile. "Turns out he just likes to make Noah's life a nightmare."

Sophie squeezed her hand. "Is he a threat to Noah? Or you?"

"Noah doesn't think so."

"And Noah'll make sure you're safe." It never took long for Olivia to find the bright side.

"Yes, he will." *Even if I did reach out to Ritchie.*

"So what brought on the baking therapy?" Sophie nodded toward the island.

Maddison's eyes dropped to her clasped hands. "It shouldn't matter. It doesn't change things between Noah and me. But meeting Daniel, it muddles my feelings. Makes me want to distance myself."

"What do you mean?" Sophie asked.

"Daniel's so much like ... *him.* I looked into Daniel's eyes and saw the same disregard for human life. The helplessness I felt, it's right here under the surface. I couldn't stop it then, and I can't stop it now. Daniel could kill someone I love because they look at him the wrong way. And I'd have to stand by and watch it ... again." The sobs returned with a vengeance. "I couldn't stop it. They were just gone, and I couldn't save them. It didn't matter that I hid the novel. It didn't matter because they were already dead."

A chair scraped across the hardwood floor, and Olivia's arms encircled her. Sophie's hand squeezed her shoulder, and she mumbled soft phrases in Spanish, unintelligible yet comforting somehow.

When the tears began to abate, Maddison sniffed back the final set and leaned back in her friends' arms. "I've been lying to myself—because the local liquidators haven't given me a second glance—telling myself it couldn't happen again. I'd forgotten how terrifying it is to be caught in a liquidator's sights, but Daniel … nothing's changed."

What if Daniel found out about Ritchie, about the resistance? Her throat tightened again.

"Not true." Sophie shook her head as she and Olivia stepped back. "Noah's part of the equation, and he can stop his brother."

"But not all of them." *What have I done?* "Noah could get himself killed. I saw it in my dreams last night, and the one before. I don't think … I can't watch that happen in real life."

"What does he say about all of this?"

"We haven't talked about it." Her eyes dropped to the table. The wood grain ridged under her fingers. "I haven't talked to him since Wednesday night. I can't. It's too much."

Sophie reached over and grabbed Maddison's vidcom off the counter. "Call him. He needs to know."

"I will. I just want some more time to process."

"Not alone. Soph and I are here if you need to talk about this, any time." Olivia smiled. "We'll even serve as your human buffers so you don't have to interact with Daniel. But no more dwelling on your fears, and Soph is right, you need to be honest with Noah."

Sophie stared her down. "We won't leave tonight until you've set up a time to meet him."

Maddison held her hand out for her com. "Fine."

"We'll pick out a movie in case he can't come over right now."

Maddison nodded her thanks and waited until the girls wandered into the den before she gave the "Call Noah" command. *Forgive me, Noah, please.* Seconds later, his concerned face popped up on her screen.

Her tear-stained face made something clench in his gut. He raced toward his car. He had wanted to give her space if she needed it. Clearly, that had been the wrong decision. "Maddison."

"We need to … I need to see you."

He took the steps three at a time. "I'm coming."

The corners of her mouth rose, and with an "okay," she disconnected. Noah quickened his pace. Should he be slower? He couldn't care less. Within minutes, he backed out of the parking lot and sped toward her door. He'd spent most of yesterday following Daniel around, thanks to his brother's insistence that they spend the weekend together. Noah quit arguing once Daniel told him that he'd already called the hospital and "politely requested Noah be granted leave." Daniel had been almost gleeful, and nothing good ever came of him smiling. Noah watched as Daniel set himself up in the penthouse at the best hotel in the area, bumping a local business mogul from the room in the process.

The livid man made his displeasure apparent to Daniel, who pinned the younger man against a wall by his neck seconds later. Noah pried Daniel away before any permanent damage could be done, and by the time Daniel had thrown him off, the young man had disappeared. Smart enough to know when to run for his life.

Daniel seemed determined to make his presence in MA-4 well known and documented. By the time Noah returned home, he fell onto the bed exhausted and disappointed that he hadn't seen Maddison's face, in person or over the com, all day. So much for a happy Thanksgiving.

He'd woken up today and rid his body of the tension by running three times his normal route. He'd considered calling her after breakfast, but he wanted to give her space. So he fumbled his way through the day, running surveillance on Nurse Walker's acquaintances.

He pulled into the last space in the driveway. Next time, he'd pay more attention to his instincts.

As if on cue, Sophie and Olivia exited the front door, loaded down with containers and plastic bags. He stepped out of the car and made quick strides to where Maddison waited, silhouetted by the lights inside. Sophie repeated Olivia's goodbye and he nodded at them, not slowing his pace. He stepped over the threshold, shut the door behind him, and met her eyes.

The pain there echoed in him, and he pulled her into his

arms, cradling her head in one hand. She clung to him and let out a tiny sob.

"What is it?" Whatever it was, he'd make it right.

She pulled back and took his hand, leading them both to the couch. She sat across from him, folded into the corner with her arms around her knees. "It's Daniel."

His blood ran cold. "What did he do?"

"He didn't do anything, well, I mean … it's what he represents." She dropped her eyes. "Seeing him, thinking he might hurt you … He's too much like the man … who killed my parents."

Her gaze shot back up, apologizing for the connection. But he understood. When she told him about the man who'd toyed with her after killing her parents, the description had sounded eerily like his brother.

"I couldn't stop him, Noah. I couldn't do anything to save them, and Daniel, his presence, makes clear what's always been true. I could lose the people I love any day of the week, and there's nothing I could do to stop it."

His eyes slid shut. He couldn't give her what she wanted, but he could try to assuage the pain in her voice. Opening his eyes, he moved closer on the couch and took one of her hands in his own. "I can't promise you'll never lose someone you love, but I will promise it won't be at Daniel's hands. And I'll do everything I can to keep it from happening at anyone else's."

Her grip on his hand grew fiercer. "That's part of the problem."

"What do you mean?"

A slight blush filled her cheeks, and she fought to keep her gaze on his. "I watched you die in my dreams the last two nights. Over and over again. The scenarios and liquidators changed, but in every one, you died protecting me or someone I love. And in every one, they made me watch." She shuddered. "I'll never get those images out of my head. Don't you see? You've become one of the people I can't lose."

He couldn't hold back a groan, pulling her into his arms. "You aren't going to lose me. You can't lose me." He'd make it true. Somehow.

"You don't know that." She mumbled into his shoulder. "You're not as strong as them. I've seen what they can do."

The guilt rose hard and fast. He should've been honest with her the day Daniel arrived. At least then, she wouldn't have been tortured by the idea of him getting hurt. Her eyes wouldn't be rimmed with dark circles.

He couldn't leave her in the dark anymore. Keeping the truth from her had hurt her. He'd been fooling himself to think she'd only be in danger if she knew. Daniel was right—now that Noah had involved her, they were both standing on the edge of a cliff. She deserved to know. She'd be less likely to lose her balance if she had all the facts.

He'd been selfish for too long. That's what it all came down to anyway, and he couldn't rationalize it away now, not after seeing the pain the last two days had caused.

He swallowed and shifted away from her. "Come with me. Leave your vidcom here." He laid his on the coffee table.

She gave him a questioning look but complied. He stood up and led her by the hand into the kitchen. The oven fan hummed in the background. Good, that would muffle their conversation even more. He sat them on the far side of the room.

"Noah, what's going on?"

He licked his lips. "What if I was as strong as Daniel?"

"What are you talking about?"

Man up and tell her, but be smart about it. "I need you to promise to keep secret what I'm about to tell you. You can react however you want, but I can't keep you safe from the Elite if you tell anyone."

"Noah, you're scaring me." Maddison ran a shaky hand through her hair.

"Promise me first." The churning in his stomach picked up speed.

"I promise."

The words slipped out of her mouth without pause. It stung. She had no idea he'd deceived her. He forced his mouth open. "I said before that I know how to pick my battles. It's true. I learned how to. Because I'm a liquidator."

The silence that followed was its own explosion, the wreckage written on her face, in her body language. Something died in her gaze. Then, "No, you can't be. You're Noah. You can't be."

"It's true. I'm in the area undercover."

Maddison shut her mouth, eyes hardening with betrayal and hurt, and he braced for the aftershock. "You lied to me. From the moment we met, you've been lying. Knowing how I felt about liquidators, knowing my history." She whispered, but the words shot through him with vicious force. "What else don't I know? What's true about you?" Her volume grew. "Does Noah *State* have a girlfriend? Is that who Callista is?"

"No." The word was as vehement as he felt. The idea of being with anyone else but Maddison made him cold. "Callista is a liquidator. I met her at the Academy, but I want nothing to do with her, never have. She can't, or won't, take the hint."

"Where are you from really?" Her lips curled in derision.

"I'm from MA-16, I didn't lie about that. I lied about my title, that's it."

She jumped up and away from him, crossing her arms around herself. "That's it? You lied about your brother being a liquidator. You lied about being a CNA. Do you realize you could have endangered patients by pretending to be a medical professional? You lied about attending the Academy. You lied about killing people. You lied about being a good man. You are a liar, Noah State, a liar and a murderer."

All true. The words had never been blacker.

"Am I part of your cover?"

"No, I might've—"

She leaned forward and jabbed a finger in his direction. "Was I part of your cover?"

He stood as well but kept his distance. "No. You took me by surprise." He gathered more courage. "I'm sorry, Maddison. You're right. I should've told you. But I had orders. Still do. And I … I didn't want to lose you."

"Get out."

The words hit him like a physical blow. "Let me explain."

"Too late. Get out of my house."

"Maddison, please."

"I'll keep your secret. If you leave." She made for the door, but he couldn't leave yet. Not if she was going to throw around threats like that.

He reached for her. She recoiled. *Forgive me for this.* He sped around her, blocking the doorway.

She gasped. "No ... ah."

"I'll leave. I will. But you have to hear me on this." He held his hands out in apology.

Fire lit in her eyes again. "I don't have to hear—"

"Yes. You. Do."

He hated this. Every single second. "You can't threaten to tell my secret. You can't tell anyone."

She stared back at him. "What are you going to do?"

He growled. "I'm trying to protect you. Let me talk."

She retreated a step. He followed.

"O ... kay." The word had none of her previous bravado.

"Your vidcom, your compad, the vidwall, they can be tapped."

"Have you been spying on me?"

"No! But they've been spying on me. It's why I left my vidcom in the other room. Why I gave you that warning several weeks ago."

Her eyes widened and her hand groped for something to hold onto. She found the kitchen counter. "Noah, those things I said ... in the beginning ..."

"It's fine. I kept you safe. You should be safe. But if they find out you know, if you tell someone the truth about me, I don't ..." He wanted to touch her, to reassure her. No, to reassure himself. "I'll do everything I can, but you have to be careful. In case they're watching." He took a step away from her. "Please be careful."

Her breathing accelerated, but she managed a nod.

"Maddison."

"Please. Go."

She had heard him out. He had no other reason to stay. He grabbed his vidcom on the way out and closed the door behind him. Then he heard her. Her sobs threatened to take him to his knees, but he forced himself on.

CHAPTER FOURTEEN

MADDISON COLLAPSED ON the floor, her shoulders shaking. The last bit of rage drifted away, and without it, stabbing pain stole her breath. A sob stuck in her throat, and she wrapped her arms around her chest. Shattered glass filled her insides, and the jagged edges caught on her gasping lungs. He'd protected her? No, he'd lied to her. He was a … How could he have fooled her so completely? Something in her soul should've known, should've rebelled. How could she have fallen for a man who killed people for a living?

Emotions flickered through her. Fear, self-doubt, shame, and grief. The grief cut the deepest. She pushed it down and bit back another cry.

Jakob thrust a wad of napkins in front of her face and sat down beside her. She mopped at her tears as he draped an arm around her shoulders.

"I heard everything."

Her gaze shot up to his. The sympathy in his familiar eyes brought another wave of emotion, and she buried her face in his chest. He patted her back, the robotic motion communicating his awkwardness. Jakob had always taken her pain on himself, listening and protecting. She lurched back and grasped his shoulders.

"You can't let anyone know you know. No one else can know." Her fingers dug deeper. "Please, Jake, for me. You have to promise. You won't take matters into your own hands. You won't, right?"

"Come on. Let's go to your room. This isn't the place to be talking about this." He pulled her to her feet, but she stood firm.

"Jakob, promise me."

"Maddie, we need to go to your room. We can talk about what's going to happen there. Taylor will be home any minute, and you aren't ready to answer her questions."

The nickname softened her pain. When had her little brother become a man? She nodded and followed him toward her room. She huddled in the pile of pillows on her bed and jerked the comforter around her.

Jakob sat cross-legged in front of her. "I promise not to seek Noah out, but …" He held up a hand to stop her. "But if he shows up here, if he pushes you, I'm going to talk to him."

"I don't think he'll come back. Can't you let it go?"

He raised an eyebrow. "He hurt you, lied to you, to all of us. I warned him. I have to look out for you. Since Dad's not here."

A fresh wave of guilt swept through her. How could she have betrayed them like this? "How did I not know?"

She pressed the crumpled napkins against her mouth, a sob building in her chest.

"No one did. He seemed real. His stories made sense. You couldn't have known he was lying, sis. We sure didn't."

She shook her head. "No. I knew the minute I saw Daniel, the minute the other one stepped into our living room. I always know."

Confusion settled over Jakob's features. "What do you mean?"

"Liquidators are supposed to wear that …" Her mouth screwed up. "Ring, but even without looking at their hands, I've always been able to identify one out of a group of people before. I know a murderer when I see one."

"Noah's not a murderer."

Her mouth fell open. She blinked once, twice.

Jakob cleared his throat. "He's a liar, but he's not like the man who killed Mom and Dad. He's not cold or vengeful. He kept you safe despite your … transparency. If he has liquidated someone, they probably deserved it."

She felt her face flush. "No one person should make those decisions. No one can be that objective." She twisted the pillow into an unnatural contortion. "Besides, it doesn't matter that he's not vengeful. He still accepted the Academy's offer. It's unforgivable."

The front door opened downstairs, and Taylor shouted a cheery hello. Jakob's eyes shot to the door. "What will you tell everyone?"

"I don't know yet." Her voice sounded small even to herself.

"I'll cover for you with Taylor tonight. Just let me know what you decide to say. And if you need to talk, well, you know." He walked over to the door, pausing halfway through. "I'm sorry he hurt you, Maddie. It won't happen again."

The last semblance of control left with him. She crawled beneath the covers and held a pillow to her face, muffling the sobs. What would she tell everyone? How would she keep this sealed up inside?

Why couldn't Noah have been who he claimed? Why did he have to be one of them? She curled into a tighter ball, wishing she could go back to this morning when she hadn't known the truth. Then, she wouldn't have the image of his tortured face seared into her mind. She wouldn't hate herself for wanting to forgive him.

*

Noah stumbled into the dark hotel room without bothering to activate the lights. He dragged his feet toward the bed and prayed he'd be able to succumb to unconsciousness and block out the sounds of Maddison's anguish.

"Exhausted after another day of saving the world?" Daniel sneered from the corner.

"Not now, Daniel." Noah sank down on the bed, head in his hands. He needed to be alone to self-destruct.

"Did you get broken up with, baby brother?" Daniel stood and walked around to look at Noah. Daniel's face hardened. He commanded the lights on and the curtains shut in a terse voice, all hints of mocking gone. "You told her."

"I'm not doing this with you. Go play your game with someone else." Noah collapsed on his back.

"What did you tell her?" Daniel took a step closer. "What does she know, Noah?"

Noah sighed. "She knows who I am and why I'm here. Happy? Close the door behind you."

Daniel cursed. "This is serious. Why did you tell her?" He paced the room. "What did you think could be gained by coming clean? Now, you're in danger of being exposed."

"She's not going to tell anyone." Noah scrubbed his hands over his face. Why wouldn't Daniel leave so he could release the pressure building behind his eyes?

"Did she promise before or after you dropped the bomb?"

"Why do you care?"

"You know, this whole throwing your life away thing? It's getting old. Now I have to save it. Again. Without thanks. Again." He headed for the door.

It took half a second for his meaning to hit Noah.

He sprang to his feet and grabbed Daniel's arm. "You're not going near her."

Daniel shook him off. "She can't be trusted to keep your secret."

Noah growled. "I said, no."

Daniel advanced on him. "Protecting her is going to get you killed. For once, turn off that weak heart of yours and think with your head."

"Stay away from her, Daniel." Noah stood nose-to-nose with him and circled a half turn around his brother to put himself between Daniel and the door.

"Maybe you should've considered my reaction before you told her." He pushed Noah. "All she has to do is say one thing to one person." Pushed again. "And it will get you killed. You'd better thank me for this one day when you come to your senses. I've done more than enough in the last four years to deserve a little gratitude from you. Now." A final shove. "Get out of my way."

Noah roared and tackled him to the ground, using an old wrestling move to pin Daniel to the floor. "You aren't going to touch one hair on her head. Because you'll have to kill me to do it." He leaned in, narrowing his eyes. "Still want to try?"

*

Noah pushed the pedal harder, speeding back across town. He had an hour head start at best. He had to reach her before then—because Daniel was serious.

Keeping her safe would be difficult. He needed to be in the same room with her, but Maddison would never allow it. He commanded the Mustang to call her residence.

Jakob answered. "You've got a lot of nerve." Ice seeped through the line and chilled the air.

"She's in danger." Noah's heartbeat echoed in the silence.

"I'll meet you across the street in ten."

"Thank you."

He looked down at the clock when he reached her neighborhood. Good, only fourteen minutes had passed. They had enough time to plan. *Please, let her house be secure.*

He slowed to a stop and got out of the car. Jakob stood

from the curb, brushing off his pants. Noah showed Jakob his vidcom then dropped it inside the car. He held out his hand for Jakob's.

Jakob opened the passenger side door and dropped his vidcom into the seat. Both doors slammed. "The minute she's safe, you'd better give me an explanation for what you've done."

He walked around the car to join Jakob on the curb. "Fair enough. You know?"

"Everything. What's going on?"

A tremor ran down Noah's spine. "You need to keep that quiet."

He huffed. "I'm not going to out you."

"No, you don't understand." Noah grasped his arm. "I don't want you on anyone's radar."

"You mean, your brother's?" Jakob shook Noah's hand off, his tone dry. "Come on, I'm not stupid. You came clean two hours ago. Unless our house is actively tapped, the one person with a reason to hurt her is your brother."

Noah nodded, clenching his fists. His knuckles turned white. "He'll have to go through me first."

Jakob studied him. After a minute, something relaxed in his face. "So, what's your plan?"

"How secure is your house?"

"It's old, but Dad had the security features updated every couple of years. The house goes into lockdown if anyone tries to tamper with a window or door. But that won't keep him out if he's determined."

"I don't need the house to keep him out. I just need it to

alert me to his presence. I can monitor everything from my position here. I won't give him a chance to get inside. It'll be harder when she leaves. She should never be alone in public. I can shadow her, but if she tries to lose me ..."

"I'll talk to her."

He released a deep breath. "I'll keep my distance, as much as I can, but if I think there's a threat ... well, I make no promises." His eyes scanned the quiet neighborhood for anything abnormal.

"What set him off?"

"That I told her the truth. He thinks she'll tell someone." Everything that had happened in the last twenty-four hours pushed Noah's shoulders to the ground. He straightened, took a deep breath. Falling apart would have to wait.

"So he wants to get to her first? Didn't you tell him she'll keep your secret?"

"Tried, but he wouldn't believe me. It doesn't matter. I won't let him near her."

Jakob chewed on his bottom lip. "Can he be stopped?"

"Once he knows I'm serious he'll give up. He needs to see I'm going to do everything I can to keep her safe, no matter how long it takes. Killing me to get to her defeats his purpose. At least I think it does."

"What do you mean his purpose?" Jakob's gaze zeroed in on Noah. "Wait, does he think her outing you would put you in danger? Is this some twisted form of brotherly protection?"

"Yes."

"Does it?"

He looked back over at Jakob. "Does it what?"

"Does her knowing put you in danger too?"

"I can take care of myself."

Jakob leveled him with a glare very much like his sister's. "Answer my question."

He nodded. "But it's my problem, Jakob."

"Maybe, but it's good information for me to have. I'd better get back, but you're going to need my number." He pulled out his vidcom, and Noah did the same. Once the devices faced each other, the information transferred in three seconds. Noah dropped his back into the car.

"Thank you, Jakob."

"You'll be here?"

"I'm not moving."

Jakob started toward the house then turned. "What about curfew?"

"Doesn't apply to me. I'll be here as long as it takes."

CHAPTER FIFTEEN

SUNLIGHT STREAMED AROUND the sides of the curtains, blinding her. Maddison slammed her eyes shut and burrowed deeper into the blue chair. She took a deep breath, searching for a hint of the sandalwood cologne her dad used to wear. She could almost pretend he held her in his arms. Almost, but not quite. Why couldn't he be here? She really wanted her daddy.

To her left, Jakob muttered something unintelligible. She squinted one eye open as he shifted, closer to the edge of the couch. A twinge of joy pulled a corner of her mouth up. At least she had Jakob. He hadn't left her side since telling her the news. She tried to stare through the door. Was Noah still parked across the street? A stab of pain twisted in her chest, and she fought back a new round of tears. When had life become so complicated?

When Jakob had burst back into her room with the news that Noah sat across the street in his car, fury and betrayal fought for dominance. She didn't want Noah outside her house or anywhere near her. And Jakob's blatant disregard for her wishes opened a fresh wound. Until he told her about Daniel's threat. Fear released a deluge of icy liquid, washing everything else in its path away.

"Are you sure Noah's telling the truth?" The question had an alkaline taste to it. He wouldn't lie about her safety, not now, but another lie seemed better than reality.

"You didn't see his face, Maddie."

Jakob told her about Noah's plan, and she had to admit it made her feel better to know he stood guard. Noah still made her feel safe. It didn't change anything, but it would help her sleep.

Or so she thought.

She'd tossed and turned for hours, seeing Daniel's mocking face every time she closed her eyes. Finally, she gave up and started downstairs to make some tea. When she opened her door, there lay her little brother, asleep on the floor. They had gone down to the kitchen together, deciding on hot cocoa instead of the cinnamon rooibos she craved. She confessed her inability to sleep, and he suggested they pull up a season of *Confidence* from the VisEnt archives for a marathon. Her favorite show about a con man always made her laugh, so he didn't have to twist her arm. Halfway through season one, she'd drifted off to sleep.

Her sleep must've been nightmare free, or Jakob would've woken her. Looking over at him now, so young and innocent in his sleep, she pondered his very grown-up behavior in the last twelve hours. He'd been her rock. What would she do without him? She hoped she'd never have to find out. Stretching, she stood and folded the blankets covering her. Jakob didn't stir, so she left him sleeping and wandered into the kitchen.

A note on the table confirmed that Taylor had left for work and would bring home some Japanese for their usual Saturday night dinner together. Maddison groaned. Taylor would have plenty of questions about the situation if Noah's car remained parked outside the house. The fact that she hadn't already begun an interrogation served as a small miracle.

Oh well. Maddison would construct her story after a shower. Heating up some scones and pouring two glasses of milk, she carried one set to the den and set it down on the coffee table for Jakob. "Jake, I'm going upstairs to get dressed. Breakfast at your three o'clock if you want it."

He muttered something, stretching the kinks out of his neck before reaching for a scone. For such an easygoing guy, he sure could be a zombie when he woke up. She headed back to the kitchen to grab her breakfast before going upstairs.

She walked into her room, and the message indicator on her vidcom caught her attention. She let it continue blinking. Stepping up to her front window, she pulled the curtain back a couple of inches.

The Mustang hadn't moved. Noah stared right at her.

*

Maddison rubbed some moisturizer over her clean face, glad it didn't feel tight anymore. She applied some mascara and a coat of lip gloss with a pursing of her lips. Her rose tunic brought out a little color in her cheeks. That would help. She managed a somewhat believable smile in the mirror. Being put together did wonders for her attitude.

Coat of armor on, she went in search of Jakob. She needed a game plan and help to come up with it. Her foot landed on the third step when she heard the extra voices—three to be exact. Her friends. Time to see if the armor held up.

Sophie spotted her first. "Are you okay? We called and called when you didn't show up for breakfast. It's not like you to not check in."

"Jakob said you had a rough night. You aren't contagious, right?" Josh smirked, but his lowered eyebrows gave away his concern.

Olivia jumped up, pointing to the door. "Why is Noah parked across the street?"

Maddison stepped back. Would they see the bags under her red eyes? "One question at a time, guys." She glanced around for Jakob but didn't see him. He must be the one clanking around in the kitchen. "I'm fine, sorry about breakfast. I forgot and overslept. Jakob and I stayed up late watching TV, and I left my com upstairs." She turned to Josh. "And no, Josh, I'm not contagious, but thank you for the concern."

"And Noah?" Olivia tapped a foot.

Maddison frowned. Why did her friends have to be so observant? "He decided to stay there after I told him about Daniel."

Olivia opened her mouth, snapped it closed.

Sophie cocked her head. "And he didn't stay in the house, why?"

Maddison took a deep breath. *Here it comes.* "Because we broke up."

"When did you start dating him?" Josh asked.

Oh. She couldn't even really say they had. No matter how much this felt like an actual breakup. "Nevermind. That doesn't matter. I don't want to talk about it."

Sophie walked over to stand in front of her. "Did he hurt you?"

Maddison locked her arms at her sides. Her fingers might itch for a lock of hair to twist, but doing so would announce her anxiety to the room. "Soph …" She sighed.

"I'll make him leave." Josh headed for the door.

Jakob strode in, a towel gripped in his hand. "He's here for a reason."

Josh's head whipped back around, and Maddison laid a hand on his arm. "He's protecting me. Jakob and I agree he can stay."

Josh sank back into the chair he'd occupied, his attention flitting from Sophie to Maddison to the door. Maddison shifted, left foot to right foot. She needed a distraction.

Sophie raised a finger. "I thought you said Daniel wasn't a threat? Is this for your peace of mind or is something else going on?"

Maddison looked at Jakob for help. He shrugged his shoulders. What would satisfy them without provoking more questions?

"Noah wanted to be sure Daniel's not a threat. He knows his brother better than Jakob or I, so we ..."

"We're following his lead, until it's resolved," Jakob said, and Maddison sighed. Beside Jakob, Olivia clasped her hands in front of her and smiled.

Sophie's face didn't relax. "And you won't tell us why? Or who initiated this?"

"It was me. I ended ... whatever it was. He's not who I thought." An image of an onyx ring flashed before her eyes, and she shivered. "That's all I'm going to say."

Josh crossed his arms, his brow lowering. Sophie planted a hand on her hip. "You'll talk things through when you're ready?"

Maddison nodded. She wanted their opinions more than anything else, but she couldn't risk their lives. "When I'm ready, I promise."

"I'm sorry, Maddie. I know how much you liked him." Olivia's quiet, sweet words dripped into the tender places in Maddison's heart, and the sorrow rose again.

She swallowed it down. "Thanks Liv."

Olivia chewed on her bottom lip, crinkling her nose. "And I'm sorry if this makes it worse, but I want to make sure I understand. You broke things off with Noah yesterday, told him you wanted nothing else to do with him, and he still stayed outside your house to keep you safe?"

"Stayed awake all night too. He hasn't left since he got here at eight thirty last night." Respect rang in Jakob's tone.

"Wait, he broke curfew for you?" Olivia's eyes could not

have been wider. "How did he … he could've got himself killed! And he's not the man you thought he was?"

Direct hit. The shards rammed into Maddison again, reopening yesterday's wounds, and she stifled a gasp. Nevertheless, she stiffened her spine. "He's just not."

Olivia marched into the kitchen, returning a moment later with a mug of coffee and four steaming pancakes wrapped in a napkin. Everyone watched dumbfounded as she opened the door and headed across the street. She didn't talk long with Noah after handing over the breakfast, and when she returned, she zeroed in on Jakob.

"I told him he could come in and use your bathroom, shower and such."

Still no one moved or spoke. They'd never seen Olivia so serious before. She always flitted along behind the rest of them, happy to go with the flow. Take charge? That phrase had never been used to describe her.

Olivia came up to Maddison and wrapped her in a warm hug. When they leaned back, Olivia locked eyes with her. "I love you, Maddie, but you're wrong. He's exactly who you thought." One more squeeze and Olivia released her, turning to usher her other two friends out the door as well.

Within a minute, the living room stood silent and less three occupants. "Did that just happen?" Maddison stared after them.

"Pretty sure she's right, sis." She whirled to face Jakob. He held both palms held out in defense. "Hear me out. I did some research last night after you went to bed."

He couldn't say anything to erase what Noah's Class

One status meant. She rolled her eyes and walked past Jakob into the kitchen, sitting down at the kitchen table and looking out at the remaining leaves on the trees, stragglers one and all.

Jakob followed with his sketch pad. "I'm not saying it's okay he lied to you, to us, but I think I understand it a little more this morning."

She gaped. "How could it be okay for him to be dishonest about being a liquidator?"

"His superiors gave him an undercover mission, and we know he's been trying to protect you. Daniel's not the only one who might be unhappy about Noah's cover being blown. Being honest with you put you in danger, and he didn't want to do that. Kinda like how we aren't being honest with Aunt Tay and your friends to protect them."

She couldn't argue with him there. She didn't want to keep them in the dark, but she understood the need to protect the people she loved. If Noah had withheld anything else, it wouldn't sting this way. "But he knew how I felt about liquidators. He should've told me then." She hated the whine in her voice.

"Yes, he should have, but I understand why it was so hard for him to come clean. Honesty meant putting you in danger, putting himself at risk—not that he seems to take that into account—and losing you."

"Wait, what do you mean, putting himself at risk?"

"Turns out liquidators aren't as free of consequences as we thought." He flipped open the sketchpad. "I copied this word for word from the government website: If a liquidator terminates a member of the Elite, that individual will face a tribunal to determine the rightness of his or her actions. Furthermore, any actions which are deemed treasonous by the Elite will result in the offending liquidator's immediate liquidation."

He paused, letting the words sink in. "Outing himself would be considered treason by the Ministry of Justice and by CSE's regional liquidator, someone called McCray. I did some reading on him as well, seems like he's not big on second chances. It's not just a matter of protecting you or me. This is bigger than us, Maddie."

She stared down at the table. Could this situation be even grayer than she thought? Maybe the decision had weighed on Noah. But would she ever be able to trust his word again? And what about the fact that he had killed people?

"Look at what else I found." Jakob pointed to the middle of the page.

The paragraph in question defined entrance requirements for the Academy, the liquidators' two-year training school. She was familiar with the information about the Gifting and Aptitude Placement but not the score necessary to be drafted.

Noah and his brother were geniuses.

Less than one percent of the population could achieve that score, and Noah and Daniel had. Her brain struggled to realign its perceptions. She continued reading until she reached the last line. "Those who qualify to enter the ranks of the Elite must accept the weighty responsibility to serve without reservation. All those who are selfish or weak enough to refuse will be eliminated."

She read the words three times before their meaning sharpened in her brain. Her breath leaked out of her lungs. "Every placement's compulsory. How did that never occur to me before?"

"Can you imagine being Noah?" Jakob ran a hand through his hair. "I thought about it last night before I fell asleep. He was my age when they drafted him, and the one choice he had—judge or die?" His eyes rose to meet hers. "Then to live every day, trying to make the right decisions. Do what no one else wants to do. To do his job and still be able to live with himself. Just to keep his head? It makes me hope I score real low."

Jakob drafted into the Academy? The thought made her nauseous. Suddenly, even Josh's placement didn't seem so bad. Noah's ability to hang onto his kind, protective heart while fighting for his life was an anomaly she couldn't account for.

"That's a lot to process, Jake."

"Tell me about it."

A hopeful voice within her cheered at the idea that maybe she hadn't been wrong about Noah. However, it went against every paradigm about liquidators she had, so she silenced the hope.

"I'm going to go upstairs, I guess. Think some more, maybe rest." She stood and squeezed Jakob's shoulder. "Thanks. For everything."

He shrugged and smiled, his cheeks coloring. "It's my

job." She made it several steps toward the staircase when he interrupted her. "For what it's worth, he really cares about you. He made it plain enough last night."

She smiled a little and opened her mouth to respond, but the roar of a motorcycle drowned her out. Moments later, the motorcycle's engine died in what sounded like their driveway. Across the street, a car door slammed.

CHAPTER SIXTEEN

NOAH EASED OUT of the car, tense and poised, and stood on the balls of his feet. Ready for action. Slamming the door behind him, he walked toward his brother. Daniel slung his leg off his sleek E Class motorbike and turned to face his brother, a mischievous glint in his eyes.

Noah stood his ground. "I was serious."

Daniel took several steps forward, coming nose to nose with him. "Obviously."

"Then what are you doing here?"

"Verifying your seriousness." A dark undercurrent rumbled in his tone. He circled Noah. "You know, you've looked better. Those clothes could benefit from a hot iron, and your deodorant is past its prime too."

"What are you doing here, Daniel?" Noah growled. This time Daniel needed to know the line in the sand had been set with concrete.

"Well, after you so rudely knocked me out and left me tied to the hotel's shoddy desk chair—it'll show up on your bill by the way—I wanted to finish our conversation. You didn't give me a chance to respond after all."

"So respond."

Daniel stopped circling and crossed his arms. "You care enough about this Maddison chick that you're prepared to fight me, your only brother, to protect her?"

"Fight *and win*." Noah clenched his fists at his sides.

Daniel leaned closer. "I see. You're making her a weakness, you know. Don't you have enough of those already?"

"Not your business."

"Fair enough." He uncrossed his arms and smiled, a switch so unexpected Noah froze. "If she's that important to you, I'll leave her silence up to you. She doesn't have to worry about me."

"Thank you, Daniel."

"Hey, you're my brother. What else would I do?" He turned, and Noah relaxed.

He shouldn't have.

Daniel spun back around and landed a right hook on Noah's jaw. Noah went down, arm outstretched behind him to catch himself. Daniel towered over him.

"Now we're even. Don't ever start a fight with me again, little brother."

He turned to nod at Maddison, who stood in her open doorway with a hand over her mouth, before getting back on his bike and speeding away.

Maddison shook Jakob off and ran to Noah, who staggered to his feet. *Be okay. Please be okay.* She skidded to a halt in front of him. "Are you all right?"

Noah massaged his jaw. "Yeah, I'm fine. Wow. That hurts a lot more than when I was twelve." He rolled his shoulders and surveyed the area before returning his gaze to her. "You, however, might not have been. Why did you open the door? He could've made it to you in seconds."

Jakob walked up to them. "I tried to stop her, but the minute you went down—"

She planted a hand on her hip. "He hit you. I thought he might try again. I had to help somehow."

"No, you didn't." A muscle in Noah's jaw rippled. "I can take care of myself. Besides, punching me could've been a diversion to get you to come to him."

"But it wasn't."

He threw his hands up. "You didn't know that." He shot a look at Jakob, who stuck his hands in his pockets. "No jumping into fights alongside me, okay? There are too many ways you could get hurt. Promise you'll let me take care of things."

Like he couldn't get hurt? Maddison shook her head. "I can't."

He paced. "Won't is more like it. I'm serious, Maddison. I can't be worried about you." He pointed a finger at Jakob. "You explain to her why it's not a good idea."

Maddison raised an eyebrow at them both. *Dazzle me.*

Jakob took a deep breath. "Well, I think Noah is trying to say that if you had gotten in the middle of things with him and Daniel, you might've gotten hurt. If you get involved, then Noah's attention is diverted. He's got to be thinking about how to defend you and how to handle the attacker." Jakob shot a sideways glance at Noah. "I'd add that both of you could get hurt if he can't concentrate on Daniel or whoever else might be a threat."

She deflated a little. "I hadn't thought about that. But." She pointed a finger at both of them. "You two need to understand something else. I'm not about to stand by and watch someone I care about get hurt."

Noah crossed his arms and planted his feet, ready to argue.

Jakob took a step between them. "So what happened? Will he be back?"

"No, he won't bother you or Maddison again. I think he got my message." He rubbed his jaw again. "And I got his."

What was he talking about? "Your message?"

"My initial warning carried its own punch and included me knocking him out and tying him to a chair." He released a small chuckle. "Guess I'm lucky there aren't any chairs here." He sobered. "But he understands you're important to me. He'll leave you alone."

"You knocked him out?" She sounded like a parrot.

"To get back here before he could, yes. And I'd do it again." He took a step toward her, his tone softening. "No one will hurt you if it's within my power to stop them. That's the truth."

She flinched, breaking eye contact. The reminder of his

dishonesty felt like a bucket of cold water thrown in her face. "No one can hurt me but you, you mean."

His face contorted. "I never meant to ... I'm sorry, Maddison."

She brushed his words off, ignoring the guilt that rose within when she saw the flash of pain across his face. "Well, I'm glad we're all okay. I guess you'll want to be getting back to the hotel to rest. I should make some plans for our dinner with Taylor tonight." She turned. He'd call out or try to stop her. Wouldn't he?

Neither happened, so she continued to the house by herself and headed upstairs for another cry.

*

Noah felt human at least. He hadn't been sure how long it would take to feel normal again. Between the emotional upheaval with Maddison, the fight with Daniel, and being on watch all night, he'd been finished. He grasped on to his fleeting reason long enough to watch Maddison walk away from him and hear her brother deliver a promised but short warning lecture. Three little words—"No more lies"—but they packed a punch when paired with the signature James glare. He'd managed a promise, appeasing Jakob who nodded and followed his sister. The drive back to the hotel took forever, or so it seemed.

Four hours of sleep and a long, hot shower helped. His synapses fired at their regular speed now, which was good because he stood on Ben Yancey's front stoop, ringing the doorbell.

The door swung open. Ben gestured him inside. "Noah, right on time. Come on in."

"Thanks." He ducked his head and entered the den. One sparse overhead light worked against the shadows. Wood paneling made the room seem even darker. He gave his eyes a minute to adjust.

"Thank you again for the invitation."

Ben chuckled. "I do believe you might be regaining some of your Southern upbringing."

"My mama trained me well."

"Well, come and meet my wife. She's been cooking all day for you." He led Noah to the left, and they entered the faded yellow kitchen. A haze separated them from the woman standing at the stove. "Ethel, Noah's here."

From the fog emerged a woman with a blonde beehive, heavily lined eyes, peach lipstick, and cigarette dangling from her lips.

"Well, aren't you a cutie?" She held her cigarette between her fingers, giving him the once over. "Ethel Yancey, but you call me Ethel, okay, sweetie?"

"Yes, ma'am." He schooled his expression, hoping to disguise his shock. She looked like she'd walked straight out of a time warp.

"None of that ma'am stuff either."

Her attention shifted to Ben, allowing Noah to study her. He hadn't expected someone so beautiful, but he sensed a hardness in her that matched the raspy quality of her voice. "Dinner's ready, just the last dish to carry to the table. Billy here?"

"Think so, I'll go check." Ben headed in the other direction.

"You go right on through the archway to the table, sweetie." Ethel pulled on some oven mitts and reached for a casserole dish. Yep, time warp fit the situation to a T.

Noah entered the dining room with its own faded wallpaper, although a chandelier gave the room a brighter glow. Every Southern dish he could list—fried chicken, macaroni and cheese, collard greens, mashed potatoes and gravy, and biscuits—crowded the small table.

Mrs. Yancey carried in a green bean casserole. "Thought you might be needing a homecoming meal, considering Ben said you've been away from this part of the country for a while and are living in a hotel."

"Yes, ma'am." She shot him a pointed look, and he gave her a sheepish grin. "Sorry. You didn't have to go to so much trouble." There had to be enough food here for twelve people.

"Oh, this isn't trouble." She smiled and motioned for him to take the seat across the table from where he stood. "I like cooking, which is good 'cause when you live with your husband, two boys, and your husband's younger brother, food tends to fly off the table."

Noah sat. "How old are your sons?"

"Jeremy's fourteen and Luke's ten. You won't be meeting them tonight. They ate earlier and headed off to a friend's house for a game of baseball."

"How do they manage when it's dark out?" He and Daniel took any opportunity they could to play ball growing up, even if they had to get creative to do it.

She laughed. "I think they have a couple older kids shine their headlights on the homemade field."

Ben reentered alone and smiled when he heard the last words. "Boys at the diamond?" He sat down at the head of the table, and Ethel sat across from him, nodding. "Those boys would play ball 24/7 if we'd let them. Don't mind too much, plenty of hard choices once they grow up."

"Billy not joining us?" Her eyes shone. With hope?

Ben shook his head. "He said he'd be along in a few. I told him we wouldn't be waiting on him." He picked up the plate piled high with fried chicken and handed it to Noah. "Let's eat."

"Sounds good to me." Noah pulled a piece onto his plate and passed the platter on. Over the next several minutes, the three filled their plates, sipped sweet tea, and found new homes for the serving dishes on the table.

After a couple bites, Ben swallowed. "How're you settling in?"

"Pretty well. I've enjoyed getting to experience all MA-4 has to offer." He turned to Ben's wife. "Mrs. ... I mean, Ethel, this is all wonderful. Thank you again."

She blushed. "You're welcome. Better get another helping of whatever you like before Billy shows up." The skin around her eyes tightened despite her light-hearted reply.

"I guess you're enjoying floor two with your pretty apprentice friend." Ben winked.

Noah started. "Maddison?" He searched the other man's face for an ulterior motive but found none. Ben's heart rate was steady. No hint of nervousness. Still, Noah remained on alert.

"I think that's her name. Maddison James? Seen you two around the nurses' station, leaving the building and such, enough to make me curious."

Noah searched for the most innocuous response he could give as another voice spoke from the doorway.

"Why don't you ask him about his liquidator brother?"

Noah shifted in his seat. The tall, glaring man could only be Billy Yancey. Like his brother, he had green eyes, but the similarities ended there. Billy had light brown hair, a long face, square chin, and what must be a permanent scowl on his face considering the way Ethel sighed. He reminded Noah of an angry bull.

"Noah's our guest, and I expect you to treat him with some respect."

Ben's authoritative tone matched the one Noah used with Daniel. It worked a little better with Billy. He rolled his eyes but sat down across from Noah without a word and began filling his plate.

Ben turned back to Noah. "I apologize. Over the summer, an executive accused one of Billy's friends at the hospital of stealing some drugs from the pharmacy. He was liquidated."

"No apology necessary." Noah didn't need the friend's name. His dossier told him he filled Matt Dooley's CNA position. Dooley had been suspected of being a player in the local resistance. His death opened a slot at the hospital and, McCray had hoped, in the group.

Looking at him now, it was clear Billy Yancey was exactly the kind of person who would seek out involvement in the resistance. Noah's gut tightened but he kept up with the conversation. Billy would never be able to hide his involvement from Ben, given the elder brother's observant nature.

Which meant one of three things. Billy's anger management problems put him on the Elite's radar and his connection to Dooley kept him there. Billy was involved and Ben knew. Or they were both involved.

The first option seemed a likely possibility, given the way Billy glared at Noah and shoveled food into his mouth, his elbows resting on the table. The brothers' relationship could be similar to Noah and Daniel's with Ben being aware of Billy's involvement but not turning his brother in because of the familial connection. That felt like a stretch though. Letting Billy live with the family put Ethel and the kids in danger too. Option two bit the dust. So, either Billy just liked to fight, or the resistance counted both brothers in their numbers.

Easygoing Ben, part of the resistance? It seemed off somehow. But Ben was smart, perceptive, and unassuming. The kind of person the resistance would want on their side. Plus there was his connection to both Lynn Walker and John Henderson. Noah shot another gaze at Billy. Had Ben been drawn in by his impetuous younger brother? He needed more information, and the tension in the room indicated this might be his one interaction in the house.

"Ask me." He met Billy's stare. "I know you want to."

Both Ben and Ethel's heart rates jumped.

"What kind of man can sit across from a murderer and eat lunch with him? I've heard about it. How your brother's caused trouble all over the MA in the last three days, and how you followed him around like a little puppy. Makes me sick." Billy's face grew red.

Anger pulsed through Noah's veins. He used it to channel his energy and didn't allow it to show. "So, you were there? Saw it for yourself?"

"Who needs to see it? I trust the people who told me."

"You shouldn't." Noah leaned forward, his elbows fixed on the table. "Because if you'd been there, you'd know. I'm never the puppy. I'm the man who keeps my brother on a leash. I don't enjoy spending time with Daniel, but doing so means people stay alive and in one piece." He studied Billy. "He likes to stir things up, enjoys picking fights." He let Billy catch his meaning and continued again before the man could interrupt. "So I have the responsibility of making sure no one gets hurt."

"We understand that dynamic." Ben shot a silencing look at his brother.

"I'm not defending my brother." Noah kept his composure and turned his attention to Ben. "What he does is unforgivable. I'm saying just because we're brothers doesn't mean I'm like him. I've had to work very hard at proving myself to people, and I don't appreciate being judged because *he's* a liquidator."

Ben nodded, his gaze sharp. "Understand that too, son."

"If you hate it so much, why don't you take care—" Billy spat.

"Enough." Ben banged a hand on the table. "I'm sure it's for some of the same reasons I tolerate you."

"How about some dessert?" Ethel stood and headed for the kitchen without waiting for an answer.

Billy pushed away from the table, still glaring at Noah. "I'm done here." He stormed out of the room.

Ethel came back in with a chocolate cake and dessert plates on a tray. The china rattled in her arms.

"I'm sorry for ruining your dinner." Ethel had gone to so much trouble, and he'd let Billy rattle them. Sure, he knew more about the dynamic between Ben and Billy now, but it'd been at the expense of everyone else at the table. "You've been so gracious to me and worked so hard on this meal."

Ethel waved him off. "Coffee or milk, Noah?"

"Milk, please." Almost twenty-one and he still couldn't turn down the offer of milk with chocolate cake.

She smiled and walked into the kitchen.

Ben laid a hand on his arm. "You didn't cause the scene. It's hard not to let them get under your skin sometimes, ain't it?"

Noah chuckled. "You'd think all my practice with Daniel would make me smart enough to not even engage."

Ben shook his head. "If you figure out how to keep your cool, let me know."

Ethel returned with a glass of milk for Noah and a pot of coffee for her and Ben. Her heart rate returned to its normal rate, as did Ben's. In fact, by all appearances, Ben seemed completely composed. Only a faint salty tinge in the air remained. What exactly made them so nervous?

CHAPTER SEVENTEEN

AS HE WAITED for his v-compad to boot up, Noah went back over the evening again. Billy wouldn't be an asset in Noah's investigation. He'd already made up his mind about Noah, and there would be no trust or friendship built between them. Ben had to be the key. If Noah could figure out where Ben stood, that would tell him all he needed to know about Billy as well.

The calm, good-natured man didn't seem the type to involve himself in such a risky venture. And that's what it was. Even with all of the group's apparent care and planning, a rebellion here wouldn't be widespread enough—McCray would send every liquidator he had, and they would kill everyone involved. Someone like Ben had to be aware of the inevitable outcome.

Billy's involvement made more sense—the angry, single man had nothing to lose. Ben would leave behind a wife and two young sons. It would be too risky for him to be involved of his own volition. Noah needed to figure out if Billy had somehow coerced his brother into helping. But Ben had been the more dominant during their interchange, and Noah couldn't see him taking orders from Billy. He could, however, see him cleaning up after his brother's messes. Like Noah.

Where did that leave him? With a bunch of questions and no real answers.

The compad's screen loaded and projected on the wall across from him. He entered his password to view the secure files and pulled up a background search on Billy Yancey.

Billy's mental aptitude scores were average, his position at the hospital menial. He couldn't be the hacker—he had no access to terminals.

Pulling up the criminal record screen, Noah found minor infractions reported but not filed. Petty theft, minor assault, and rumors of anti-government slander littered his past. Why hadn't he been visited by a liquidator?

He entered a more complex search algorithm. It proved more helpful. Billy had in fact been visited, several times, by a stationary liquidator. One named Gary Bullard. Every report ended with a warning and minor fines but no major punishments. Strange.

He clicked on Bullard's name so he could set up a meeting with the man to ask his own questions. The uploaded page told him Bullard died of natural causes two months ago. No way to follow up there.

Maybe the ARL in charge of stationary liquidators for MA-4 would have more insight. Otherwise, he had no way of figuring out what had taken place between Bullard and Yancey. Had Yancey been able to pay the liquidator off? The practice happened, but Yancey didn't look like the type to have money for it.

Shaking his head, Noah made a note in the notebook to follow up on Billy's financials and make contact with ARL Watkins later. He pulled up background information on Ben and found his suspicions confirmed here as well. Ben had no criminal background. His record remained white as snow. The man never took a sick day, showed up to work on time, paid his taxes, and even attended PTA meetings.

Noah needed to do more digging. He opened the surveillance program and split the screen between Billy's bedroom and the Yancey living room. He didn't like spying on people he knew, but if he didn't succeed in finding the resistance himself, a lot of people would die, and Ben could be one of them, guilty or innocent.

A message notification popped up. Clicking on the message from McCray, he found what he expected. A terse e-mail demanding more action along with the threat of "help." Noah typed a quick reply and attached Billy Yancey's file. He promised that he'd made headway and reminded the RL about the finesse required because of just how underground this particular group had gone. He ended with his own reminder that the presence of more liquidators would only derail his progress. No help would be necessary.

He sent the message and left the surveillance program playing in the background. So many lives hung in the balance. And he needed to keep an eye on Maddison. And Callista. And Daniel.

I've done more than enough in the last four years to deserve a little gratitude from you. The words had been on constant loop in his head. What had Daniel meant? They hadn't even been in contact during Daniel's years at the Academy. What could he have done for Noah when Noah was sixteen?

Sixteen. His stomach dropped. No.

Daniel wouldn't have been able to … there was no way he could've influenced Noah's placement. He was just a cadet at the time. He couldn't have. But. Daniel had risen through the ranks quickly. Almost as though he had the ear of someone powerful.

No, it wasn't possible.

Dread multiplied. There was only one way to know for sure. He grabbed his official vidcom off the bed. "Call Ryan."

Ryan Lutz appeared on the screen before the second ring. "Hey, kid."

"You do know I'm twenty now, right?"

Ryan's dimpled grin grew wider. "Aw, shrimp, you're always going to be Daniel's annoying kid brother to me. Kidding about the annoying part, of course."

Noah rolled his eyes. Despite his climb through the Regional Classification Office in MA-16, Ryan was himself all kid. "How ya been, Ry?"

"I'm great, kid. Didn't I tell you we'd be ruling the world one day? I place 'em and the Seforés keep 'em in line."

He fought off a grimace. Yeah, same old Ryan. "Well, speaking of placing people, I need your technical expertise."

"Are you going to ask me to do something illegal?" His blue eyes twinkled.

"Ryan."

"Sorry. Serious face. What do you need?"

"I need you to check out my GAP file."

"What exactly am I looking for?"

Good question. "Um, it is possible to see who viewed my results and who verified my placement?"

"Sure, that's a breeze. I'd look for you now, but I can't access those files from home. Should I ask why you need me to dig up the past?"

Noah sighed. "It's probably nothing. I just have a hunch. I'll tell you all about it once you've seen the file. Okay?"

"Sure. No problem. I'll give you a call as soon as I get in it."

"Thanks, Ry."

"Take care of yourself. And tell your good-for-nothing brother to call me, will ya?"

He smiled. "Will do."

They disconnected, and Noah flopped back on the bed. Nothing would come of it. Ryan would call back tomorrow with nothing out of the ordinary to report, and Noah would feel like an idiot. But at least he'd know. Then he could put it out of his head.

And focus on the ten other things vying for his attention. Like Callista. He groaned. He should call her, but right now, he wasn't in the right headspace to placate her. First thing tomorrow he'd call. He cracked his neck and exhaled. The tension in his spine hardened like iron. Sooner or later, Jakob or Maddison or Lynn or someone else would fall out of his grasp and get hurt.

He couldn't keep this up forever. He wasn't strong

enough. If he'd made better choices in the past, he could ask God for help. But he hadn't.

Now, he would fail, and they would kill him.

It was only a matter of time.

*

Maddison stared at the clock, waiting for it to click over from 6:59 p.m. to 7:00 p.m., time to sign out. Time had dragged by without Noah's company the last two days. Angry with him or not, she had to admit it. Was she angry still? The more she thought about what Jakob had showed her and the night he'd spent parked outside her house …

But how could she trust him? How would she ever know if he lied to her again? He had fooled her the first time—couldn't he be pretending even now?

That didn't matter. Not today. She'd finally heard back from Ritchie. Through a coded message stuck underneath her windshield wipers this morning. They were meeting tomorrow night. She was invited. A week ago, she wouldn't have thought twice. But now? With Daniel in town and the knowledge that the Elite could tap anyone, anywhere? Now she wanted to be careful.

A hospital janitor whizzed by her, making for the stairs. The chatter on the floor picked up as well. She turned to the head nurse on duty. "What's going on?"

"I heard a liquidator showed up outside a couple minutes ago and has a CNA cornered."

Noah. Maddison didn't wait to hear the rest. She signed out and raced for the steps. Within sight of the exit, she jumped the last two steps and pushed out the service entrance door.

Daniel stood about twenty feet away. He held a man up in the air by his throat. *Not Noah.* A small crowd had gathered around the perimeter.

She sighed, relief trembling in her fingers and toes. Guilt pricked her conscience. A man was still in danger. What could she do? As she looked around for help, a weapon, some answers, a car door slammed behind her. Noah strode past, face fixed on Daniel.

She shifted closer.

"Let him go, Daniel." Noah stood, feet planted, hands on his hips.

Daniel looked over at Noah and smirked. He actually smirked. She wanted to wipe that look off his smug face and took a step forward. No, remember what Jakob said. Noah already had to focus on two targets without adding her to the mix. She pressed her heels into the ground, willed herself to stay there.

Noah stood his ground, and Daniel opened his hand. The man fell, choking and holding his throat, but he didn't try to run. Oh. Daniel's foot pinned the man's jacket to the asphalt.

"You're interfering with government business."

"What's his crime?"

"Insulting me." Daniel eyed the individuals in the crowd with a threatening glower. They all shrank backward but didn't leave. Maddison took another step forward when he looked at her.

Noah leaned down to talk to the hospital employee. "What's your name?"

The man's voice came out in a dreadful rasp. "Ralph Emerson."

Maddison groaned. Of course, the mouthy CNA from the fifth floor that all the nurses dreaded having shifts with. Everyone in the hospital described him as a pain in the neck. The story made total sense. Why hadn't he known better than to provoke a liquidator?

"And did you insult him, Ralph?" Noah maintained the same patient tone. The man nodded. "What did you say?"

Ralph's eyes slid away to the right, his head bowed against his chest. "Under my breath, I ... called him a power-drunk twerp."

"Not your best idea, huh?" Noah's question had to be paired with an eye roll.

Daniel waved a hand at the man. "See, he needed to learn my lesson."

Noah stood and crossed his arms. "I think he knows now. A near strangulation seems punishment enough, don't you think?"

Daniel shook his head, kicking the man to the ground when he tried to get up. "Can't have people thinking I'm growing soft. Then where's the respect for our Elite? They," he surveyed the crowd again and Maddison didn't lower her gaze, "need to know I mean business."

Noah's arms uncrossed, his eyes fixed on Daniel. "No one is going to die today."

"You don't even know him. What do you care?" Daniel pulled the man up by his arm.

Noah took another step closer. "I care because it's wrong. I won't let you."

"On what authority?" Daniel tilted his head and smirked again.

"Mine."

The smirk fell off Daniel's face. When he spoke again, he used a voice she'd have nightmares about. "I told you not to pick a fight with me, brother. This is not your business. Walk away."

"No."

"Then keep your distance." In a flash, Daniel stood behind the shaking man, arms wrapped around his head, ready to break his neck. "It'll be quick."

Noah lunged forward, knocking the pair off balance. He yanked the man out of Daniel's grasp. Emerson wasted no time getting out of there. Noah jumped back to his feet, but Daniel waited for him. Grabbing Noah by the arm, Daniel swung him into the stone wall. Noah's breath left his body in a hard exhale.

"I told you to walk away." Daniel punched Noah's jaw for the second time in as many days. Noah managed to push him off and deliver a couple hits of his own, but Daniel seemed unfazed, answering with a right upper cut that sent Noah staggering. Daniel took advantage. His fists flew into Noah's stomach, sending Noah doubling over in pain. Maddison's hands flew to her face. Quick as lightening, Daniel's hand sliced between Noah's shoulder blades, and Noah fell to the ground. He tried to get up, but Daniel kicked him in the stomach. Maddison's hands dropped from her face. Without the screen of her fingers, the scene sharpened. She took several steps forward, hearing Noah's warning echo in her head.

Daniel's leg swung forward again, but Noah's hands caught it and knocked Daniel to the ground. He pinned Daniel with his knees, hitting him in the face several times. The reversal sent Maddison skittering back toward the crowd.

Noah had the upper hand until Daniel anticipated his next move, dodging the fist and then head butting him. Daniel regained the ground he'd lost with added zeal, pinning Noah and throwing several vicious punches.

Maddison rushed forward, screaming, "Stop."

Daniel jerked back, eyes scanning for the distraction. He spotted her and prepared himself for her attack, but that hadn't been her plan. She knew she couldn't fight him, but standing still hadn't been an option. She threw herself over Noah's upper body and braced for the impact.

Nothing happened.

She dared a look up at Daniel. He stood motionless in front of them. For a moment, he seemed perplexed, but then his nonchalant mask reappeared. He shrugged. "I didn't want to get blood on my boots today anyway." He walked through the crowd, which parted before him.

Noah didn't move.

CHAPTER EIGHTEEN

PANIC CRAWLED UP Maddison's throat. "Noah!" She tapped his shoulders with the heels of her hands.

Nothing. He had to be all right. He just had to be. She scanned his face for eye movement underneath his closed lids. For facial twitches. For any sign of life.

"Wake up, Noah, please." She leaned over to listen for breath and take a pulse. Relief flooded her when she found both.

"Maddison?" His breath floated across her cheek.

She shot up and grabbed one of his hands in her own. His beautiful eyes blinked open, shut, open and took a moment to focus.

"Are you okay?" *Really? That's what you ask him? Idiot.*

His eyes locked on hers, and his grip tightened. "What are you doing here?"

"Later. Anything broken?" She looked him over once more. He did not seem placated. She didn't care. "Any floaters in your vision? Do you have feeling in your extremities?"

"I'll live."

Relief filled every pore. She wanted to laugh, cry, and, most of all, kiss him.

So she did.

When she leaned back a moment later, his free hand touched her cheek before brushing her hair behind her ear. The surprise and joy in his eyes made her want to dip down again, but he needed to be checked out.

"You didn't answer my question." His fingers trailed along her jaw.

"Can you sit up?"

He rolled his eyes but complied. Putting one hand on the ground to brace himself, he sat up with a pained groan. She shifted to put an arm around his back for support and waited for his breathing to settle back into a normal rhythm. "Do you think you can stand and walk? Or do you want me to have them bring one of the gurneys?"

His gaze flew to hers; something determined and fearful lay in his eyes. "I'm walking to my car."

"You were knocked unconscious." The instinctual response came out sounding hysterical, so she cleared her throat. "Which we can talk about later, because I'm not buying your 'Daniel isn't a threat to me' philosophy at the moment. You need to be examined. No more male stubbornness."

"I'm not being stubborn." He scanned the surroundings, including the remaining onlookers who hadn't moved a step. "They'll want to do an MRI. The results would be problematic." His eyes drilled into hers.

"Because of who you are?" she whispered. How would

an x-ray highlight the differences between a liquidator and a CNA?

He nodded.

She added this question to the list she would ask later and took a deep breath. Refusing treatment really wasn't in his best interest. "You could have internal injuries. Please let someone look at you."

"I'll be fine if you help me to my car. I promise."

She rolled her eyes. "Fine." Standing, she held out her hands to help him up. He ignored them, pushing off the ground with both hands. He swayed, and she stepped over, sliding an arm around his waist.

He squeezed her hand. "Thank you."

"You're sure you can make it across the lot? I could bring the car over."

He shook his head. "You're not in the system. I can make it, I promise."

"I'll hold you to that." The words slipped out of her mouth, catching her off guard, but she didn't regret voicing them.

He smiled, catching the openness in her tone. "You do that."

They shuffled their way forward, the silent crowd parting for them. She wanted to shout at them to go away. The gaping onlookers. Wanting to take in the drama of watching one man beat another to death. Even now, they kept their places. Like someone had scripted this 3-D event for their entertainment. She glared at them all, forcing each one to break her gaze in embarrassment.

Noah squeezed her arm, his face still pale and strained. "Don't be too hard on them. Most of them are in shock."

"Shut up."

He chuckled but didn't say anything else. That laugh released a little tension in her spine. The rushing adrenaline of the last twenty minutes began to drain away, leaving an exhausted numbness in its place. The image of him striding into the crowd remained imprinted on her brain.

The little voice inside her shouted the obvious differences between him and Daniel, between him and any other liquidator she'd met. Noah didn't fit the stereotype—he turned it inside out. She let the knowledge fill every part of her and embraced it.

When they reached the car, she led him around to the passenger side, waiting while he deactivated the locks. She opened the door and helped him ease down into the seat. He slid the seat back as far as it would go and swung his legs in, sweat running down his brow. She ran around the car, settling herself in the driver's seat as he opened the glove compartment.

"Would you close your door?" He pulled a small case from underneath the owner's manual.

She complied. "What's in the box?"

"The reason I don't have to be checked out." He deactivated the lock on the case as well and opened the lid to reveal a large syringe, several vials of clear liquid, and packets of alcohol swabs.

She cocked an eyebrow. "So it's a magical healing potion, is it?"

"Something like that." He lifted up his shirt and cleaned a small area on his abdomen. With precision, he slid one of the vials into the syringe then passed off the case with his free hand. He plunged the syringe into the disinfected area and emptied it. Inhaling a long breath, he pulled it out and looked over at her. "How much do you know about the physical enhancement program?"

She stared at him. "Only the rumors."

"They probably aren't rumors. We're chosen for being smart and strong, the top tenth of a percentile in both physical ability and mental processing, but to further the propaganda and maintain control, candidates undergo a steroid and DNA-based regimen. It's designed to heighten abilities and enhance strength to the cellular level. We are stronger and faster than anyone else. Our senses are perfected as well."

Memories flashed through her. "That's how you took John Henderson down so quickly. And your ability to balance all those dishes while clearing the table. I've been so jealous of that."

He chuckled.

"What else?"

His eyes lit with boyish excitement. "I can pinpoint your vanilla perfume from thirty feet away and lift two hundred fifty pounds without breaking a sweat."

Two hundred and fifty pounds? Her hearing must be malfunctioning. "Serious?"

He nodded.

"Well, I'm drafting you to carry the Christmas boxes down from the attic then." Again, the words escaped without being checked, and she opened her mouth to correct them. Shut it. She did want him, alive and well, to be a part of Christmas this year. Why deny it?

"You're taking this well. You name the day, and I'll move anything you want me to."

Reaching over to take his hand in hers, she returned his smile. "The thirteenth. Jakob's birthday is the twelfth, and we've always waited until the day after to put up the tree, decorations, and stuff. That falls on Friday this year."

"Done," he said with a nod. The color returned to his face as they spoke, the sweat gone from his forehead.

"So." She tapped their hands on the box still sitting in her lap. "What does your super strength have to do with this?"

"It's an experimental regenerative drug. It boosts the immune system and speeds tissue repair."

Her mouth gaped open; she stared down at the closed box. "It *is* a healing serum."

"It speeds the natural process up. I'll still be bruised and sore but not for as long." Noah sat up in his seat, stretched, and twisted, wincing for a millisecond. "It helps he didn't break any bones."

He couldn't be serious. "You say that like he did you a favor. He still knocked you unconscious. I thought you said he wasn't a physical threat."

"He wasn't … isn't, I'm not sure." He frowned. His forehead creased. "Can we talk about this somewhere else? I don't want any company."

She looked in the rearview. A couple of stragglers still stood at the corner between the employee lot and the ER entrance. "We'll go to my house. Jakob's there, but Taylor's working today." She adjusted the seat and mirrors so she could see. "Okay?"

"Perfect. That'll give you and Jakob the chance to ask whatever you want." He leaned his head against the headrest and closed his eyes. "It'll be nice to be honest with someone besides Daniel for once."

He sounded worn down, discouraged. It must be exhausting to have to keep parts of yourself secret. To carry that burden. An image of Josh's blistered flesh flashed through her mind. The Elite wrecked more than she'd known.

"We're still going to talk about how you got involved."

She rolled her eyes. "When we get to the house. Wanna start the car?"

*

Jakob pointed a thumb toward the kitchen. "You sure you don't want an ice pack for your jaw?"

Noah shook his head. Pain exploded and radiated down his neck. *Don't cringe.* He took a deep breath. "Couldn't talk with it." He shifted on the couch, one hand against his ribs while the other readjusted the pillow he leaned against.

From her spot beside him on the couch, Maddison raised an eyebrow. "You could use it and some rest. You've already lectured me on getting involved. We can talk about Daniel later."

"I wouldn't rest, just lie here and try to figure out Daniel's motivation. I might as well talk it out with you guys." His initial surprise and anger at Daniel swinging him into the wall had receded. Leaving in its wake a nagging concern. What didn't he know? Why the sudden shift in Daniel's boundaries? "Something else has to be going on. Something I haven't pieced together yet."

"What do you mean?" Jakob leaned forward in his chair.

"It doesn't make sense. He loves to make my life miserable, but he's never done more than throw a punch at me. I mean, we fought growing up and he'd overpower me, put me in my place." He tapped a finger on his leg. "But not this, and he's never physically fought me over a punishment before." He wanted to stand and pace, but even the thought exhausted him.

"Do you think it's because you provoked him in front of so many people? That he just lost it?" Jakob asked.

Noah ran a hand over his face. "No, he was in complete control."

"Which makes it worse." Maddison's face bloomed with color.

"No, he aimed like he wanted to cause minimal damage. And he was moving slower than normal as well, we both were."

"This is minimal damage?" She crossed her arms across her chest.

"He could have killed me. He's been taught all of the ways to do it, in three moves or less. I'm just as strong, but he knew I didn't consider him a lethal threat and that I couldn't use my enhanced senses. If he'd wanted to cause permanent damage, he would've."

So, why? Was it payback for his loyalty to Maddison?

That didn't seem right, but what other reason would Daniel have for provoking a fight with him?

"That's more than necessary," Maddison said. "I know he's your brother, but I think you need to start considering he's lethal, even to you."

"There's something else. I know it."

Jakob clapped his hands together and swiveled to lock eyes with Noah. "Does he know the specifics of your mission? Could this be related somehow?"

"Maybe? But I don't know how."

"What exactly is your mission?"

Telling them meant sharing his deadline, something he didn't want anyone to know, but he'd promised not to lie. He stared over at the vidwall's right hand corner, making sure they'd disconnected it, for the fifth time.

"Coastal South East has a resistance, a volatile one, that got the attention of the Council. It started out with computer hacks and some vandalism, but they've escalated. They bombed their last target. I was sent in to find and infiltrate them before February seventeenth."

"They've hurt people?"

"What happens February seventeenth?" Jakob's question overlapped with Maddison's disbelieving one.

Noah gave Maddison his full attention. "Yes. I've seen the reports."

She shook her head, trying to come to grips with the idea he guessed. "What happens in February?" Her repetition was a whisper.

Deep breath. "RL McCray wants me to liquidate everyone involved or he'll liquidate me."

"What?!" Jakob shot to his feet.

"Noah!"

"Well, I'm not going to do it."

Maddison grabbed his hand. "No. I … know. But you can't …"

Jakob paced. "So what is your plan then?" The tension in the room was palpable.

"I knew my days were numbered even before this." He squeezed Maddison's hand. "They haven't been happy with my approach from day one. The mission only gave me an exact date to plan for. If I'd outright refused, McCray would've initiated plan B. It would've been a blood bath." Recognizable dead bodies piled up in his head. He pushed the thought away. Not helpful. "So I've been working to clear as many people as possible. I might not be able to save everyone, but I can make sure no one innocent gets liquidated."

Jakob stopped pacing. "And you?"

He met the teenager's gaze straight on. "McCray was very clear, Jakob."

Maddison tugged on his hand. Hard. "Noah."

He huffed. "I don't want to die, okay? But the only way McCray is going to let me live is if I liquidate everyone involved with the resistance. And I'm not, I won't do that."

Their faces fell. Jakob sank back into his chair.

Maddison twirled a strand of hair, pulled it tight. "Think outside the box. Not probable, but possible. Just for a minute."

He sighed. "I've done all this. Over and over again."

Her gaze hardened. "What's the most likely scenario that includes you being alive on February eighteenth?"

"If," he stressed the word. "I could find them, I might be able to punish and scare the lower ranks into giving up and keeping quiet. I'd have to build an airtight case proving to the Council and McCray that the people who built the bombs and started the fire were the only ones involved. If I could do that, they might let me live."

Maddison's face lit up.

"But."

The light went out.

"I'd have to liquidate the people I took to McCray. I don't know that …"

Jakob leaned forward, arms on his knees. "Even though they've hurt people themselves."

Andrew's face. Noah blinked. Gone. He couldn't add to the list. "I don't think so, Jake."

"We'll have to keep thinking then." Jakob shook the hair out of his face. "Back to the more immediate problem. Does Daniel know about the deadline?"

"No. If he knew…" Noah cringed, and pain shot through his ribs. Bad idea. "You saw how he reacted before. Daniel can't know."

Maddison continued twining the strand of hair through her fingers. "Would McCray have told him?"

"I don't think so." Then he remembered Daniel's cryptic remark from the first night. "Wait, he has his own orders.… McCray thought he might be useful."

"If a number of the hospital employees are part of the resistance, the fight today would be enough to clarify where you stand and grant you some respect with them."

Noah stared at Jakob. How had he not thought of that first? Maybe it was the bass drum pounding in his head. "Sounds about right."

Maddison threw her hands up in the air. "That sounds crazy to me."

"No, it makes sense."

Her arms trembled, her face a shade lighter than normal.

He reached over to capture one of her hands. "You're scared for me again."

She nodded, her eyes filling with tears, and he pulled her closer, ignoring the stab of pain running down his side.

"What if we can't ... what if you're wrong about Daniel?"

"I'm not." He wrapped an arm around her shoulders.

"How do you know?"

"Because Daniel's protectiveness is the one thing that's never changed."

CHAPTER NINETEEN

"TELL ME ABOUT him then. The before Daniel."

Noah sighed. How far back would he have to go to give her a true sense of the brother he remembered? Seven years? Too long.

Jakob stood. "I'm going to head out before I have to endure any more PDA."

Maddison straightened. "You don't have to go."

He waved her off. "I know all of the important stuff, and Noah can give me the condensed version of this later on. Besides, somebody's got to figure out what we're eating for dinner." He headed for the kitchen.

"He's very mature, your brother," Noah said.

Settling back against him, she nodded. "I have no idea when it happened."

"That's pretty normal, I think."

"Are you okay? Comfortable? I can move." She began to shift, and he used the arm around her shoulders to pull her back toward him.

The weight of her body did hurt, but he would never admit it. "Don't go anywhere."

"Okay." She reached out for his left hand to weave her fingers through his. "What was it like, being his little brother?"

A small smile escaped despite the pain that came when talking about what used to be. "It was kind of awesome. I've always been the quiet one, but Daniel drew a crowd, the proverbial life of every party. He could make anyone laugh—except our father, but I can't ever remember him smiling. So I'm not sure he counts. Growing up, Daniel could make our mom smile even on the worst day. He had friends everywhere, charmed the teachers and, in secondary, the girls. I wanted to be him.

"He's the one who taught me how to throw a football, to swing a bat, to fix a car." Looking down at Maddison who'd been studying his face, he wanted to convey how empathetic Daniel had been. "He was my best friend."

"I can tell."

"He scored a spot on the football team his third year of secondary school. He'd come dragging into the house after practice every afternoon, muddy and banged up. Didn't speak to anyone until after he showered and ate dinner." He smiled. "But after we finished cleaning the kitchen, he'd pull me outside and run drills with me. He'd plow into me, knocking the wind out of me, and then rib me when I didn't bounce back up ready for another play. I thought he just wanted to make up for all the times he got tackled himself, but one night he clued me in. 'It's going to be great when we're on the team together,' he said. 'The other teams won't stand a chance against the Seforé brothers.'" The brothers united—all Daniel ever wanted.

"So that really is your last name?"

He nodded.

She squeezed his hand. "What changed?"

"The day I entered the Academy, the day he graduated …" Frustration mounted, and he tried to expel it with an exhale. "Did you know that during the two-year training period, you can't have contact with the outside world?" He clenched his mouth shut, swallowing down the anger that flooded his throat. "It's criminal, that protocol. They did send word about my parents, but I couldn't see or talk to Daniel, not once, until I graduated. We had already gone two years without communication because of his time in training." He pounded his fist against the top of the couch. "They should've given us fifteen minutes, something. By the time I found him, it was too late."

She rested a hand on his leg. "I'm so sorry."

He kept his gaze fixed on the wall; moisture gathered in his eyes. "Thanks."

"What happened?"

His eyes slid shut, but he couldn't block the memory of finding Daniel drunk and unconscious in his trashed bedroom. The encroaching darkness, the shards of glass littering the floor, and the burn marks along the wall by the metal trashcan. He could almost smell the smoky after-effects in the curtains.

"On the day our parents were killed, the one person

190

besides me who could've saved Daniel, who should've cared about him, only added to the devastation. She destroyed him." Hatred flickered to life. He squashed the flame—it did no good to hate her.

"He loved her?"

"Very much," Noah whispered. Daniel had been so excited about his and Avery's plans the day before he'd been bused off to the Academy.

"He pushes everyone away so he can't be hurt again?"

Noah opened his eyes. Though Maddison's face still held skepticism and mistrust, a sympathy glimmered there as well. He nodded. "The problem is, I know who he used to be, and I won't let him forget it. I hold him to a standard, remind him he's going to account for his actions someday. That's why he pushes my buttons. It would be easier for him if I'd leave him alone or become like him."

"Would it be easier for you?"

"To leave him alone?" The muscles in his jaw and neck tightened on reflex. "Yes. He's less my brother each time I see him. That day destroyed something in him, but the way he lashed out in response—and still is lashing out—it could never be okay." The stiffness moved down into his spine.

She cocked her head at him. "What?"

"The thought of spending the next two months pulling him out of a drunken stupor or away from his ego-driven fights. It makes me angry." He wanted to hold the next words back, but he wouldn't. "Sometimes, I think I hate him."

"But he's your brother." Maddison gave his shoulder a little nudge. "And you can't let him go."

"He's family—all I've got. Somebody's got to look out for him."

"And you're all he has." She turned in his arms. "That's why he can't kill you."

"I hope so." He brushed a lock of hair behind her ear.

"Me too."

But what if … should he trust Daniel now?

"I understand. I wouldn't expect anything else from you." Her fingers slid over the bruising around his eyes. "I don't like him. I don't trust him." She paused and sucked in a long breath. "But I trust you."

He shouldn't do it, but he leaned closer, cupping her face with the hand tangled in her hair, and kissed her. Her hands fell to his chest as he pulled her further into his embrace and deepened the pressure on her lips. When his breath quickened, he released her. Her lungs must be screaming for air.

She sighed. "You're much better at that than I am."

"Not possible."

He rested his head on top of hers and let his eyes close. Her fingers ghosted over the knuckles of his left hand. "You don't have a tan line where your ring should be."

"It's on the other hand." He laid that hand over hers. "Third finger."

"Does it feel weird to not have it on?"

Weird? Never. "It feels freeing."

"Tell me about finding out, about being drafted, I mean."

He pulled her closer, needing the light she provided to go back there, to the worst day ever. "When Daniel's results came, I got nervous. I'd hoped to score well enough for Class

Three. Knowing what a small percentage separated it from Class One made me second-guess my plans. I wanted nothing to do with the Elite. I decided to fix my grades, not fail—because that would've been noticed—but bring my scores down low enough that I wouldn't be inducted."

"It didn't work." Her words were soft and slow, full of regret.

He shrugged. "Maybe the grading computers can spot cheating, I don't know. Both the physical ability and intellectual aptitude tests came back with almost perfect scores. It has to be due to the brain wave indicators and not your actual answers. That's all I can figure." His mouth turned sour at the memory of his dad announcing the results. "I'd never seen my parents so proud, both sons scoring in Class One. I wanted to talk to Daniel. He would understand, but he'd been at the Academy for a year and a half at that point. So for the next three months, I sat in my room and considered my options."

Her mouth fell open, and she clutched his hand. "Noah."

"I never wanted this. Never. But I told myself continuing to breathe gave me enough reason not to refuse. Lot of good it's doing me now."

"Don't say that." She sat up and held his face in her hands. "You made the right decision. Don't think anything else."

She didn't understand. Letting the Elite end his life at sixteen might've saved them. Maybe even God could've accepted him then. Before the blood, before wrecked lives, before orphans and widows … maybe heaven wouldn't have been out of reach.

He took her hands in his. "You don't know what I've done, Maddison. Lives aren't ever the same after I've visited someone." He looked into her eyes. She had to see the seriousness of his offenses. "I've killed. Other people don't breathe because I do."

"Because of their own actions."

"Not theirs alone." His head dropped. An accusing whisper recited the names.

Her hands gripped his. "Tell me." Her voice wobbled. "About your first … liquidation, I mean."

A weight dropped in his stomach. He'd never wished for a rewind button more.

Andrew's face, so like Jakob's, flashed to center stage. "He was fifteen." He sucked in a deep breath. "And distraught. His parents had been liquidated three weeks before." The similarities between Andrew and Jakob, between him and Maddison, hit Noah in the gut. He braced himself for her inevitable rejection, pulled his shoulders back, steadied his breath.

"Go on." Her nails scraped his skin, her hands so clenched around his own.

He widened the memory, pulling back from Andrew to see the larger scene. "I had graduated from the Academy and sped back to MA-16. I spent a month trying to sober Daniel up. Andrew spotted me coming out of the grocery store, loaded down with cleaning supplies, coffee, and pain reliever. I remember because when he yanked the bag out of my hands, the pill bottles bounced on the ground around our feet."

"He picked a fight with you?"

"A liquidator took his parents away without batting an eye. He'd been sent to live with his aunt and uncle who didn't want him. Life had spun out of control, and he wanted to reassert some power over it." The kid's shoves didn't even put him off balance, which riled the young man more. "He wanted someone to punish. Someone to blame, and I happened to be the first liquidator who crossed his path.

"I tried to calm him down, to get him to walk away." Noah forced his eyes up to hers. He needed to watch her face as he finished. "He kept pushing me. The constant guard duty over Daniel had left me exhausted …" Tension built in his shoulders as it had that day. "I didn't see his uppercut coming, but the moment he made contact, my training kicked in. The drills made my countermove second nature." He swallowed and forced the next words out. "I snapped his neck before I could stop myself."

Maddison's eyes grew wide and frightened. Something fractured inside him, and darkness clawed its way into the new fissure.

Her lungs stopped working. Her body froze. Her brain repeated his last words: Snapped his neck. Snapped his neck. Snapped his …

Stop!

She rubbed her hands over her face, willing away the refrain and the images—of her own rebellious actions after her parents' liquidation, of the young man who'd taken Jakob's face in her mind.

Noah's movement caught her attention. He'd stood and crossed the room, placing as much distance between them as possible. His eyes darted between her and the ground, his shoulders stooped.

She wished they could go back to before she'd asked for answers. She didn't want to know he might be dead in two months. She didn't want to know this.

It was a terrible accident, and anything but. An action that could never be taken back. Her fingers twisted a lock of hair tight against her scalp. She braved another glace at him and caught his eyes dead on. Defeated, broken eyes. He knew. More even than she did.

"Maybe I should go."

Everything moved in slow motion. "No." Her head shook. He needed to stay here. "We'll finish … talking. I just need a minute. To process."

"I'm sorry. If I could go back …" His voice broke off. She could almost see the pain oozing out of every pore. "I'd make it right if I could."

Of course he would. Everything about today, every action today proved it. She reached out for him. He came closer and took her hand, furrowed eyebrows matching his frown.

She pushed the words out. "I know."

"Didn't you hear anything I said?" He tried to release her hand as he spoke, but she clung tighter.

"Yes. And it's horrible. It's all horrible." She tugged his

hand closer. "I wish it'd never happened—I wish you'd never been drafted—but Noah, you aren't that guy anymore." He opened his mouth to interrupt, but she held up her free palm. "The Noah I know isn't a recent graduate of the Academy. He has honed self-control. He steps between liquidators and innocent people." An image of John Henderson arguing with his son. "He stops non-liquidator bullies from terrorizing weaker people as well.

"He has complete control even when that bully takes a swing at him. The Noah I care about, as he's so often told me, knows how to pick his battles."

He sank to the couch, his eyes closed. A shudder ran through him. His voice cracked. "He was just a kid. He needed help."

She ran a hand through Noah's hair. "So did you." He tried to pull away, but she held firm. "Listen to me. You, Noah Seforé, have changed my life, for the better. And I don't think I'm the only one."

In the other room, a vidcom rang, and Noah sat up. "I have to get that one."

She didn't release him. "Okay?"

He sighed. "Okay."

Noah walked into the kitchen. His official vidcom vibrated in a circle. The caller ID? Ryan Lutz. He picked it up and headed for the hall bathroom. "Hey, Ry."

"Noah. I'm in your file." Ryan's voice held none of its usual exuberance.

Noah shut the bathroom door and turned on the fan. "What'd you find?"

"There are no scores. In your file. No academic grades. No athletic notes. No psych eval. Just the placement into Class One."

Noah's knees gave out.

Clicking noises echoed in the background. "I thought maybe a set of files had been corrupted. Maybe a problem to do with your testing group or something…." Ryan's Adam's apple bobbed. "Your file's the only anomaly. Everyone else has a complete workup. What's going on, Noah?"

His mouth was dry. The room seemed to spin. When had he breathed last? He sucked in a long breath. Exhaled. The floor and ceiling righted themselves.

"Noah?"

"Who's been in my file?"

Ryan frowned. "The last two entries were Commander Westin, head of the Academy, and … Regional Minister of Classification Joy Barnhardt. That's weird. She never signs off on individual reports."

His stomach rolled. He forced another breath. It was true. Somehow Daniel had known. No, been a part of it. His head dropped back against the wall.

"Noah." Ryan's voice demanded his attention. "What is going on?"

"I think Daniel had someone fix my placement. I don't know how, but …"

"What makes you think that?"

"Something he said. About me being ungrateful for what he did four years ago."

"When he was at the Academy."

Silence filled the space between them.

Ryan sighed. "It doesn't necessarily change anything, hypothetically, I mean."

Blood pounded in his ears. "It. Changes. Everything."

CHAPTER TWENTY

MADDISON AND JAKOB stared at the bathroom door. The vidcom in the bathroom had been ringing for ten minutes. Something—else—was wrong.

"This is all you, sis," Jakob whispered. He took a step back toward the kitchen.

She knocked on the door. "Noah?"

No answer.

She tried the doorknob, not locked. "Noah, I'm coming in unless you tell me not to." Still, no answer. She twisted and the door the swung open.

Oh. Noah sat slumped on the floor, his legs awkwardly wedged between his torso and the bathroom cabinet. He didn't acknowledge her presence. The vidcom spun on the floor beside his hand.

"Noah?"

He blinked. She reached for the vidcom. His hand shot out toward it. "Don't answer it. Turn it off. Take the battery out too."

"Okay." She sat beside him and picked up the phone, following his instructions. "Who was it?"

"Daniel's best friend, Ryan."

"Did something happen to Daniel?"

A dark chuckle escaped him. The reality of it went against everything she knew about him. He shouldn't be able to laugh like that.

"Something happened to me."

Okay, she was officially scared. She grabbed his arm. "Noah, what happened?"

He turned to look at her, his eyes shuttered. "Daniel. I think Daniel got me placed in Class One."

No. That wasn't possible. He couldn't have …

"Ryan works at the Regional Classification Office near our home. He looked at my file. Someone tampered with it. Someone at the office or at the Academy."

Someone had deliberately put Noah in his worst nightmare? Not even Daniel would do that. Right? "How do you know it was him?"

Noah clenched his fists. "Friday night. When he threatened to kill you. He told me he had to save my life again, that I'd better be grateful considering I haven't thanked him for anything else he's done for me in the last four years." His chest rose and fell, rose and fell. "Maddison, we've only been back in contact for two years. He shouldn't have been able to do anything for me when he was at the Academy."

She needed to play the devil's advocate here. It could've been Daniel, but all of this info was circumstantial. "Maybe—"

"Ryan thinks Daniel could've done it."

Shit. Daniel got Noah into the Academy. Daniel made Noah a liquidator. That kid was dead because of Daniel. Noah was haunted because of Daniel. They were going to kill Noah because of Daniel. Her vision went red.

"I could kill him."

Noah shook his head and straightened. "Whoa. What just happened with you?"

Was he serious? She sat up on her knees. "Everything is Daniel's fault. Everything."

"Well …"

Her hands curled into fists. "Why aren't you angry? I want to punch him. I want …"

"Hey, guys." Jakob appeared in the doorway. She glared at him. "Taylor'll be home any minute, so um, we should probably shift gears."

She could do damage with her words right now if she wanted to, the anger felt that sharp.

"Maddie."

"Give me a minute." She spit the words. There had been too many revelations this afternoon. One too many. She closed her eyes and counted to ten. Unclenched her fists. Got to her feet.

She opened her eyes. Noah stood beside her. "I'm fine."

Sure.

He took her hand. "Come on, let's get back to the living room."

Jakob led the solemn procession. "What's our cover story?"

Noah kept his mouth shut but inclined his head to her. She considered the possibilities for a moment, searching for the best option. "We'll tell everyone the truth."

Both guys froze.

"That I overreacted about *his* arrival and lumped Noah in with him." She pushed the anger back down. "But he's not like *him*—parking outside our house on Friday night and defending a total stranger proved it to me."

"I don't like it." Noah shook his head. "It makes me seem innocent. Can't we come up with a way to even the scales a bit?"

"But that's what happened, minus what we can't tell them. Olivia already suspects that I'm to blame." Olivia and Sophie would chalk the situation up to Maddison's suspicious nature, and Josh didn't need another reason to dislike Noah.

"I think she's right." Jakob drummed his fingers on the back of the couch. "It's the easiest solution. Besides, we're talking about Aunt Taylor and Maddie's friends. They'll overlook a mistake of hers. You wouldn't come out of it so unscathed."

Exactly.

Noah did not look convinced. "Are you sure?"

She couldn't be more sure. "Positive."

"I still don't like it, but I'll go along with it."

"Let me do this," she said, giving his arm a light slap. He winced. Had Daniel hurt him more than he let on? How much pain was he still in? She put her hands on her hips. "Okay, you lay down. I'm going to go get an ice pack. You should at least rest until dinner gets here."

He opened his mouth to argue, but she deepened her glare and pointed his head to the pillow. Once he complied, she headed for the freezer. How had it never occurred to her that some liquidators might be different? That maybe some of them could be victims too?

She'd been so wrong.

Grabbing several frozen bags of vegetables from the top shelf, she headed back to the living room. Noah lay down, one hand resting on his left side.

"Can you take over the counter pain meds with that shot?" She handed him the vegetables.

"I'm fine." He held the frozen peas to the swelling on his right cheek and rested the bag of corn against his ribs.

"How much?" Maddison moved for the bathroom cabinet. He muttered something in response. "What did you say, dear?" She infused the question with a healthy dose of sugar.

"Four hundred milligrams."

She brought back six hundred and a glass of water.

He glanced down at the number of pills in her hand. "Are you going to be difficult often?"

"If necessary." She thrust her open palm toward him.

With an eye roll, he took the pills in one hand and swallowed them. He ignored the outstretched glass.

She smiled. "Thank you."

The lock mechanism clicked. All three of their heads swiveled to face the front door. A disheveled but alert Aunt Taylor came through it seconds later. Maddison took a step forward. She needed to head Taylor off, and quick.

Taylor brushed past Maddison and observed Noah. "I

don't know why you didn't seek treatment at the hospital but you won't refuse it here. I'm going to examine you." She stared at his pupils and grabbed his wrist to take a pulse. No one spoke or moved. After thirty seconds, Taylor released him with a nod and faced Maddison. "But first, I need to talk to my niece about throwing herself into a fight with a liquidator."

Don't roll your eyes. That'll only make it worse.

Noah began to sit up and protest, but Taylor pushed him back down. "Jakob, look after him. We'll be back downstairs before too long." Her tone brooked no argument. She led Maddison upstairs.

This was not going to go well.

Once her bedroom door had closed behind them, Maddison turned. "Noah already lectured me about getting involved."

"Well, hear it again." Taylor paced in front of the door. "I heard you rushed in and threw yourself over Noah. What in the world possessed you to do that?"

"Someone had to stop Daniel. Noah could've died."

"You could've too." Taylor's voice raised in volume to match her own.

"So, what? I was supposed to stand by with every other person and watch?" Her hands flew to her hips as she stood in Taylor's path.

"I just want you to think. You could've called for help. Or tried to distract his brother another way."

Maddison let the rage cool into a controlled and derisive tone. "Who would've helped? Did you hear about anyone else rushing out to help Noah or Ralph Emerson? Hundreds of doctors and nurses, people twice my age, filled the hospital, and no one moved a muscle to help them. The ones outside all stood by and watched, like helpless sheep." Her voice dropped another note. "Well, they weren't. And if you want me to tell you that's what I'll do when someone I care about is in trouble, you're wasting your breath."

Taylor leaned away from Maddison, her eyes wide.

Maddison's arms slid off her hips, and her shoulders dropped. "I will make you the same promise I made Noah and Jakob. I won't get involved unless I am one hundred percent certain there's no other option. If someone else will step in and help. If Noah or Jakob or you can handle yourselves, I'll make myself stand still and watch. Because it's what you want. But not if it means watching someone else I love die if I can do something about it. Liquidator or not."

Taylor sank down on the bed, her head bowed. "That's what worries me. I don't want you getting yourself killed trying to prevent something you can't. Like with your parents." Her last words tiptoed into the room, and Maddison leaned forward to catch them. She wished she hadn't.

"I know now I couldn't have saved them." She sat down beside Taylor. "But today was different."

Taylor sighed. "His brother did that to him?"

"Yeah." And so much more.

"How is he taking it?"

Maddison fidgeted with a throw pillow. With that revelation? "Better than I would be. But he's had longer to adjust to the idea."

"So, what about you?" Taylor laid a hand on her shoulder.

An image of Noah thudding against the hospital wall flashed before her eyes. Another of Daniel kicking him. Her throat tightened. She sucked air in. "He could've died, Aunt Tay."

He could still die. A sob forced the air back out. Fear clogged her airway.

"The fight keeps playing over and over …" Her voice cracked.

Taylor's arms encircled Maddison. "One little breath at a time. It's going to be okay." Taylor's hand moved up and down her back. "Take another for me. In. Out. Good. He's okay. Noah's okay."

After several minutes, her lungs quit screaming. She took two more deep breaths. The panic faded away. "He won't tell me how much pain he's in, but I think it's bad. I gave him six hundred milligrams of anti-inflammatory right before you walked in the door. He refused anything before then."

"I'll make sure he's going to be okay." Taylor brushed Maddison's hair off her shoulder and down her back. "How are you feeling about everything else?"

She brushed the tears away with a frustrated swipe. "I've been such an idiot."

"He doesn't seem to think so." Taylor smiled at her. "You know, I think that boy would walk through fire for you."

He already had.

*

Noah glanced up at the ceiling again. "They've reached a compromise."

Jakob laughed. "I bet they're crying on each other's shoulders."

"You sound like an expert."

"My dad gave me some pointers, but if you want to survive living with two women, you pick up on things quick. They'll get it out of their system and be fine when they come back down. You," he pointed a finger at Noah, "might be a different story. Maddison's bossiness is genetic. I think Aunt Taylor has a gold medal in getting her way. She'll only be satisfied with a complete examination."

"I'll consider myself warned."

A physical examination wouldn't be a problem. He just needed to avoid the computer-monitored tests and their ability to display the increased brain activity indicative of a liquidator.

"I have to take my placement exam next week." Jakob's voice held an anxiety Noah had never heard from him before.

Just a placement. His file. Daniel. His life. Noah pushed himself up into a sitting position. *Focus on Jakob.* "What tier do you want to score in?"

"Third."

The tier he'd tried to … No. "Education. What do you want to teach?"

"History."

Me too. He weaved his fingers together. "You know there's no way to prepare for the test. You heard me talking about that?"

Jakob slumped in his seat. "How did you know?"

"Lucky guess. You've eavesdropped before."

"Fine, you caught me." Jakob studied his hands.

He knew the answer but asked anyway. "Are you nervous about scoring too low or too high?"

"Too high." With a slow, circular motion, Jakob pushed his cuticles back. "What if I score top tier?"

Noah stood up and walked over to him. The fear was all too familiar. Realistic or not, it could still gut a person. Ignoring the pain, he knelt in front of Jakob and put a hand on his shoulder. "Then I'll help you prepare as much as I can. And on the day you graduate, I'll be waiting for you."

Jakob stiffened. "Couldn't I run? Go underground?"

Noah sighed and sat on the coffee table. He turned his back toward Jakob and pulled his shirt collar down. "See the gray bruise?" He pointed to the square on his left shoulder blade. "The day you arrive at the Academy, they insert a unique, GPS-tracking microchip under your skin. To protect their investment." He dropped his hand and faced Jakob head on. "To keep tabs. It monitors your heart rate, among other things. If you flat line, because of death or because you disconnect it, a distress signal is sent to the regional headquarters. A local team is dispatched within seconds. Their response time is less than fifteen minutes."

He rubbed at the tan line on his right hand. A tan line he shouldn't have. "I'll never be free of them, Jakob, and if you run, neither will you. Even if you could elude their grasp before being shipped off to the Academy, you could never stop running. The Elite are very good at hunting down their enemies." He locked eyes with Jakob and inclined his head toward the stairs Maddison and Taylor had disappeared up. "And they'll use every means necessary to do so."

Jakob's eyes dropped. "I wouldn't put them at risk."

"I know. I'm just making it clear: the one choice you have is how you handle your commission. So if you end up needing my help, you have it."

"Why?"

"Because you're important to me—and not just because you're Maddison's little brother. I promise, if the worst happens, to stand by you anyway I can."

Jakob met his gaze and nodded. "Thanks."

"You're welcome."

The doorbell rang, and Jakob shot up. "Has to be the pizza. I'm starving." He turned back to face Noah. "I can't protect you if they catch you off the couch."

CHAPTER TWENTY-ONE

SUNLIGHT SLANTED INTO the living room, casting shadows on the 3-D wall. Stupid shadows. Maddison groaned and pushed off the couch to close the blinds. "Play next episode." The "downloading from VisEnt" message flashed on the wall before being replaced by *Metro Seven*'s opening montage.

Noah slumped on the couch. "I still can't believe you've watched every season of this. Don't you get enough of doctors and nurses during your shifts?"

"That's why I watch them." She settled back into his side. "It pokes fun at everything absurd about hospitals. Like the cocky med school interns being instructed by the nurses assisting them. And, it still manages to be medically correct."

"Oh yes, please save us from an inaccurate depiction," he muttered.

She jabbed his side. "Nobody's making you stay, you know."

"I didn't say I wanted to leave."

"Last episode, I promise." She laid her head on his shoulder.

"Whatever you say."

His lips brushed her hair, and her eyes slid closed, grateful. He seemed so much better today. She owed Taylor big for letting her use a sick day to stay home and take care of him since he'd had to call in sick himself. Maddison reveled in the peace and quiet. No interruptions, fights, or tension.

Just the knowledge that he'll be dead soon. And that it's his brother's fault.

Tucking her feet up under her, she sighed. "Do you want to talk about it now?"

His whole body stiffened. "No."

"Noah." She pulled away enough to look at him. "We need to talk about it. You need to talk about it."

The muscles in his jaw were taut. "No, I don't."

He was like a high-end bank safe. Closed, locked, and impenetrable. The moment she'd gotten angry yesterday, he locked himself away. No, that wasn't quite right. He'd locked it away. Compartmentalizing better than any man she knew. Maybe they taught that at the Academy too.

A pounding on the door startled her. Noah's eyes were already trained on the door. "Expecting anyone?"

She shook her head. "Jakob's with Ethan, and Taylor wouldn't be pounding." Worried voices filtered into the house, two female and one male. Not now. She dropped her head on his shoulder. "Maybe they'll go away."

He chuckled. "Doesn't sound like it."

The voices grew more insistent, proving his point.

"I'm not ready to share you." It sounded childish, but the calm before the next storm hadn't lasted as long as she'd wanted it to.

"Come on, they're worried about you."

She paused the sitcom. "Fine, but I'm not getting up."

His arms tightened around her. "I wouldn't have let you anyway."

A laugh escaped. She commanded the door to unlock and raised her voice. "It's open."

The door burst open. Sophie and Josh elbowed their way in but froze when they spotted her and Noah on the couch. Olivia brushed past her friends and came to sit across from the couch. "Hi, you two."

Noah's lips curved up into an indulgent smile. "Hi, Liv."

Maddison's head swiveled back to him. "When did you start calling her Liv?"

"Just now. When she brought me breakfast, she told me she expected me to use it the next time we saw each other."

Gratefulness filled her. For Olivia's faith in Noah and in her. She locked eyes with Olivia. "Thanks, for everything."

Olivia brushed her words off, pulling her knees up into the chair to get more comfortable. "I knew you'd come around."

"Come around?" Josh shouted, startling her and Olivia. Beside her, Noah tensed, but Josh chugged forward, gaining speed. "He comes to town with a liquidator brother following, misleads and hurts her, and then gets her pulled into a fight with his brother, and you think she should 'come around'?"

Anger rose like a flash flood. She shot to her feet, hands clenched. "First off—"

"First off," Sophie said, "are you guys okay?" She shot a silencing glare to Josh, who deflated like a helium balloon.

Maddison let Noah tug her back down on the couch but didn't relax.

"When I signed in this afternoon, everyone asked me if I knew about the fight and recapped it for me. I knew the details had to be exaggerated at this point, but we hadn't heard from you, and you weren't there. I worried the entire shift. Maybe we overreacted."

Noah nudged Maddison, a bump asking her to calm down. She let her shoulders fall. "I'm okay. Noah's the one with the bruised ribs and sore face."

Sophie looked over at him. "You'll be okay?"

He smiled. "I'll be fine. Thanks for asking."

"So what's the real story?" Leave it to Sophie, ever the investigator.

"You know Ralph Emerson?" Maddison waited for confirmation from Sophie, who nodded. "The idiot picked a fight with Daniel. Noah had to get involved, saving Emerson's skin but riling Daniel in the process. I just rushed in and yelled at Daniel to stop. He did but had already knocked Noah unconscious at that point." Her last words didn't hold the uninvolved tone she'd begun with.

Noah squeezed her hand.

Josh glared at Noah. "Serves him right."

The blood rushed to her face, and she opened her mouth

to tell him to get out when Noah responded with a simple, "Yes, it does."

Josh closed his mouth and dropped into the chair. Placated, but only for a moment. "She could've gotten hurt because of you."

"I got word my brother had someone cornered. I was too focused on defusing the situation to note her arrival. But you're right—it would've been my fault if something had happened to her."

She shrugged away from Noah, and his self-loathing, and stood glaring at them. "You both are ridiculous jerks." She fixed Josh in her sights. "You, more than him. Did it ever occur to you that I'm a woman with a brain and self-will? Do you think someone lured me into this fight like a defenseless twit tied to some archaic train tracks?" Behind her, a giggle escaped from Olivia. "I weighed the risk and chose to get involved all by myself. I'm suggesting you quit making Noah the villain in this scenario because we have enough of those already."

She faced Noah, pointing a finger at him. "Quit trying to take responsibility for me."

The calm demeanor fell from his face. "Not going to happen. I'm not about to stop protecting you."

"Then quit trying to stop me from doing the same." Her hands fell to her sides. "I know you want me to stay out of the way, and I will try to respect that. But I won't," stupid tears filled her eyes, "I can't stand by and watch you die."

He stood, wincing, and wrapped an arm around her

shoulders. "Okay, I hear you." He pulled her closer. "I hear you."

But he didn't make any promises about the future. Her arms slid around his waist, clutching him close.

"So, I guess you two have made up," Sophie said.

Olivia burst into giggles. "The cuddling on the couch wasn't clear enough for you? I think your powers of observation are slipping, Soph."

Sophie threw a pillow at Olivia but laughed as well. Maddison and Noah joined in as they broke apart. Even Josh cracked a smile.

Olivia bounced in her seat. "So, what are we going to do now that we're here?"

*

Maddison waved at Noah and waited until his car disappeared out of sight before heading over to hers. She didn't have long before the meeting with Ritchie. She deactivated the locks and slid into her driver's seat. "Start ignition."

"Identify destination, please."

When she'd decoded the message yesterday, the address was one she knew well. The park at her primary school would be deserted at this time of night. Nonetheless, she'd parked a street away. "Two hundred Cedar Birch Way."

"Destination accepted." The GPS calculated her route and estimated she'd arrive at 8:58 p.m. Two minutes before the meeting would start. As the car pulled into the street, she glanced back at the house. Neither Taylor nor Jakob stood in the windows. Good. The last thing any of them needed tonight was another fight.

She'd almost decided not to go tonight. With Daniel's presence in the metro area and the threat of Callista's surveillance, not to mention Noah's injuries and revelations. But that's what made up her mind.

Noah. If they were going to have a prayer of keeping him alive, he needed to get in touch with the resistance. And she could do that. The rest of the plan would come, she knew. But first, she had to make contact with them, and she would. For him.

It was almost like fate.

She looked out at the houses as her car pulled into the neighborhood bordering her old primary school. They were all lit up at this time of night; the people inside going about their normal lives, unaware of the trouble brewing around them. At least most of them were.

Her car slowed down and pulled over to the curb. Across the street, two streetlights lit up a fenced-in basketball court. Several guys bounced a ball between them, but no one made for the hoop. A girl approached the court from the other end. Seven people in all.

8:59 p.m. This was it. She shut the car down.

Don't.

The admonition sounded like Noah's. Weird. She reached for the door handle.

Don't do it. Stay in the car.

Definitely Noah's voice, but maybe a little deeper? She

looked at her vidcom in the center console. The screen was clear. When had her conscience started sounding like Noah?

9:00 p.m.

She didn't move. The risk suddenly seemed much bigger than her justifications warranted. Noah would be furious with her when he found out. Stupid. Reckless. Impulsive. That's what this plan had been. No one even knew where she was. She should've told him or Jakob. They were supposed to be a team. She had to remember that.

But she was stuck now. If she powered the car on, her headlights would shine toward the court and draw everyone's attention. So she sat and watched the entire meeting from a street away.

When the meeting ended, everyone scattered. One guy walked straight toward her. He wore a long gray coat with the collar popped up around his neck. As he came closer, he shook blond hair out of his face. His blue eyes met hers. Brandon? His pace stuttered for a second, but he kept on going right past her car.

How had Brandon met Ritchie? And how had he gained an invite into the group in such a short amount of time?

*

Noah closed out of the surveillance program, opened the *Innocent and Uninvolved* file, and typed in the twentieth name: Barbara Whitlock. If only the list in his notebook wasn't three times as long. He cracked his neck and stretched.

Noah State's vidcom rang. He glanced at the screen. Callista. He answered anyway.

"Congratulations." Manic glee danced in her dark brown eyes.

"For what?" He got the feeling he didn't want to know.

Her smile grew wider, white teeth flashing, like a piranha. "Your tip. We caught them."

Don't react. "And?"

"Problem solved."

And that was why he hadn't wanted to pass his instinct on to McCray. At noon yesterday, a janitor had walked past him in the cafeteria whistling the childhood jingle, "The Wheels on the Bus." At four, he heard the same tune out in the hallway while he charted the patient in 204's blood pressure. By the time he overheard it in the parking lot that night, he had a decent hunch. The resistance hadn't interfered with anything in the Ministry of Agriculture, Industry, and Transportation yet, and disrupting the public transit buses would get plenty of attention and cause lots of chaos. He only called it in because a bomb anywhere in the public transportation system would mean major casualties.

When no phone call came last night or this morning, he breathed a sigh of relief, assuming he was wrong. "How many?"

"Only three."

Three lives. He sighed. "Did they have a bomb?"

"Not this time, but the hacker headed straight for the computer mainframe." She sneered. "They planned a metro area standstill, complete with in-vehicle entertainment. But thanks to you, we were there to stop it. McCray's ecstatic we got the hacker, bragging to whoever will listen. More importantly, that should cut the head off their organization."

"Unless they're like a hydra."

Callista rolled her eyes. "Please. This is a victory. Quit being such a downer. You need to lighten up. Take a lesson from your brother."

Pain erupted. Nope. Not going there. He had too much on his plate. He didn't have time to indulge in what Daniel's betrayal meant.

Callista tilted her head, and long black curls fell over her shoulder. She licked her lips. "I could come over."

Shudder. "No. You couldn't."

Her eyes narrowed. "Because of Little Miss Class Four?"

Careful, man, be very careful.

"Callista, I'm undercover. I'm not supposed to have any contact with the Elite. If the wrong person were to see you here, it would ruin months of hard work."

"Daniel can see you."

"Daniel's my brother. You know that's different."

She huffed. "Sure. Fine. Whatever. I'll just go celebrate with the rest of the team then."

"Sounds good." He forced a smile. "Have a good night, Callista."

She gave him a small smile in return. "Night, Noah."

CHAPTER TWENTY-TWO

HE LOUNGED AGAINST the hotel wall. Like an angsty teen idol, complete with dark look and leather jacket. Maddison quickened her pace toward him. "What are you doing here?"

His eyes danced. "I'm here to see my baby brother. Maybe take him out for a bite."

"What are you up to, Daniel?" She stood in front of him, arm cocked on her hip.

He threw his hands up. "Oh, alright, you caught me. I'm really here to snag his keys. Got a hot date tonight and need a car for the evening."

She narrowed her eyes. "You're here to pick another fight, aren't you?"

He stood up, leaning forward inches from her face. "You should go inside and wait for your boyfriend."

That stupid smirk of his ticked her off. After everything he'd done. Enough was enough. "No."

"Go inside, Maddison."

"What's your plan? You want to add to his three bruised

ribs, black eye, and concussion? Maybe do some permanent damage this time? Damage a kidney, break those ribs, and leave him in a coma?"

Something worked in his jaw. "You. Need. To. Leave."

"Why? Does it make you uncomfortable to be called on the pain you've inflicted on your own brother?"

"Stay out of it. You don't know all of the circumstances, and you could get hurt."

Like Noah?

"Oh, but I know enough. You make his life miserable because you can't stand to be miserable by yourself. For a while, watching him clean up your messes filled that sick need, but something's changed. Now you have to play with his head and knock him around too. Sound about right?" She might not have any physical advantages, but she had perfected the withering glare and steel-laced tone over the years. "What, it wasn't enough that you condemned him to a life he hates? It's not enough that they are going to kill him because of you?"

"What did you say?" His tone was ice.

She cursed herself. Noah hadn't wanted him to know.

Noah turned the building's corner. Maddison and Daniel stood toe to toe in front of him. A crack split the veneer inside him. "What's going on?" He fixed his brother with a warning stare.

"Your little girlfriend," Daniel spat the last word, "seems to think someone's going to kill you and it's all my fault."

Well, she'd be right. Noah's hands curled into fists.

"Maddison, get in my car." For once, she didn't argue but headed around the corner where he'd parked.

"Obedient little thing, isn't she?"

Noah growled. "You. Shut up."

Daniel took a step forward. "What was she talking about?"

"Did you get me placed in Class One?" Adrenaline pulsed through his veins. Part of him catalogued the fact that there was no one within twenty yards of them. No one to see him use his full strength. Another part noted the gravel scattering the pavement—he'd have to move with that in mind.

Daniel frowned. "What?"

"You heard me." He stared Daniel down.

"Noah—"

"Ryan tells me someone fixed my file. If you want my 'gratitude,' you'll have to 'fess up to it."

"Says the shortsighted kid who thought fixing his own scores was a smart idea. Class Three? Please. I saved you."

He would've been Class Three? It had worked? His right fist flew out and connected with Daniel's face. Daniel stumbled back. Noah advanced. Left hook. Right hook. An uppercut with his left. Daniel hit the ground. Noah reached out and grabbed Daniel's shirt collar, pulled him up, and hit him again. Once more.

Daniel kicked Noah away, using all his body weight. Noah landed several feet away. They both shot to their feet, circled each other. He and the brother who was the cause of every single minute of panic and regret in the last two years.

The brother he'd defended and made excuses for. He jabbed. Daniel ducked away.

Daniel spat a mouthful of blood on the ground. "Only you would be angry making millions of dollars a year and having unlimited power."

Noah lunged, his shoulder connecting with Daniel's midsection. They both went down, but years of wrestling training gave Noah the position of strength. "And the cost was just my soul." He landed a right hook.

Daniel used Noah's momentum against him, rolling them over. His face drained of emotion. His hand closed around Noah's windpipe. "I've been enhanced longer than you."

"Well, I'm angrier." He reached up and grabbed Daniel's hand, twisting and applying enough pressure to snap bones, then head-butted him, knocking Daniel off.

Noah sat up on his knees, leaned back. "Get out of my life." He delivered the final blow, exactly on target. Daniel lost consciousness.

He stood. Brushed himself off. Walked away.

*

"Hey, Seforé, wait a minute."

Evidently, his shower and evening plans would have to wait until he dealt with whatever John Henderson wanted. He about-faced and made eye contact with the towering man.

Henderson's mouth scrunched in disgust. "I don't much like you."

"Feeling's mutual then."

The man huffed, staring at the ground. "Well, don't change much, but what you did the other day … it was alright."

"Noted." Did Henderson consider that an olive branch?

Fierce brown eyes locked with his. "Don't make it easy for a man to own up, do you?"

Noah crossed his arms.

"I might've been wrong 'bout you. If you'd step in to help somebody you don't even know, you can't be that bad."

Noah let his arms fall to his sides. The man's demeanor irritated, but his intention seemed sincere. "I appreciate that."

"You run interference with your brother before?"

"More times than I'd like."

"He always beat you unconscious?"

Noah raised an eyebrow.

Henderson's eyes flickered around the desolate parking lot before locking gazes with Noah for the first time. "You have problems with all liquidators or just him?"

"Daniel is the least of my problems."

Henderson nodded once. His frown evened out. "Reckon Lynn read you right after all. You open to meeting some people?"

"Anytime."

"Okay, then." Henderson turned and sauntered away without a backward glance.

Something had finally gone in his favor. Why did it make his stomach churn?

*

Maddison opened the door to a frowning Noah. The pointer finger on his right hand tapped against his pant leg. What had happened at the hospital today? "Hey, what's wrong?"

Noah shut the door behind him. "Doesn't matter. Tonight I want to be normal: carry some dusty boxes down from the attic, put up your Christmas tree, and drink some coffee."

"I think we can do that. Wanna start with the coffee and some ginger snaps?"

His posture relaxed. "Yes, ma'am."

Once in the kitchen, she grabbed a clean mug from the dishwasher, filled it with coffee, then turned to face him. He leaned against the island, staring. Heat filled her face.

She held the mug out, and he took it, placing it on the counter beside him. His other hand encircled her wrist, pulling her into his arms. She rested her head against his chest.

"I missed you today," he whispered.

"Is that what brought this on?"

"Are you complaining?"

"Nope. Just making an observation."

He pulled her closer and buried a hand in her hair. "You smell like cinnamon and oranges."

"It's the orange cranberry muffins I made earlier."

His head dropped down again, and he kissed her, his hand cradling the back of her neck and tilting her head to the side. His lips met hers at this new angle, and he deepened the pressure of his kiss. Warmth spread through her, and she leaned against him, grateful for the arm around her waist keeping her upright. When he drew back, he smiled, his fingers trailing along her jaw. "Taste like them too."

She raised an eyebrow. "You complaining?"

He swept down and captured her lips again. "Making an observation of my own. Where is everybody?"

"Taylor took Jakob and Ethan to a baseball game for his birthday." She fingered a button on his shirt.

The smile fell off his face, and his arms slacked. "Did he say anything when he got home last night?"

Before she could answer, the front door clicked open. Taylor entered the kitchen first, arms loaded down with take-out bags. "Jakob wanted Thai, so we picked some up on the way home."

Jakob shuffled in a minute later, anxiety written on his face. "Do we have any coffee? I'm going to need some with dinner if you guys are going to boss Noah and me around all night."

Noah picked up his cup and handed it off. "Here. I haven't touched this. You start on it, and I'll pour another cup."

Jakob gulped some down and made a horrible face. "That's awful. Didn't you put anything in it?"

Noah laughed, shook his head. Maddison pulled the sugar container from the countertop and passed it to Jakob with a spoon. Taylor busied herself by sticking serving utensils in the containers she set on the island.

"Hey, why isn't there Christmas music on yet?" Jakob wandered off to the living room and the sound system.

Maddison took a step to follow him, but Noah laid a hand on her arm. "I don't think he wants to talk about it yet. He will, when he's ready."

Taylor nodded. "You're right. When Ethan ribbed him today, he always changed the subject. It'll do him no good to talk about it now anyway." She piled a plate with food and handed it to Noah before starting another. "So, let's get cracking on those Christmas decorations."

Maddison giggled. "Cracking?"

"Oh shut up," Taylor said. Strains of "White Christmas" filtered through the house.

"Are you guys eating without me?" Jakob poked his head back in and grabbed the plate being passed between Taylor and Maddison.

"Hey, get your own." Maddison tried to snatch it back. No luck.

"I thought I did." He gave her a cheeky grin and headed back into the living room. "Hey, Noah, you do know there are twenty-three boxes of decorations, right?"

"Is he being serious?"

Maddison pushed him toward the living room. "Of course not, it's just nineteen."

Noah groaned, but his eyes twinkled. Taylor followed them in with a tray stacked full of mugs, the coffee pot, a plate of cookies, and her own dinner. She sat down and addressed Noah. "What is your favorite part of Christmas?"

He put down his plate. A moment later, his adorable lop-sided smile appeared.

"Every Christmas Eve, Mom would bundle us up in coats

and blankets and give us huge steaming cups of cider. Then Dad would drive us around the historic district to look at all the houses lit up and decorated for Christmas. We had the heater on full blast and the windows rolled down so we could smell the fresh pine and hear the carols blaring from a house on the corner." He shook his head, a wistful look on his face. "My dad always tried to make it educational, spouting off about the historic nature of each house, but at some point, my mom would shush him and weave her arm through his.

"The last year we went, I was thirteen. Daniel was ..." He sank back into the couch. "Well, it was a long time ago."

Maddison reached over and squeezed his hand. He was so far from okay.

"Would you mind ..." Taylor tucked a piece of hair behind her ear. Her eyes darted around the room. "Re-creating your tradition with us this year? It wouldn't be the same, I know, but our historic district does the same thing. We'd love for you to celebrate with us and include some of your traditions with ours."

Maddison felt emotion creep up her throat. For Noah, who would've celebrated Christmas without anyone for the last four years, unless Daniel decided to crash his party of course. For her aunt, for making such an effort to include him as a permanent part of their little family.

Noah cleared his throat. "I'd like that."

"Great." Taylor brushed her hands off on her pants and stood. "I expect you to join us for all of Christmas Eve and Christmas Day as well." She headed for the kitchen.

Noah stared after Taylor. "Did she...?"

Maddison nodded.

He looked back and forth between Jakob and her in a daze. "Okay then."

Jakob bounced up. "How about we start moving those boxes?"

Noah's smile returned. "Lead the way."

CHAPTER TWENTY-THREE

NOAH DOUBLE-KNOTTED HIS laces, more than ready for his morning run. Waiting on Henderson or Nurse Walker to contact him about meeting had begun to wear. A faint buzzing filled the room. His official vidcom. Don't be Callista. Don't be Callista. Don't be Callista.

He fished it out of its hiding place. Worse. He accepted the call. "Hello, sir."

McCray's face appeared on the screen, vein in his forehead already bulging. "You'd better have some news for me, boy, because those terrorists torched five public transit buses this morning."

A reprisal for their failed attack on the fifth. He'd anticipated it. "Was anyone hurt?"

"No. They did a shoddy job for once. The depot was deserted, and the security guard alerted us before the fire drew any more attention. Stupid kids."

Wait, kids? How did McCray know that? "Why do you—"

"But a plan like that shouldn't have gotten past us.

Doesn't Westin train anyone how to do his job anymore? Bunch of incompetents." His gaze speared Noah. "You going to prove me wrong, Seforé?"

"I've only been in Metro Area Four two months. It's going to take time for me to build inroads and trust with these people."

McCray's face purpled with rage. "I don't want to hear excuses. And don't you dare lecture me. Need I remind you that two months from today I'm going to break your scrawny neck if you haven't fixed this problem?"

His stomach dropped. "No, sir."

"Prove it." The regional liquidator grabbed a bottle of scotch and took a long swallow. "Tell me exactly what information you've acquired in the last seven days."

"I cleared ten more hospital employees of suspicion. I continued my surveillance of Billy Yancey and several other suspects."

"Idiot. None of that is progress."

Noah bit his tongue but kept his face clear. He scrolled through everything he'd been doing. What else could he give McCray without risking anyone innocent? He'd have to give up Henderson. "I wasn't finished. Sir. On Friday, I was approached by a potential member about my interest in meeting with a group."

McCray slammed the bottle against his desk. "Why am I just now hearing this?"

"One individual asked me if I had problems with liquidators and would want to talk to some others who did as well. I don't have a place. I don't have a date. I don't even know if the invitation is legit. In fact, there's no way to know right now if this man is connected to the group setting fires and building bombs."

"What's his name?"

Noah straightened his shoulders. "I'm going to withhold that for now."

McCray cursed at him. The vein bulged again.

"With all due respect, sir, we don't know that he's done anything against Patrisia's interests. He hasn't even said anything disloyal yet."

"Listen here, you, you twerp, don't think because the Council signed off on this mission that I can't have you replaced. You aren't untouchable. You got it?"

Ice floated through Noah's veins. "I'm well aware of that."

The regional liquidator sneered. "Well, maybe not aware enough. You get me some results. Or even better, you give me a list of offenders in twenty-one days or I'll send in someone else to help you."

Absolutely not. "Sir, another liquidator won't help. The MA's already flooded with them."

"Well, you'd better have a productive couple of weeks then." McCray signed off.

Noah growled. Now he really needed that run before his shift. He threw the vidcom on the bed and pushed out the door.

All of his hard work would be wasted if McCray didn't back off. It mattered too much, to McCray and to himself.

*

"How ya doing, son?"

Noah looked up from the table to see Ben standing across from him, tray in hand. He motioned for the older man to sit down.

"You took quite a beating a couple weeks ago."

"Yeah." *But then I gave him one of his own.*

"Stepping in for Ralph that way took guts."

"You were there?"

Ben nodded. "Ralph's never known how to keep his mouth shut."

"Daniel's never been known for his self-control either." He shifted in his chair, pushing his lunch tray back. "He went too far with Emerson. I'm hoping I didn't make things worse. Daniel likes to push my buttons, and I can't be sure he didn't start with Emerson because he wanted me to remember who's in control."

"Haven't heard Emerson's name on the Liquidation Updates this last week, so you definitely didn't make things worse." Ben took a sip from his coffee. "And you've become quite the hero around here because of it."

He glanced to the left and the right—people watched him and Ben. The furtive whispers and respectful nods he'd received in the last two weeks told him everyone knew what he'd done. He shook his head. "I didn't do anything heroic. It was the right thing to do, and I did it."

"Maybe in these times, that's all it takes. Heard you broke up a similar fight between Henderson and his boy Stephen."

Noah shrugged his shoulders. "I'm a sucker for the underdog."

Ben leaned back in his chair. A slow grin appeared on his face. "Henderson didn't appreciate it too much, but you should've heard him change his tune after your fight the other day. Emerson is his brother-in-law, you know, and he managed to admit his misjudgment of you. I never thought I'd see the day."

"Will it keep him from terrorizing his son?" *Doesn't matter unless it will.*

"I don't think Stephen's mom will give him a chance to."

He nodded. "Good."

"Must be rough having a liquidator for a brother."

Ben had no idea. "I wouldn't wish Daniel on anybody." Lavender and vanilla, the scent he'd come to associate with Maddison, wafted his way. He forced himself not to turn around and look for her. "How're your boys doing?"

"Oh, they're good. Driving their momma and me crazy about what they want for Christmas, but that's pretty much par for the course." Ben chuckled.

Noah laughed as well. "From what I remember, yes."

"Mind if I join you?" Now he could turn. Maddison took the last four steps their way, coffee cup in hand.

"You're early." He pulled out the chair next to him.

She sat, leaning over to kiss his cheek. "I think the teachers are as antsy for winter break as we are." She inclined her head to the older man. "Good afternoon, Mr. Yancey."

"You call me Ben, sweetheart." He smiled at them both as Noah rested his arm across the back of her chair. "How many more days do you have 'til break?"

"Two. It seems like it can't get here soon enough."

"I remember that. What days do you have off next week, Noah?"

"The twenty-third through the twenty-fifth. Don't know how it happened, but I'm not complaining."

"I wouldn't either, son." Ben gathered his things. "Well, I'm not going to take up any more of your time since Maddison's here. You two have a merry Christmas if I don't run into you before then, okay?"

"Same to you, Ben."

As they watched him walk toward the tray return, Maddison scooted her chair closer. "I like him."

"Me too." The pressure of McCray's demand descended again. He needed to figure out Ben's involvement. Soon.

She laid a hand on his arm. "Hey, what's the matter?"

"Let's take a walk." He stood and pulled her to her feet. She didn't question him, grabbing her cup off the table and following him toward the door to the climate-controlled garden outside. It was dormant but private.

They meandered through the leafless bushes and trees in silence for several minutes while he surveyed the area. He listened for any signs of life other than theirs and found none. "My superior called this morning. He's not happy. I need to make some progress or he'll send someone else. Things could turn nasty."

"What does that have to do with Ben?"

"His brother's been identified as a potential member."

"And you think he's involved as well?" The question trickled into the air as quiet as the fountain behind her.

Rubbing his hand over his face, he nodded. "If I can't get out in front of this, well, I don't know who they'll send in."

She shivered beside him, and he pulled her closer with the arm around her shoulders. "I'm not cold."

"I know." He sighed, hating everything about the conversation. He cursed McCray for forcing him into this position. "The idea of turning in anyone who's yet to commit a crime makes me sick, but if I can't give McCray a list of names in three weeks, innocent people will get hurt."

He felt her back straighten, and she sucked in a deep breath, staring straight ahead. "Any new leads?"

His shoulders dropped. "One. Maybe."

Her gaze flew to his. "What do you mean?"

"A hospital employee approached me after my shift on Friday. He's part of a group and indicated I might get an invitation."

She took a step out of his embrace. "That's why you were distracted when you showed up the other night."

He gave a slow nod. Why the sudden shift in her mood? The fear he sensed a minute ago had morphed into something shrewd. Did she think he'd lied to her again? "Are you angry? I didn't mean to keep it from you. I just wanted to enjoy the evening without the shadow of the mission hanging over our heads."

"I'm not mad."

But she wouldn't make eye contact. Her eyes flitted from a bench to the mulch and back again. Her posture radiated tension. He reached out to take her hand. "Are you sure?"

"I'm not upset." Her feet shifted back and forth, and she took a deep breath. "Um, I have something to tell you."

"Okay."

She looked away. "I have a contact in the resistance."

Oh no.

"His name's Ritchie Callum. He's a couple years older than me."

"Tell me."

"After my parents died ... I wanted the liquidator to pay. I wanted them all to pay." Her words sped up. She started gesturing. "Ritchie was a senior, brilliant with compads, and I heard a rumor he'd hidden anti-government messages on some of the terminals at school. I contacted him and told him what had happened. He asked if I wanted to stop it from ever happening again. I jumped at the chance, so he gave me a meeting place, some signs to look for, and a time.

"Taylor caught me sneaking out. We had the worst fight. She was terrified. I know that now, but I said some horrible things. Unforgivable things. Jakob." Maddison's eyes flew up to his. "Jakob threw a fit. He yelled and got up in my space. Well, you know my brother. He doesn't do that."

She was right. Noah couldn't imagine Jakob raising his voice, not even as a twelve-year old kid. "He changed your mind?"

She kicked at the mulch on her right. "Yeah. He was terrified he'd lose me too. I couldn't ... I wanted revenge, but not if it cost me the family I had left. I knew going through with Ritchie's plan would hurt Jakob, so I avoided Ritchie the next day at school and promised myself to stay out of it for Taylor and Jakob's sake. Only later did I realize I could've put them in serious danger by joining."

Thank you, Jakob. Noah sighed. That wasn't so bad. He needed to find a way to check her file again, make sure no one else knew, but she should still be safe.

"That's not all."

His head whipped around to stare at her.

"After Josh got blinded, I was so angry, and I wanted to do something. So … I reached out to Ritchie again."

"Maddison." Her name came out as a groan. What had she done?

She bit her lip. "Then you got hurt and you told us about your mission and that they're going to kill you, and um, twoweeksagoIwenttoameeting."

Time froze. Sound disappeared. "I'm sorry. I heard you wrong."

Her face flushed. "I didn't go. I mean, I drove there, but I didn't actually meet them. I sat across the street and watched them. I knew you'd be angry, and it was a really bad idea, I know that now. That's why I didn't get out of my car. I couldn't leave by that point. But if you wanted me to introduce you to Ritchie, I'm sure we could come up with a way for him to trust you. Or, well, I don't know. Noah? Say something. Please."

They'll know. Somehow, they'll know. Of all the stupid …

She reached for him, but he shrugged her off. Stood. Paced.

"How could you? Maddison, you knew…. You knew

Callista could be watching you. I'd warned you. You just …
Forget saving me. I have to figure out how to save you now."

She gasped, but he couldn't look at her. Maybe they
didn't know. Maybe Callista hadn't been watching. After all,
she hadn't taunted Noah with that info, so there was a chance
no one had seen Maddison.

He stopped in front of her, locking gazes. "No more contact with Ritchie. None. Do you hear me? No more secrets.
No more meetings. No more trying to solve this on your
own. Okay?"

"I'm sorry."

"Okay?" She nodded, and he exhaled. "Did anyone see
you there?"

She glanced away for a moment, and when her eyes met
his again, they were narrowed. She looked thoughtful. "Yes.
The new kid from school. Brandon. Ross, I think? Noah,
something's not right with him. He's only been here two
months. I don't even know how he would've met Ritchie."

All his intel proved that the leadership of the resistance
was cautious. How had a newcomer been vetted so quickly?
"When did he start? Do you remember?"

Her mouth dropped open. "The day I met you."

CHAPTER TWENTY-FOUR

NOAH LEANED BACK against his seat, navigating around the other cars on the interstate. His fingers drummed a beat in time with the Mustang's digital playlist. Montreal's Muse never got old, even on constant loop.

"Are you sure this is a good idea?" Maddison asked from the passenger seat as they raced east.

He cut his eyes to the right, grinning at the focused look on her face. "You really don't like surprises, do you?"

"It's just … with the deadline hanging over your head …" She fidgeted with the scarf in her lap. "I'm wondering if there's a better way to spend the day before Christmas Eve."

"In the last week, I've done everything I can to strengthen my relationship with Nurse Walker and investigate Ritchie, Henderson, and Billy Yancey's acquaintances. Everyone will be with their families for the holiday. So you and I aren't going to talk about work, not today."

"But—"

"Maddison, if this is my last Christmas, I want to spend a day in my favorite place, with you."

"Don't say that."

He took her hand. "Please. Just a day."

"Okay." She leaned over and dropped her head on his shoulder. A minute passed. *Thank you.*

"I'd enjoy it a lot more if I knew our destination."

A laugh rumbled out of his chest. "We're headed east, that's all the information you get for now."

Pouting, she sat back up. "You're no fun." A sign whizzed past them, and her eyes narrowed. "Wait a minute, did that sign say Metro Area Six ten miles?" She spun to face him. "Are you taking me to the beach?"

"Yes, Miss Intuitive, I am. You told me it'd been years since you've been, and I've missed it."

Leaning over, she kissed his cheek. "You're the best."

"You haven't even heard the agenda yet."

"Are we starting with lunch? 'Cause I'm starving."

His smile grew. He'd guessed that she wouldn't eat before he picked her up. "We are. At the best sandwich shop downtown. I thought we'd start there and then wander the streets, explore the area."

"I love this day already."

"I hope you will."

She grew silent as they crossed over the first waterway bridge, rolling down the window to smell the ocean. He took in a deep gulp as well. It'd been too long since he'd stuck his bare feet in the sand and watched the ocean crash on the shore. As he made his way downtown past the waving grasses and flowing canals, he snuck glances at her. Her eyes darted back and forth along the scenery. The joy in them, which in the last month had been shadowed with anxiety, confirmed he'd been right to plan this. The tension from their conversation last week had faded but not vanished. She still grappled with the Elite's injustice, and he still wasn't sure how to save everyone. But they also needed a reminder of goodness and fun, a reminder of what exactly they were fighting for.

He parked the car and shrugged out of his jacket. "This is why I love the beach, sixty-five degrees even in December."

"But that cuts out the possibility of snow." Maddison stepped out on the sidewalk and took a deep breath before leaving her own jacket and scarf behind. "It does feel wonderful though."

"Told you." He held his arm out to her, and they walked the four blocks to the landmark sandwich counter. Settling in by the window, she ordered a vegetarian wrap while he ordered a cheeseburger, despite the waiter's huff at his choice. As the guy walked away with a raised eyebrow directed toward her, she giggled.

"He's wondering how a smart vegan like me can stand to sit at a table with you and your vile animal-killing ways."

"Do you want to clue him in to your horrible omnivore lifestyle?" he whispered.

"Nope. I think we should let him stew." She laughed again and reached across the table to take his hand. The last bit of tension in his spine melted away as he cupped her small hand in his own. Within minutes, their waiter returned with their waters and meals. His eyebrow rose higher when he spotted their entwined hands.

Maddison pulled a piece of bacon off Noah's burger and munched on it. The waiter turned away in disgust. "Oh, this is too much fun." She tugged her hand out of Noah's grasp to pick up her wrap.

He stuffed several fries in his mouth. "You're going to be a troublemaker all day, aren't you?"

She swallowed her bite and returned his smile with a mischievous one of her own. "I think so."

He chuckled and went to work on his own food. They ate and people watched, narrating the conversations of those who passed by the window. She stole more food off his plate. He pretended to mind. After paying the bill, they headed back outside where they wandered through several shops and past the dilapidated *USS North Carolina* museum.

As the sun began to dip toward the water, he led them back to the car. They picked up their coats and the bag he'd stowed in the trunk and navigated their way down to the sand. He surveyed the beach, empty but for two fishermen in the distance near the pier then dropped the bag on the ground and pulled out a blanket for them to sit on. The waves crested and disappeared without much fanfare. The sun continued its descent, dipping a toe in the dark ocean.

"Thank you for today." She leaned back against his chest, looking out over the water.

He ran his hands up and down her arms, breathing in the silence around them, and kissed her hair. "It's not over yet." He moved toward the bag and pulled out a box of pastries, fruit, and a thermos.

"What all do you have in that bag?"

He shrugged and schooled his face to hide his excitement. "I came prepared."

"Just when I think you can't surprise me anymore …"

His chest filled with pride, and his shoulders rose. "I must be doing something right then." He handed her the thermos and pastry box, so he could snag her Christmas gift from the bag. He sat down beside her, their shoulders touching, and placed the small box in her lap with his free hand.

She smiled a secret smile of her own and leaned forward to pull something out of her purse. "I thought we might be exchanging gifts today." She handed him a rectangular package. "You go first. Please?"

He couldn't say no to her. He tore the wrapping paper away from the box and tossed it to the side. Removing the lid, he found a sleek digital frame. She reached over and turned it on. The screen filled with an image of them kissing on the sidewalk outside her house. It faded away to be replaced by another of them putting the star on her Christmas tree, him holding her up by the waist so she could reach the top. The next showed her dragging him through the art archives. Olivia had snapped that one with her vidcom, capturing the playful smirk Maddison couldn't see. Tears clogged his throat.

"What do you think?" She didn't give him a chance to answer the hesitant question. "You don't have any pictures in your room, so I didn't know if you didn't like pictures or if you didn't have any you could carry around with you.

This seemed like a good option. Taylor and the girls helped me collect the pictures. There's an extra memory card in the frame if you wanted to put any on your com or compad, but you don't have to if you don't like it. It's a stupid idea, isn't it?"

"No." The word burst out. He couldn't tear his eyes away from the screen. "It's great. I couldn't bring myself to take any of the surviving frames from Mom and Dad's, and … It'll be nice to see your face when I wake up in the morning. It'll make the room seem a little more like home." He met her gaze. "Thank you."

"I'm glad you like it."

"Very much." He crossed the remaining inches and kissed her, his lips brushing against hers. When he leaned back, he tucked a strand of hair behind her ear and nudged her package. "Your turn."

She picked up the small box and unwrapped it one corner at a time. His breathing accelerated, and he bit his lip. When she opened the box, her eyes widened.

The platinum ring and chain he'd picked out for her lay nestled in blue velvet. "Noah, this is beautiful." She fingered the delicate chain and turned the ring around in the waning sunlight. "Is there something engraved on it?"

He freed the necklace from the box. "*Non puoi perdere me*. It's Italian."

"Which means?"

"You can't lose me."

She grabbed the hand holding her necklace and pulled him forward. Her lips crashed into his. Wow. Once he recovered from the shock, he brought his other hand up to cup her neck, kissing her back just as fiercely. When he pulled away, she took a deep, trembling breath. He rested his forehead against hers and waited for her breathing to slow.

"I'm going to do everything I can to make that true."

"Shut up, it's already true."

He sighed. "Maddison."

"Say it."

"You can't lose me."

She kissed him hard. "We're going to make it true."

CHAPTER TWENTY-FIVE

MADDISON MUST BE a liquidator magnet. No other explanation accounted for the stranger making her way toward the nurses' station. The exotic woman moved like a panther, slinking forward with controlled ease and power. Her signet ring caught the light, drawing the attention of everyone in the area.

When she came to a stop before Maddison and the nurse on duty, her perfect curls settled on leather-clad shoulders. "I'm looking for Maddison James." She sneered as though it was beneath her to speak to mere mortals.

"You found me." Maddison clenched her teeth shut to keep from saying more. She'd pushed enough buttons in the last three months, and even Daniel didn't seem as dangerous as this woman.

The woman's gaze drifted over her. "Hmm." She turned to the nurse, holding up her hand and waving the finger with the signet ring. "I'm going to borrow Miss James for a bit. Excuse her for the rest of the day."

Nurse Tuttle gaped, shooting a wide-eyed look in Maddison's direction.

The catwoman released a harsh laugh. "She'll be back tomorrow. Probably."

Good sense warned Maddison to act submissive, but she couldn't watch the liquidator toy with Nurse Tuttle. She swiped her card. "Have a good weekend, Sandy. I'll see you when you get back Sunday." She turned to Catwoman. "Where to?"

The other woman's face hardened. "The elevator will do."

Maddison walked past her toward the elevators. Her fingers twisted a strand of hair. She forced herself to release it. When the first set of doors opened, they entered, and the liquidator pushed the emergency stop button.

"I'm not a woman to be played with. I expect you to answer my questions and nothing more. Got it?" She stood, hands on her hips. Her eyes pinned Maddison in place.

Maddison nodded.

"What is your relationship with Noah State?"

"I'm his girlfriend."

"So, he did tell you who he is." The woman sighed; a hand dropped off her hip. "Daniel told me you weren't a threat. He didn't mention you knew."

Why hadn't she considered acting surprised, playing it cool? What was Daniel up to? "He told you the truth. I'm not a threat to Noah's cover."

"I didn't ask your opinion." Catwoman paced. "McCray thinks the relationship is a strategic layer in Noah's cover."

She huffed. "He doesn't know Noah as well as I do." She spun to face Maddison. "Did he tell you or did you figure it out?"

"He told me."

"Which means he's losing objectivity. I should liquidate you now."

"But then you'd have to answer to Noah. I don't think you want that."

Catwoman growled but made no move toward her. "I don't want Noah in any more hot water with McCray either. And you aren't making that easy, distracting him from his mission." Her eyes narrowed. "He's good at his job, but no one's bulletproof. He needs my help."

Her impassioned tone clicked like a puzzle piece into place beside the one labeled *aggressive behavior*. Maddison could just decipher the picture—the liquidator was jealous.

She stamped down the triumphant smile. Envy made the woman more dangerous. "I haven't been distracting him."

A frozen smile appeared on the liquidator's face. "Of course you have. You have to know that, don't you?" She took a step forward, raking her eyes over Maddison again. "You're a distraction to fill his time here, but when the mission's done, he'll move on. Why wouldn't he?" She gestured to herself. "When he could settle down with someone genetically superior like me?"

Maddison bit her tongue, tasted the copper slipperiness of her blood.

"But let's put logic aside for a moment, and talk legalities. Even if he doesn't settle down with me, Noah won't marry you." Catwoman shook her head. "And you, my pet, should already know why. He may be a liquidator, but no one's exempt from the marriage statute. He'll marry a member of the Elite, or if he's slumming, someone from Class Two. But you? Class Four?" Her smile turned menacing. "It's forbidden."

The world stood still. How could she have forgotten? Her fingers clasped the ring lying on her heart. It should mean something. It should matter.

"See, you can't deny it. So, I'm going to do everyone a favor." She backed Maddison up against the wall. "You are going to stay away from Noah. I don't care what it takes, but you leave him alone and make sure he does the same. He needs to focus on hunting down the terrorists McCray sent him here to find." She ran a finger down Maddison's cheek. "And if you don't, I'll liquidate you and your family, starting with that promising little brother of yours." Backing away, she released the emergency stop, and they lurched downward. "Understand?"

Maddison could only nod.

The doors opened with a ding, and the smile on the liquidator's face became even more predatory. "Good. Nice meeting you, Maddison."

*

The outer door swung open. Noah froze. Until he picked up the faint whiff of leather and whiskey. He rubbed the towel through his hair one last time and threw it in the sink. "How did you get in here?"

"It's a perk."

"I thought I made my position clear." He grabbed a brown knit shirt from its hanger and walked out of the bathroom.

Daniel leaned against the bed's headboard, flipping through one of Noah's books. "Is Maddison working at the hospital today?"

Noah froze mid-motion, shirt clenched in his fist. "Why?"

"Guess who paid me a visit today." Daniel waited several beats for a response. "What? Not interested?" He rolled his eyes. "Oh, all right, I'll tell you. It was Callista, and we had the most interesting conversation. She had tons of questions about you and Maddison." He gave Noah a pointed look over the Steinbeck. "Anyway, you know how delusional Callista is about you. I told her Maddison couldn't be classified as a threat, but she had that huntress look in her eye. I don't think she listened."

Noah tugged the knit over his head and punched his arms through the sleeves, starting toward his vidcom across the room. "Why didn't you call? She has a head start on me now." Something cold coiled in his gut.

Daniel sat up. "Yell at me later. Put your shoes on so we can get out of here."

Noah growled and stomped into his boots before grabbing his keys and heading for the door. He swung it open and almost knocked Maddison over.

"Maddison." He crushed her to his chest and dragged her back inside, slamming the door with his foot. The breath rushed out of his chest. She was here. She was okay.

"You're crushing her air supply." The evenness of Daniel's comment embodied disinterest.

He loosened his grip. She shook in his arms. "Are you okay? Did I hurt you?" He led her over to the bed where she sank down, trembling like a frightened swallow.

Her gaze found Daniel, who lounged against the wall. "She came."

Noah froze. Beside him, Daniel became a statue.

"What happened?" Noah asked.

"Callista? At least I think that's who she was." Maddison folded her arms around herself.

Noah slipped an arm around her shoulders, pulling her close. "Tall with dark hair and eyes?"

Maddison nodded. "She's obsessed with you." Another round of tremors passed through Maddison, and her teeth chattered.

Daniel came around and sat in the chair across from them, all seriousness. "She really got to you, didn't she?" Maddison managed another small nod. His face hardened and he raised his eyes to Noah's. "She's in shock, pull the blanket around her. You need to get her warmed up."

Noah stood up to pull at the bed covering. She clutched at his hand, and her breathing became more erratic. In seconds, he wrapped her up and sat back down, pulling her into his lap.

"You're safe now. Hear me, Maddison? You're safe." He took deliberate breaths, inhaling and exhaling at a normal rhythm, and rubbed a hand up and down her back.

After several moments, her breathing matched his,

bringing the color back to her cheeks and causing the shaking to lessen.

"I'm sorry." Her voice regained some of its normal confidence. "I don't know why I let her get to me."

Noah brushed a hand through her hair. "What did she threaten?"

"To kill us if I didn't stay away from you."

A growl escaped from deep within him. "Where did she go?"

"Hold on." Daniel raised a hand in warning. "Hear the whole story, so you know what you're dealing with." He addressed Maddison. "Start from the beginning."

Noah tried to shut off the rage pounding inside him. He needed to tap into detective mode and gather the facts, but the thought of Callista threatening Maddison overrode his senses.

Maddison took a shaky breath. "She figured out I knew. About Noah's identity, I mean. Because of the way you phrased your warning. I confirmed her suspicions without realizing it. She wants me dead more than you do." Her gaze shot up to Noah's. "She *likes* you. In fact, she thinks she's protecting you, just looking for an excuse to liquidate me."

The blood roared through his veins. "She's not going to get the chance."

Maddison's hand shot up to grasp his arm. "What if she knows I came here? What if she follows through with it?" Her breathing quickened. "She said she'd start with Jakob."

"I'm going to make sure she can't follow through on anything."

But he couldn't take Maddison with him. Or leave her alone. Only one option existed. He stared at Daniel. His brother didn't break eye contact. Noah took a deep breath and stepped out on the proverbial limb. "I need to take care of this situation, but Maddison and her family shouldn't be left alone tonight. Take her home and stay with them until I get there?"

Daniel stood. No snarky comeback.

"I'm serious, Daniel."

"I heard you. Go on."

He looked down at Maddison. "It's going to be all right. I promise."

"Okay."

He kissed her temple and ran a hand through her hair one last time. Releasing her, he stood and pulled her to her feet. "I'll be at the house as soon as I can."

The other two nodded. He curbed the rage with his training, beating the emotion into a useful weapon as he pulled open his bag and found his ring. Daniel took a step forward. "Don't do anything stupid."

"I won't, but she has to know I'm serious. This ends tonight." He headed for the door but turned back to catch Maddison's gaze another time. "See you soon."

She managed a small smile. "Soon."

As the door swung shut, Daniel said, "So, Maddison, have you ever ridden a motorcycle before?"

CHAPTER TWENTY-SIX

MADDISON TURNED AWAY from the open screen door and headed back to the blackened cookie sheet in the sink. The acrid smell of smoke wafted throughout the kitchen.

She hadn't even heard the oven timer. Too many distractions—Callista, the looming deadline, the marriage statute and her and Noah's lack of a future. And she had three days' worth of ruined baked goods to prove it. She scraped the burnt remains off the cool pan then watched the running water sweep them down the drain.

"Don't you know it's not safe to leave doors wide open considering the Area's political climate?"

She spun and found herself feet away from Callista, who slid the door shut behind her. The spatula clattered to the floor, sending water droplets flying.

"I'm on my way out of town, but I decided to make time for a quick visit with you first. Don't you feel flattered?"

Maddison raced for the front door. The liquidator

flashed in front of her, blocking her path and forcing her to slam to a stop.

"Where do you think you're going? I took time out of my very busy schedule to come all the way over here for a chat, and now you're not being a very accommodating hostess." She took several more steps forward, and Maddison backed away and around the couch. Callista gestured to a chair. "Why don't you sit, Maddison?"

"I think I'll stand." She straightened her shoulders and resisted the urge to wrap her arms around herself.

"Your choice." Callista replied in the same taunting tone. "Do you mind if I do? No? Good." Settling on the arm of the couch, she blocked the one clear exit to the kitchen or the stairs.

"Why are you here?" Maddison's left hand flew to the ring around her neck. Praying somehow Noah would sense the trouble and come. But he was on duty, and Taylor had been called in today for a mandated shift. Jakob would be at baseball practice for two more hours. Her vidcom sat on the dresser in her room. There would be no rescue.

"Do you know the term the Elite use for those who don't obey?" Callista's eyes glazed over with hatred. When she spoke again, her low voice sent a tremor down Maddison's spine. "We call them traitors, enemies of the state, but you already know that. It's written on your parents' graves. Oh, wait, they didn't deserve graves."

Rage bubbled up inside Maddison. "Don't talk about them."

"Oh, I'll talk about whomever I want. Because I am

the one in control here. I am a chosen member of the Elite. My directives are to be obeyed. And if they aren't, I have the authority and the responsibility to liquidate you." She stood up and took two slinking steps toward Maddison, the predator cornering her prey. "Having a liquidator boyfriend doesn't exclude you from the rules. You, unlike me, are no one special. If you'd stayed away from Noah, I wouldn't be here today."

She pressed closer, backing Maddison up against the wall. Nowhere to go.

Stepping back, Callista surveyed her. "I don't know what he sees in you, but that won't matter after today. Someone needs to step in before he puts himself in jeopardy, and if Daniel won't do it, I will. Once you're gone, he'll focus on his mission. He'll remember who he is, and he'll make McCray happy. And I'll be with him every step of the way to make sure of it."

Maddison clutched the necklace tighter and inhaled a deep breath. If Callista planned to kill her, she might as well have her say. "You're wrong. Because if you really knew Noah, you'd know that being a council-pleasing liquidator has never been a priority of his. He doesn't want your future. And he doesn't want you."

"If that were true, I'd be dead right now." Callista ran a finger along Maddison's jaw. Dropped her hand to Maddison's neck. "But I'm not, so I guess you are." She began to squeeze, forcing Maddison's windpipe closed.

Maddison clawed at the hand and kicked to no avail. Her head spun. Need oxygen. Now. The edges of her sight darkened. Suddenly the pressure was ripped away from her throat. Falling to her knees, she blinked several times. The room swayed back and forth like a pendulum. Now two black clad figures danced in the living room.

"How did you get in?" Callista screeched from across the room, in a boxer's stance.

"The glass door. You didn't lock it behind yourself. Sloppy, sloppy." Daniel's back faced Maddison, but she could hear the smirk in his voice.

Callista growled and lunged toward Maddison, but Daniel anticipated the move and used her momentum to spin her into the wall on the other side of him, trapping her with his arm against her chest.

"Let me at her." Callista spit the words at him. "She's not worth it. You know it."

Daniel didn't even glance back at Maddison where she cowered by the couch, wheezing and coughing, hoping he didn't agree.

"Get past me first." He leaned into his captive's face. "Come on, Psycho Stalker, I haven't liquidated anybody in days."

She screamed and pushed him off, her fist flying toward his face. He ducked, his own expression terrifyingly blank. When he retaliated, bone shattered. Callista spewed curses at him. Maddison's eyes couldn't track their lightning-fast movements, but she felt the effects—the coffee table crashed to the floor when Callista threw Daniel into it, the walls shuddered when he kicked her into one. Plaster fell from the place her head hit. A vase shattered against the mantel, inches from his face.

Maddison's feet were rooted to the floor. She wanted to run upstairs and grab her vidcom or put her head between her knees and wait for the earthquake to pass, but she couldn't tear her eyes away from Daniel. If she moved, he could lose his focus and Callista would gain the upper hand. He seemed to expect each of Callista's moves, buoying Maddison's hopes.

Until a glint of metal caught her eye.

Daniel dodged the knife and grabbed a broken plank from the coffee table. Callista dove forward, and blood appeared on Daniel's neck.

No. Time slowed down. Callista couldn't kill him. If she won … Maddison shrank back against the couch, willing Daniel to win. His eyes connected with hers.

He struck. Another sharp crack and Callista howled in pain. The knife fell to the ground. His hands flashed. The snap of her neck echoed throughout the room. She crumbled to the floor.

Maddison could only stare at the body in front of her, shocked beyond belief. Relief crashed over her.

Daniel stepped over Callista's body. "Come on." He put an arm around Maddison's shoulders and guided her into the kitchen.

Her eyes lingered on the dead body behind them. Once around the corner, he released her, and she fell back against the island. His hands came around her face, forcing her to look at him.

"How much does it hurt to breathe?"

"She … You …" The room spun under her feet, and the world went black.

When she woke up, she lay on her bed, a wet hand towel against her forehead. Daniel leaned against the opposite wall, no trace of blood on him. "Don't sit up. I think you'd better let your body get its bearings first."

Her hand flew to the dripping towel, pulling it off and dropping it on the floor. "Did you carry me up here? How long was I out? Is she…?"

"Yes. A couple of minutes. And yes."

"How did you know?" She pushed up to a sitting position. He studied her. It made her nervous.

"I've been following her."

"You've been … Wait, her signal … How long until the response team gets here?"

"They don't know she's dead." He picked a snow globe up off the dresser, turning it around in his hands like a baseball. "I disabled her chip last night."

"How?" It hurt to talk. The question came out with a rasp.

He passed the globe back and forth in his hands. "Let's just say I'm awesome like that."

But if he'd disabled her chip last night… "How long have you been planning to kill her?"

"Generally? Nine months. Specifically? Since Noah waved her off the other day." He threw the globe up in the air, following it with his eyes until it landed in his hand again. "I warned Noah months ago that she was unhinged.

I told him it was only a matter of time before she realized he was never going to go for her, and when that happened? Well, you've heard the saying about a woman scorned and all."

The globe flew up in the air, down into his hands. "When he delivered his warning, he essentially picked you over her. So I had to kill her."

"Why did you stop her?" She swallowed hard. "It would've made life easier for you. To let her kill me first. We both know you want me dead. And I haven't given you any reason to change your mind."

"You're important to Noah."

But that hadn't mattered when he'd threatened to kill her himself. "Well, thank you."

He rolled his eyes. Someone pounded on the front door. He set the globe down on her dresser. "That'll be Noah, I suppose."

She shot him a perplexed look, and he continued. "I called and left a message for him after you fainted. You know, it's a good thing he doesn't need his job at the hospital 'cause he seems to miss a lot of work because of you." He headed out the door but called back, "And contrary to popular opinion, I haven't wanted you dead in weeks."

A strangled cough escaped.

Downstairs she heard Noah's frantic voice asking about her and what had happened. Daniel's version seemed short on details, so she swung her legs off the bed and headed for the door. The room tilted a little to the right. She held her left hand out for balance. When she came around the corner, shock at Noah's appearance rippled through her. His hair stood in every direction, rumpled and jagged. His face was devoid of color.

"I'm here." Her voice caught and squeaked.

His eyes fixed on her, and within seconds, he'd scaled the stairs and pulled her into his arms. "You're okay." He sighed. "You're okay. You're okay." She tightened her arms around his neck, and he lifted her off the ground and crushed her closer.

A cough at the bottom of the stairs drew her attention. Daniel pointed back toward her bedroom. She nodded and released Noah to pull them back toward her room.

Noah sat down on the bed, pulling her against his chest. He dropped frantic kisses on her head. She pulled back to look at his face. Tears swam in his eyes. Reaching up, she laid her palm on his cheek. "Hey, I'm all right."

She wanted to say more, but he winced when he heard her voice. His hands traced the red flesh of her neck. "Does it hurt to breathe? Or swallow?"

Tilting his face up to hers, she mouthed, "A little. Better soon."

"Do you need water? To go to the ER? I can call Taylor." The pace sped up with each question.

She shook her head to all three. "Just you."

He didn't wince so much that time, pulling her back to his chest. "I thought my heart stopped beating when I got Daniel's message from the nurse. It took forever to get here, no matter how fast I drove. I shouldn't have left you. I'm so sorry."

"It's not your fault. You couldn't have known she wouldn't heed your warning."

"Daniel did."

Daniel's behavior made no sense, but the calculation behind it terrified her. "Don't let go, okay?" She threaded her arms around Noah's waist. "I need you here." She wanted to tell him how much she'd wanted him earlier, but that would only add to his guilt.

He kissed her forehead again. "I'm not going anywhere."

And that's what brought the tears. His presence meant she was safe and unleashed the floodgate of emotion she had attempted to shut off when she first saw Callista. Burying her head in his chest, she let the sobs take control. Hot tears raced down her cheeks and soaked into his scrubs.

He held her closer. One hand came up to cradle her head. "You're safe. She can't hurt you. You're safe with me." Once her sobs abated, he kissed her forehead one more time and leaned back to look at her neck again. "You should take something to reduce the inflammation and help with the bruising."

"Does your healing serum work on me too?" she asked with a raised eyebrow.

He chuckled and shook his head. "I think some regular anti-inflammatory will be fine. Bathroom cabinet downstairs, right?" He stood and waited for her nod before leaving. A moment later, he raced back in with several tablets and a glass of water.

"Did you use your super speed just now?"

"Maybe." He didn't look a bit chagrined.

It shouldn't have struck her as funny—not in this moment—but her emotions bubbled so close to the surface. She couldn't help but let a giggle escape.

*

Noah's vidcom buzzed once before Daniel's voice rang out in Maddison's bedroom. "Pick it up. Now. Quit wasting my time."

He rolled his eyes, making a mental note to change his password again, and pulled the vidcom out of his pocket. Daniel's annoyed face appeared on the screen. One lone street lamp in the background shone over his brother and the trash bins around him.

"If anyone asks you in the next twenty-four hours if you've heard from Psycho Stalker, you should tell them she said she was headed to the Center to get her chip repaired. That'll fit with the official record." A grimace crossed his face as something shuffled along the ground to his right.

"Wait a minute, what did you do with Callista's body? You didn't just dump it in an alley, right?"

"Of course I did. We can't bury her, you idiot. She'll have to be found because they're going to notice she's missing in twelve to eighteen hours. Don't worry, I removed all traces of my DNA first." He tilted his head. "Hmm, the rats should help destroy the evidence as well."

Maddison let out a jagged exhale across the room, but Noah couldn't tear his attention away from the vidcom, his free hand clenched at his side. Had Daniel lost all respect for humanity? Did he have no fear of God? "You make me sick."

"Add it to the list of things you judge me for."

Noah growled.

"Would you rather I'd not killed her? I mean, I assumed you wanted your girlfriend alive. But if I was wrong …"

You're not sorry. You're relieved she's dead. His head dropped to his chest, eyes sliding shut. He was a horrible person.

Daniel misinterpreted his reaction. "So we're agreed then. I leave her here. Someone else finds her in a couple days. In the meantime, if anyone asks, we think she's at the Center."

"Why didn't you talk with me about this before you acted? We could've found another way to handle every-thing." Agreeing to Daniel's scheme added Callista's blood to his hands. So much blood.

Daniel's eyebrows lowered. "There was no other way. I've run through every potential scenario in the last three days. This was the only option."

"Wait, what do you mean every scenario?"

"Come on, I knew we were in trouble after you gave her a lecture about not hurting her competition." He pointed a finger at the screen, spearing Noah with his glare. "For the record—not your smartest idea. Crazy woman thought you leaving her alive meant you cared more about her than Maddison."

Noah stared back. "You should've told me."

"So you could do what? Threaten her again? I took care of it. Be grateful and move on." His face disappeared, and the com chimed a disconnect tone.

It began to sink in—the danger had passed. Callista couldn't hurt Maddison or anyone else he cared about ever again. Daniel had guaranteed them safety. But at what cost?

You chose this. Just like Daniel.

The image of Callista's body flashed in front of his eyes, and his stomach lurched. He raced for the bathroom, heaving into the toilet not a moment later.

He slumped against the floor when the tremors stopped. He'd fallen so far.

Religious or not, two truths had become strikingly evident in the last five years. One, God existed—Nonna's stalwart obedience and the beauty in the world hinted at the reality. The nightmares, blood, and guilt proved it. And two, God would judge him … and Daniel. No excuses, no rescue, no counter-balancing of wrongs. It didn't matter how much good he tried to do, it never outweighed the bad. He would never regain God's favor, no matter how hard he tried.

*

He opened the bathroom door. Was there water running in the kitchen? Walking into the room, he found Maddison loading the dishwasher. She had changed into a high-neck, pink sweater.

"It's a good thing the weather is cold this time of year. I can bundle up in turtlenecks and scarves for the next few days." She gave a cookie sheet a final vicious scrub before dropping it in the bottom rack.

"What are you doing?"

"Making sure the kitchen is clean, so Taylor and Jakob

don't ask questions. Would you carry the table remnants to the curb, please?"

He came over and placed his hands on her shoulders to stop her movement. "Are you suggesting we keep this from them?"

"I don't want them to freak out. If everything, myself included, looks normal when they get home, the fact that Daniel stood between a rogue liquidator and me won't scare Taylor to death. I can't fix it all, but I don't want them to know how close Callista came to …" Her eyes drifted back toward the living room, and she shuddered. "All they need to know is that she showed up and Daniel stopped her." Her stony face didn't shift, but her next words came out in a pleading tone. "Please go along with it? I'll be fine. And she's not coming back. Jakob's been so worried. Can't we act like everything's fine?"

"What about your voice?"

"I'm going to make some hot tea with honey. It'll help the raspiness. If they ask, I'll say I don't feel great, which is true, but the medicine's already helping. I'll be good as new in a couple days."

"Okay." Pile it on. One more lie to add to the growing stack. "But you have ten minutes to make your tea while I survey the living room."

"I'll do it in eight." She reached up to kiss his cheek before heading for the cabinets across the kitchen.

He squared his shoulders and stepped back into the living room. The coffee table lay in large splinters. Shards of a vase and some picture frames littered the floor. A chunk of drywall and plaster dust lay like snow on the dark carpet.

He tried not to piece together the fight as he cleaned, not wanting to contemplate what would've happened had Daniel been less paranoid. He carried the larger pieces of table out to his car and dropped them in the trunk before filling a trash bag with the other debris. He vacuumed the room, pulled the couch back into its normal spot, and straightened the remaining pictures on the mantel, then headed back to the kitchen. Maddison leaned against the island, drizzling honey into a tall blue mug.

"Okay, time's up. You need to rest." He held out a hand to her.

She slid the honey back into the center of the island, grabbed her mug, and took his hand with a small smile. "I promise."

He led her back up the stairs so she could avoid the living room until tomorrow. She smiled and squeezed his hand. He watched in wonder as she settled in the middle of her bed, surrounded by pillows, and covered herself with a down blanket while balancing her cup of tea in the other hand. Not a drop spilled. He sat at the foot of her bed, one leg pulled up in front of him, the other dangled to the floor.

She took a sip of the steaming beverage. "Do you think Daniel saved me so you would cut him some slack?"

He frowned. "Daniel has his own reasons for everything he does, and I'm very bad at guessing what those are. But most of them are selfish, so I wouldn't give him the benefit of the doubt at this point."

She stared down at her tea. "Do you want to talk about him now?"

About Daniel condemning him to this life of blood and guilt? "No."

She sighed his name.

"I can't." He fought to form the words. "It's done. Talking about it won't help me. It won't change anything. All I can do is move forward."

CHAPTER TWENTY-SEVEN

THE PERFECT SOLUTION had finally presented itself. Noah frowned. Well, not perfect, but he could use the situation. He pulled out of the exit lane and back onto the interstate. Callista's hotel was ten miles away. Her ARL wouldn't know she was missing until she didn't show up for the med appointment in the Center, which gave him a little over nine hours.

He needed thirty minutes. Assuming she'd left her compad behind, and he'd bet just about anything she had. She didn't carry a purse or bag and often bragged about her ring, vidcom, and a tube of lipstick providing her with the tools to do anything she needed.

He glanced at the clock on the dash. 10:30 p.m. The front desk clerk would likely be bored and distracted, but anyone coming in at this time of night would get undue attention. The exit marker loomed ahead. He signaled and pulled over into the exit lane. Who could he be? Maintenance? Transit worker? The hotel owner's son? Playing a spoiled rich kid had perks the other two personas couldn't provide, but he'd used that strategy last year. This plan would have be to completely different. Nothing about tonight could point back to him.

The five-star hotel came into view, and Noah parked in the only shadowed space in the lot. Of course, Callista would stay in the most expensive hotel in CSE. A person would have to be Class One or Class Two to even contemplate such accommodations. Perfect. Thanks to Daniel and Ryan, Noah knew all about those people. He reached into the back seat, grabbed the set of extra clothes he kept on hand, and changed. He didn't have a suit jacket, but he could work with what he had. He got out of the car and slipped on his leather jacket. Time to go to work.

He pulled a bored expression and took his time walking towards the entrance, twirling the distinctive Mustang key around his finger. The valet rushed forward to meet him. "Sir, we would be more than happy to park your car for you in the future."

Noah looked down at him with a raised eyebrow. "Do I look like the kind of person who wants just anybody in my car?"

The valet paled. "No, sir. I'm sorry, sir."

He didn't acknowledge the man's reply or break stride toward the entrance. The doorman opened the door with a bow. At the front desk, a tall wiry man straightened in his seat. "Good evening, sir. How may I help you?"

He put his arm on the counter and leaned against the side. "I have an appointment with Callista State. She left a key for me."

The clerk didn't move. "And you are?"

"Mark Abbott."

"Abbott, like the ministers?"

Ah, there's the reaction he wanted. Both John and Barbara Abbott held positions on the Council, as the minister of education and minister of classification respectively. They also happened to be from this part of the country.

"One of their grandsons. Are you going to give me the key or not?"

"I'm sorry, sir, but Ms. State didn't leave a key. I can call up to her room if you'd like."

He waved his hand. "If you must."

The clerk dialed the room extension, number 214. The phone rang four times. No one picked up. Good, the room was still clear. "Ms. State doesn't answer. Perhaps your," he gulped, "appointment was for a different time?"

Noah straightened. "Do I look like the kind of person who misremembers appointments? Especially ones that take place after curfew?"

"Mr. Abbott, I do apologize. It's just, Ms. State isn't answering, and she didn't leave a key. It does put me in an awkward position, you understand. If you could verify your identity, I would feel more comfortable."

"I can do better than that. Although I think you'll wish I hadn't." Noah pulled his vidcom out of his pocket and pushed the code for Ryan.

"Calling Ryan Lutz. Personal or classification office?"

"Personal."

"Connecting now."

The clerk waved a card at him, his face white as a sheet. "That won't be necessary. I apologize Mr. Abbott. Here's the key you requested."

"Good call." Noah took the keycard and walked over to the elevators, silencing the phone with a swipe.

Phase one, complete. Now on to phase two. The elevators doors opened, and he stepped out on the deserted second floor. *Please don't be a waste.* He spotted 214. Unlocked the door. Stepped inside.

What a mess. Clothes and shoes littered every surface, but on the bed, a corner of her compad peeked out. Great. He pulled a pair of gloves out of his jacket pocket, slipped them on, and picked up the compad. It sprang to life, requesting Callista's passcode.

Okay, Seforé, think. What would it be? Nothing too obvious, like her birthday or birthplace or mother's maiden name. Not his birthday. Shudder. What was important to Callista? What would she want the reminder of? Then he knew, but how to say that in less than eight characters? Wait.

Spencer. He typed it in, and the screen unlocked. He rolled his eyes. She really had bought into the propaganda hook, line, and sinker. He used the same password to get into her account on the Ministry of Justice server. At the bottom of the screen sat a file that didn't show up on his account: Confirmed CSE Resistance Members. He double-clicked on the file.

Fifty names filled the page. Fifty. How did they have confirmation on that many people? He scanned the list, looking for familiar names. Yancey and Henderson were of course on it. Two thirds of the way down he found the name he'd dreaded. Maddison's name sat underneath Ritchie Callum's.

He scanned the names again. No, he hadn't overlooked it. Brandon Ross, attender of Ritchie's covert meeting, was not on the list. Maybe he needed to pay the kid a visit after all. But first, finish here. A couple clicks allowed him to delete the entire file. A minute more and he'd destroyed all related files and their back-up copies on the server. He signed out of Callista's account and laid the computer back down where he'd found it. It might not be a permanent solution, but for tonight? It felt good to set McCray back several steps.

*

Brandon Ross closed the door to his house and sauntered toward the garage. Halfway there, his posture changed. He stuck his hands in his pockets and slumped his shoulders. Like a kid undercover for the first time realizing someone might be watching even this. Noah opened his car door without taking his eyes off Brandon. The street was quiet, but from twenty yards away, the noise would be undetectable. Unless someone happened to be a liquidator. Sure enough, Brandon tensed.

Noah swung out of the car and headed straight for the fresh out of the Academy liquidator. "I think it's about time you and I had a talk, don't you?"

Brandon turned, waiting in the middle of the front yard. "Do I know you?"

"Don't play dumb. You know who I am, and now I know who you are, Brandon State."

"Could you keep your voice down?"

Noah rolled his eyes. "Use your senses. There isn't anything living in earshot, let alone anyone."

Brandon's arms came out of his pockets and crossed behind him. "I take my job seriously. That means I'm always careful."

Earnest Academy graduates were the worst. "Well, then, maybe you should've set your posture before you exited the house."

"I'm not the one who might be dead in a month. What's it like to be watched like a common criminal?"

"Such a transparent shift, rookie." Noah stuck his hands in his pockets. Man, it was cold this morning. "And don't think for a second they aren't watching you too."

"Well, that kinda comes with the territory, doesn't it?"

"The smart ones always keep that in mind. I assume the couple watching from the front window are liquidators as well and not your real parents?"

"Yep."

"And I hear you managed to ingratiate yourself right into the resistance." Which stung. Here he had to take a public beating to get an invitation, and this blond poster boy waltzed right into one.

Brandon smiled. "All I had to do was play the poor little outcast who didn't want his Class Two placement, and they came to me. Evidently the usefulness of having someone inside the Elite was too good to pass up."

Ah, yes, that did make sense. Especially to an ambition-driven young adult like Ritchie Callum.

"Must've been pretty good 'cause your girlfriend bought it."

Noah laughed. "Oh, she might not've known you were a liquidator, but she knew something was off. There's also the fact that my friend Liv doesn't trust you. She's an excellent judge of character, that girl."

Anger flashed in Brandon's eyes.

Noah took a step forward. "Don't be stupid and punish either one of them because you aren't as good at your job as you ought to be."

"Fair point." Brandon's jaw relaxed. "I have to ask. How did you manage to flirt with a resistance member on the first day? I mean, are you that lucky? She must be a gold mine of information."

Don't let the kid get to you. "I can't claim that one. But you're right, she has been very helpful." In ways you'd never guess.

"If only we all were that lucky. My first month here I subsisted on the intel from McCray's office. If they hadn't brought in fifty of us to actively survey CSE, I wouldn't have had a clue who to approach."

Wait. What now? McCray had extra staff running feeds?

"There can't be room for that many people at the RL office. It normally holds what, twenty people?"

"Oh yeah, they're crammed in there. It's ridiculous. I don't know how they do it."

Noah clenched his fists in his jacket. Fifty extra people surveilling Coastal South East. Six days a week. Ten hours a day. Deleting that list wasn't going to help as much as he'd hoped.

CHAPTER TWENTY-EIGHT

MADDISON TURNED TO the cabinet to pull out some cinnamon, catching Noah's gaze as she did. "I'm beginning to believe making snickerdoodles is a ruse. Admit it—you just wanted an excuse to stare at me."

His smile widened, mirth dancing in his eyes. "Would that be so bad?" he asked, sitting on the kitchen counter.

She laughed. "No, but you could 'fess up to it." She mixed the cinnamon and sugar to dust over the cookie dough.

"Where's the fun in that?" He made a grab for her sleeve when she passed him on the way to the sink. She let herself be caught. He drew her into his arms. "You smell nice." He dipped his head down to capture a quick kiss.

She melted into his embrace, grateful for a moment of peace. Taking in a deep breath, she savored his cedar and peppermint scent. "You don't smell so bad yourself."

"How're your bruises today?" He fingered the collar of her sage turtleneck.

Pulling the collar down, she showed him. "Almost gone.

By tomorrow, I'll be back in my scalloped neck tops. So no frowning, okay?"

"A week's a long time to carry bruises like that. Makes me worry about tissue damage."

"You sound like an actual hospital employee." She smiled. "It's fine. I promise."

He nodded, but the furrows on his brow didn't disappear. He brushed an errant strand of hair behind her ear.

She cupped his face in her hands. "No worrying tonight, remember? Callista's gone. I feel fine. Daniel hasn't caused any, well much, trouble, in the last week. And McCray's been so busy ranting about how the resistance got to Callista, his team hasn't been working on recreating that list. Let's enjoy the brief reprieve we have, okay?"

"Okay." He kissed her forehead.

"Help me roll this dough, so we can get the cookies in the oven before everyone arrives." She hit his knee to get him moving off the counter and over to the island where the pans and sugar mixture waited.

He smiled, coming over and rolling up his sleeves. She had to focus on the cookie dough to keep from staring at the corded muscles of his forearms. Thinking about them caused her to blush and bite her lower lip.

"You can stare too, you know." He winked.

A laugh bubbled up and out of her, and she swatted at him with a towel. "I'll keep that in mind." She pointed at the bowl filled with snowy, sticky dough. "Roll."

He saluted and went to work. He formed the balls, and she rolled them in cinnamon sugar, placing them on the cookie sheets. Working in tandem, they finished in a matter of minutes; the sounds of AnnMarie Michaels' crooning filled the house. She slid a full pan into the oven and turned around to begin cleaning up the mess. Noah leaned over to kiss her cheek. "You've got cinnamon on your cheek."

"Thanks for the heads up." As she washed her hands off, she caught her reflection in the window over the sink. The doorbell rang. "Would you let whoever that is in while I clean up real quick?"

He headed for the door. "Don't be long."

She dashed to the bathroom to splash cold water on her face and twist her hair back into the loose braid she'd fashioned earlier. She grinned at her reflection in the mirror. Tonight's carefree Noah made her happier than she could put into words. She imagined it was the way he would act if they lived in a world with no Elite or liquidators. She'd never see enough of this Noah.

When she reentered the kitchen, Noah leaned against the island while Olivia pulled out napkins and Sophie programmed the coffee maker.

"Do you want some?" Sophie glanced her way.

"Nope. I'll be up all night if I do."

Sophie nodded and hit the start button. Maddison had never said yes. Still Sophie never failed to ask. Seconds later, the smell of brewing coffee mingled with the vanilla and cinnamon scents wafting from the oven. The timer dinged, and Maddison pulled the first pan of cookies out while slipping a second in. Jakob and Josh filtered into the kitchen, right on cue.

"So what's on the agenda tonight?" Jakob grabbed a cookie off the hot sheet, cradling it in his hand so it wouldn't break. Josh snatched one as well, throwing it in his mouth and drifting to Sophie's side.

"How you two manage that without burning your fingers or the roof of your mouth astounds me." Maddison leaned against Noah's side.

"The burn's worth it," Jakob said around a mouthful of cookie while Olivia transferred the remaining cookies to a cooling rack.

Sophie poured steaming mugs of coffee. "What are we doing tonight?"

"Well." Olivia smiled. "It was my turn to choose the movie."

Josh groaned, and she shot him a look.

"And I did take into account the guys' feelings about my touchy-feely, artsy movies, as they've labeled them."

"So, what is it?" Maddison snagged two cookies and handed one off to Noah.

"I chose …" Olivia paused, drawing everyone closer with a raised eyebrow. "*Inception*. Remake of a classic."

"Perfect," Noah said, earning him beaming approval from Olivia. Jakob agreed, and Josh shrugged.

Weird. Three weeks ago, Josh wouldn't have admitted to agreeing with Noah on anything. Maddison took another look at her friend, who leaned against the island, holding his coffee cup in his left hand. Wait. He was right-handed.

Her eyes flew to the other side, expecting an injury.

Shock rippled through her. His right hand was intertwined with Sophie's.

"When did that happen?" Maddison pointed at the clasped hands.

All conversation stopped. A slight red color crept up Josh's neck. He opened and closed his mouth without words, looking very much like a fish.

"New Year's Eve." Sophie's answer was bland enough, but her shoulders stiffened. "We'll talk about it later. Back to the movie, isn't it the intellectual mystery with the artsy twist? By the director you adore?" She hadn't understood the last two movies by this director and evidently didn't want to spend another evening watching a movie without a clear storyline.

Who cared? How had Sophie and Josh gotten together? Did Sophie's parents know? And why hadn't anybody told her?

"It has Michael Hudson in it." Olivia smirked.

"We're in," Maddison and Sophie answered.

"Keep in mind that I'm sitting right beside you as you watch." Noah's lips brushed her earlobe, sending a shiver down her spine.

She stuttered out an okay, all thoughts banished from her head. Heat crept up her neck and face, earning a chuckle from Noah and stares from everyone else.

The timer began beeping again. Thank goodness. She grabbed the second pan out of the oven and set it on the cooling rack. Jakob pulled the milk from the fridge, filling the glasses Olivia put on the counter. Everyone filled napkins with handfuls of the hot, spicy-smelling cookies and grabbed their milk or coffee before heading toward the living room.

For the first time since last week, Maddison didn't flinch when she came around the corner and spotted the mantel and wall she'd been pinned against. Noah noticed and nudged her hip in encouragement. They settled in the loveseat by the front window while Jakob stole the oversized, blue chair she'd begun to think of as his now. Olivia settled on the floor while Sophie and Josh dropped on the couch. Maddison couldn't pull her eyes away—she needed answers. After two years of pining, she'd thought it would take a huge disruption in their lives for Josh to voice his feelings. They looked so at ease together, like they'd been a couple for years. She had to get Sophie alone later.

"Hey, do you guys have plans on the thirty-first?" Sophie asked.

Olivia and Josh both murmured no. Maddison nodded her head. "Noah and I have the pig pickin' at the Yanceys'."

"Ben Yancey? The one who works at the hospital?"

"Yeah. He and his wife invited us out since Noah's missed Southern food so much. Ben said it's turned into an all-day event."

"Oh, okay." Sophie turned her attention to the others. "Do you guys want to do dinner at my house that Friday? My nana, mom, and I'll be making enough tamales for the whole year, and we'll do a big dinner at the end of the day."

Jakob and Josh jumped in to accept the invitation, speculating on how many tamales they could each put away.

Olivia chimed in her RSVP as she found the movie on the VisEnt database.

Maddison leaned back against Noah's shoulder as he slipped an arm around her waist. Her mind wandered forward two weeks. Noah had been skeptical about her attending the cookout, not wanting to put her in a potentially dangerous situation, but she'd overridden him. Noah's actions had set the Regional Liquidator's Office back, but McCray hadn't budged on Noah's deadline. They had thirty-one days to figure out how to save everyone, Noah included, and a trip to the Yanceys' could be key.

CHAPTER TWENTY-NINE

"**H**AVE WE DONE something to get on Ben's bad side?" In Noah's periphery, Maddison stared out the passenger window at the barren landscape. He didn't dare take his eyes off the winding country road, waiting for the Mustang's GPS to signal an end to the maddening curves they'd experienced in the last thirty minutes. "Why do you ask?"

"Because this looks like the kind of place you take someone to kill them without anyone knowing."

The car traveled yet another mile down the tree-lined road. They hadn't passed a business in at least twenty-five minutes, and the houses sat farther apart. He couldn't help but agree with her assessment.

"I think Ben's family owns some land out this way." Noah shifted his gaze over so he could read her expression. "Are you nervous?"

A smile broke out on her face. "With you? No. Just remarking on the desolation around here."

As they rounded a corner, the GPS indicated a right turn

ahead, and he spotted the lone green street sign in the distance. The odometer confirmed they were on the right track. Slowing down, he made the turn. The terrain changed from pavement to dirt. Dust swirled up behind them as the car traveled between the dead trees guarding the road.

"Admit it, it's kinda spooky." Maddison nudged him with a finger.

"Okay, it's a little weird."

She raised an eyebrow. "Meeting Ethel better be worth this drive."

He chuckled. "Oh, I promise, it'll be worth it."

Spotting an opening ahead, he drove forward. His mouth fell open. A field lay in front of them, bright with sunshine and complete with a restored twentieth-century farmhouse in fire engine red.

Beside him, Maddison froze. Probably for the same reason he did. The picturesque scene didn't surprise him—no, the wet cement filling his feet and creeping upward was courtesy of the sheer number of people in the field. How could this many people gather without raising a red flag with the RL's office? How had they gotten here? Only twelve cars sat to Noah's left.

"There have to be three hundred and fifty people here," she whispered.

He resisted the urge to back out of the opening before someone spotted them. "Stay close."

"Okay."

Her instant compliance heightened his anxiety. He maneuvered into an open spot with the Mustang's front end pointing toward the road. In case they needed to make a quick exit. As soon as he powered down, a fist rapped on his window.

Ben grinned and stepped back so Noah could open the door. "You guys made it. We'd almost given you up for dead."

He nodded. "I didn't realize how far out we needed to come until I plugged the address into my GPS, and by then it was too late to adjust. You didn't tell me you'd invited the whole MA."

"Just everyone important." Ben smiled over the car at Maddison. "Including you two. Come on, let's get you some food."

They agreed and followed Ben, Maddison's hand reaching over to take Noah's. Ben led them toward the throng of people. His sons and Stephen Henderson were throwing a football around. The teens wore knit shirts and jeans. They must've been playing for a while because everyone else still sported coats.

Several people nodded at Maddison as they passed, including a couple of janitors from the hospital. At the back of the house, the barbeque grill smoked and food filled dozens of tables. Billy Yancey leaned against the farmhouse wall with a snarl on his face but didn't come over. It seemed the universe could throw a small favor Noah's way every once in a while.

Ben turned to Maddison. "Ethel's in the house dealing with some female drama, but I'll make sure to introduce ya later. You two fill on up and mingle. I'm sure you'll run into quite a few people you know."

Maddison clutched Noah's hand. "Thanks."

He called after Ben's retreating figure. "We'll catch up with you later?"

"Oh yeah, I'll be around. Putting out fires. Get this many people together, and somebody's bound to hurt someone else's feelings." Ben laughed. "Have fun. I'll find ya in a bit."

As Ben walked away, Maddison leaned in. "Feel like eating?"

Noah shook his head. "No, but we might as well."

"To blend in."

He'd never been so glad for her perceptiveness. Three hundred and fifty people didn't gather in broad daylight without questions being raised. Odder still, in the last week, he'd talked to at least twenty of the people they'd passed—no one had said a word about the event, which made no sense.

Come on, this isn't a social gathering, and you know it.

He sighed and prepared for confirmation. They filled their plates and looked around for somewhere to sit.

Nurse Walker waved them over from her blanket on the ground. "Unless you get enough of me on the job, I'd love for you to join me."

"No, a familiar face would be wonderful." Maddison sat down on the blanket. "It's a little overwhelming."

She nodded with a wave of her hand. "Ben never warns newcomers about this bash. They all show up wide-eyed like deer in headlights."

"Thanks, Nurse Walker." Noah settled in next to Maddison.

"I thought I told you to call me Lynn."

He smiled. "Lynn."

Today her voice held no traces of either the in-control supervisor or the anxious victim. Her eyes sparkled with humor, her posture relaxed.

"How long have you been coming to these?" Maddison took a bite of the steaming chopped pork. "Wow, this is good."

Lynn laughed. "A couple of years. Ben took pity on me 'cause I don't have family in the area."

"Same with me," Noah said.

"He's great at taking orphans in and making them part of his family. Life would be much lonelier without him and the rest of this group." She took a sip of the hot chocolate she'd been nursing and smiled, but it didn't reach her eyes.

"Where are you from?" Maddison asked.

The nurse mentioned she'd traveled around a lot but grew up in a metro area in Upper North East, an area fascinating to Maddison. As Maddison peppered her with questions, Noah surveyed the crowd. Teens gathered on the edges in gaggles while parents stood around sipping coffee and chatting. A group of older men guarded the grill, arguing and gesturing. College-aged youth huddled around a campfire, leaning in and exchanging whispers.

To that group's right, he spotted an anomaly.

Coastal South East's Regional Directors of Agriculture and Education stuck out like sore thumbs in their business suits. Why would they be here? He needed to get closer. Laying a hand on Maddison's shoulder, he interrupted her and Lynn's conversation. "I think I see an old friend from MA-16. Mind if I go hunt him down?"

Maddison shook her head and locked eyes with his. "I'm not going anywhere."

He squeezed her hand. "I'll be quick. I promise." He stood and nodded at Lynn before heading into the crowd. Weaving through the groups allowed him to pick up pieces of their conversations. Parents talked about their children's education and future. Some discussed the food. One group murmured about God and the Bible.

Their topic brought him up short, and he pushed himself to keep on walking without a shift in his facial expression. Marcioni's ban on the practice of religion made mention of it a liquidation-worthy offense. But he wasn't supposed to be able to hear anyone's speech from that far away. He would stop and observe them once he finished eavesdropping on Directors Beckett and Mason.

Passing the Elite members, he stood on the fringes of a group about fifteen feet away and listened to the two men. Impatience rang in their voices. Definitely not here for the food or company. They kept circling a topic but never naming it. *Come on, give me something.*

A booming voice joined the dialogue. "Gentlemen, don't you think you ought to take your coats off, loosen those ties, and leave the business alone for a little while?" A warning rang in the man's undertone.

Fabric rustled, and the Regional Director of Agriculture said, "Oh, quit with the liquidator stare. You aren't one anymore, or don't you remember?"

Noah froze. When the jovial voice spoke again, Noah paid even closer attention to the accent and cadence. "You don't forget faking your death, Beckett. And you don't stop being who you are because you're on another side either. I'm still a mercenary, and you're still a pompous paper pusher."

Beckett sputtered but came up with no response.

The third voice, Mason, chimed in. "I think we'd better change the subject or take our conversation somewhere else. This is a party, remember?"

"As I've already said."

Their voices began to fade away, and Noah turned to get a look at the trio. His pulse raced. Presumed dead liquidator Gary Bullard walked away from him with an arm around both companions' shoulders. His presence proved two things: He'd been in league with Billy Yancey for some time, explaining why Yancey had never been punished, and the Elite no longer held his loyalty. Faking his death to escape them proved it.

Noah quickened his pace back as much as possible without drawing attention. Maddison sat on Lynn's blanket, alone and looking panicked. Making eye contact with her told him she'd put the pieces together as well.

Standing, she grasped his hand, her eyes wide. "I saw Ritchie and Brandon."

"I watched one of your MA's dead liquidators walk away with two other regional officials."

"I see you two have figured it out." Lynn walked up to them with a serious look on her face. "I told Ben you should've been informed the minute you arrived, but he thought you might want to enjoy the party before he let you in on the secret. I'm sure you have questions for him to answer."

"Why Ben?" Maddison gripped Noah's hand.

"Well, as the leader, he'll be the best one to fill in the blanks racing through your heads."

Ice trickled through Noah's veins. Ben Yancey was the leader of the resistance? The smart but country janitor corralled these three hundred some people into a movement? It wrecked Noah's brain.

Maddison swayed beside him. He needed to keep her close. Look for an exit. He had to protect her. Ben hadn't invited them out here to kill them—he must think they would welcome the opportunity to join, but Noah couldn't bet on that. Nothing would separate him from her side, and he'd fight their way out of here if necessary.

He hoped it wouldn't be.

"Noah? Maddison?" Lynn sounded unsure, the last thing they needed.

He forced a calm tone. "Sorry, that's a lot to process all at once, but lead the way. We'll follow wherever you go."

Her smile returned. "I knew you guys would want in. Some people had their doubts, but I told Ben you were okay."

"And Lynn has great discernment. She's never been wrong about someone." Ben walked up to the group, familiar smile in place. His speech, however, had a sharp, distinct cadence it'd lacked before. He stood taller somehow. "You'll forgive me for investigating you both a little before we invited you. Several of our members, Billy included, had some reservations because of Daniel. You understand. I wanted to assuage their fears."

The earth shifted on its axis. Ben had been spying *on him* for months? The thought made Noah's throat dry, and he attempted a swallow. Ben had crafted a very convincing cover persona.

The older man set his gaze on Maddison. "Lynn and Ritchie Callum both vouched for you some time ago, but we wanted to let you come to us."

Maddison stiffened, but Ben didn't seem to notice.

"Ritchie told me you'd expressed interest several years ago. Because of your parents, I assume? He thought you backed off to protect your brother. An admirable decision, and since then you've proven you'll go toe-to-toe with any liquidator with the way you've handled Daniel and the new female liquidator. We knew you would join us when the time came."

Ben trained his gaze on Noah and clapped him on the back. "Especially once you became involved with Noah. You two seem to give each other courage, and that leads to action." His face took on an almost apologetic look. "I knew you were one of us from our first conversation, but I haven't spent the last five years being cautious to grow careless at the end. I know you must have been frustrated with Lynn and John giving you hints then leaving you with more questions than answers. I needed to be certain, considering you're not from around here, and I wanted to see how you would react to their hints. See if you could be cautious too." He beamed. "I'm proud to say you passed all my tests. I'd like you to join the leadership. We could you use a young man with your convictions and self-control. I'll vouch for you myself. What do you say?"

Noah's head swam, trying to process all the information thrown at him in the last ten minutes. He wanted to walk away and recover from the blows. Instead, he planted his feet and met Ben's stare with a confident one of his own. "I'm in."

CHAPTER THIRTY

"**M**E TOO." MADDISON straightened her shoulders, not a hint of trepidation in her voice despite the death grip she had on his hand.

A subtle tension dropped off Ben's face, and a wide grin replaced it. He clapped Noah on the back again. "So glad to hear it. You two are just the kind of people we need, standing on the cusp of your futures. You should have the world at your fingertips. And we're going to make sure it happens."

Someone called out to him from a makeshift stage Noah hadn't noticed before. Ben nodded before turning his attention back to them. "You guys stick with Lynn. I'm going to want your opinion after a while."

"Of course." Noah's anxiety ebbed a little. He might not have picked up on Ben's secret, but then neither had Ben guessed his. His cover remained intact. At least he had that in his favor, for now.

"Great." Ben gave them another huge smile and headed for the platform where Ethel and the boys joined him. As he stepped onto the platform, the crowd shifted as though gravity pulled them toward Ben. Families stood together, one unit. Voices tapered off, even those of the children. A rapt silence fell around them. Eerie.

Noah pulled Maddison in front of him, wrapping his arms around her waist. Her arms covered his, and she leaned back against his chest.

Someone handed Ben a bullhorn. "I'm glad everyone could be with us today. Each one of you has become like family to me over the last five years, and today is the celebration of the end of that season. A labor which has been hard, grueling, and never ending. One we've worked in darkness. But soon, no more. Five years ago, ten of us met—ten men who remembered what most of you cannot recall. But those of us over forty retain the knowledge of what it was like before Potentate Marcioni changed our dear republic into a prison. Even if we were just children or teens at the time, we remember what freedom felt like and we remember how the bloody months stripped us of it." Someone in the crowd sobbed. "And five years ago, we made a decision that our children ..." He turned to look at his sons who stared at him while Ethel beamed from her place behind them.

"Our sons and daughters would not be saddled with futures they didn't want and couldn't free themselves from. They deserve to choose what their careers will be, where they live, and who they will marry. Our children deserve the freedom to thrive or fail at something they love. And it is because of my boys I stand before you today."

The last piece of the puzzle clicked for Noah. He'd thought Ben had too much to lose, but Ben sired the movement for that exact reason. In fact, it made him the perfect leader. To Noah's right, John Henderson laid a hand on his son's shoulder. Other fathers and mothers called out in agreement or pulled their children closer. Maddison shifted in his arms.

"We made careful plans. We knew what the fallout from hastily thrown together protests and coups had been." Ben's eyes darted to Billy for a split second. "To succeed, we would need time, organization, and support on our side. And support began to come—from others who wanted freedom of expression, of speech, of industry, and from classification."

People in the crowd hissed.

"We found those calling out for democracy, both young and old." He pointed at a young man, at Director Mason, and, right up front, at Gary Bullard. "You want freedom for yourselves, for your loved ones, for the community, for our nation. And you have been patient, trusting in our passion and vision enough to be circumspect until the right time."

Ben lowered the bullhorn for a moment, resting it on his hip and sucking in what appeared to be a shaky breath. "And, just when we thought we were ready to move forward, a group of people found us." His eyes shot to the back of the crowd. "Those who've lost the most because of this regime. The Christians, Jews, and Muslims who were falsely accused of starting this whole mess and then driven underground or killed. You, my friends, have the most reason to want freedom, a livelihood, honesty, and the free exercise of your religions. I must apologize again that we did not come to find you first."

Beside them, Nurse Walker's face ran with tears. She made no move to wipe them off, chanting under her breath.

"But I promise the wait is almost over." His voice grew. "The days of the so-called Elite are numbered. The common man will regain his voice. Many of you will taste freedom for the first time. And they will never again underestimate the Masses." Rumbling and shifting began to grow in the crowd. "The day is dawning, and when it does, all will see the regime for what it is. And we will rise up and the nation with us, and we will take back control. Watch for the dawn, my friends. When you see it, you will know the waiting is over, and the time for action has begun. There will be no doubt. Watch for the dawn. Morning comes."

Applause broke out. The clamor of voices yelling and feet stomping joined in, and Noah forced himself to clap as well. Maddison's hands shook as she mimicked him. What did she think about all of this?

Across the crowd, he spotted Brandon standing with Ritchie Callum. The liquidator stared at him, eyes wide, and shook his head in disbelief.

These people would follow Ben wherever he led, like blind cattle waiting to be driven on. Once the stampede started, there would be no stopping it.

Noah wanted to grab Maddison and slip away before anyone noticed, before they could be swept along with everyone else. However, the push of the crowd made movement impossible. He held her closer.

She leaned her head back, and her wide eyes met his for a moment. She lifted her mouth to his ear. "This is madness.

They don't even know what to look for. What if they act before they're supposed to? What if some of them get themselves killed thinking they've seen 'this dawn'?" She paused. "It feels cult-like, doesn't it?"

"That's what makes it so dangerous."

He shot a glance over to Nurse Walker. She was enthralled along with the rest of the crowd and hadn't noticed he and Maddison didn't join the hysteria. After several minutes, the applause began to die down, and Ben descended the steps. The group began to disperse as though there'd been a dismissal at the end of Ben's speech. He stopped to speak with Bullard and his brother, pointing back at Noah and Maddison, before making a beeline for them.

Noah pasted on a smile for Ben and shook his hand. "Observant, wise, and charismatic? Ben, you are definitely the man for this job. I can't believe I didn't see it before." He tilted his head. "But then, maybe you didn't want me to?"

Ben chuckled. "Being cautious, young friend. I'd like to introduce you both to some people, if you'll stay."

Maddison's grip grew viselike. He squeezed back. "We'd be honored."

"Wonderful." Ben nodded. "Lynn, why don't you go on ahead then and let the group know of our additions. We'll follow slower so I can answer any questions these two might have."

The nurse beamed and turned toward the farmhouse, making her way through the dispersing crowd. Once she disappeared from view, Ben gave them his full attention.

"I assume you two have questions."

As they walked, Maddison asked, "How does such a large group meet without discovery? I'm sorry, that must seem impertinent, but a crowd of people this size tends to garner attention."

"Not impertinent at all. It's a very perceptive question." He surveyed the crowd. "Well, for one thing, over the last five years, each one of these people and their families have been vetted, like yourselves. We didn't want revenge-driven or hasty actors. We needed people we could trust, and every person here proved their trustworthiness. They, and their children, know not to speak about their convictions or our meetings outside of these times. Second, most of the crowd today either hiked several miles to get here—there's a nature park three miles to the west—or they parked at one of the houses in the area and one of the leadership ferried them in. The cars on the property belong to those men and, of course, my family. Gary Bullard circumvented the GPS tracking on our vehicles for the day. To the computers it appears like the cars are parked in our respective driveways." He spread his hands out across the area they passed through. "Plus, between my family and the other leadership, we own everything within a twenty-mile radius."

Maddison's mouth gaped open. "Are you serious? How did you manage that?"

He laughed. "Well, the homestead has been in my family for generations, and it's five miles wide. And as I said, we've used the last five years for careful planning. Different members bought up the surrounding land over the course of three years, so we could begin meeting as a group. It's been invaluable. Plus, we're so far out, no one pays much attention. You came in on major highways, right? By the time you made your first turn off, the population had already begun to dwindle, and six minutes after that, you drove onto the beginning of our land."

"Genius," Noah mumbled. Yet another reason the Elite had been hard pressed to locate the resistance.

"Thank you, Noah." Ben nodded and smiled as he led them around the side of the house.

Billy hadn't moved, still leaning against the side wall, near what looked like a root cellar. He straightened when he spotted Noah and Maddison. "I don't like it." He glared at Noah. "He's tied to the Elite through his brother. Who's not dead despite Noah's supposed loyalties to our cause." He spit on the ground.

"You've been outvoted." Ben motioned to the cellar. "Let's go."

Billy cursed but opened the doors and descended first. Ben held out his hand for Maddison and Noah to go on ahead. He went first, stepping sideways along the narrow steps to help Maddison to the bottom.

When his eyes adjusted, he bit back a curse of his own.

They'd entered a war room, outfitted with lighting, digital cable, and a conference table scattered with maps. Chairs filled one side of the table, and a satellite compad projector and camera sat in the middle. Bullard, Beckett, Mason, Ritchie, and Lynn stood off to the side. Another group of men and women conversed near the blacked out wall, which Noah assumed would project the action plans Ben had designed. As his eyes drifted over the group, he recognized a local manufacturing CEO, a retail chain president, and the area's banking director.

Ben and his leadership had laid their groundwork with brilliant vision. The resistance not only had numbers on its side, it also represented every industry and class in the population.

Taking out the resistance leadership would cripple the MA for months.

Ben cleared his throat, and the room went silent. "If everyone will take a seat or find a place to stand where you can see the wall, we'll get started." He extended a hand for Noah and Maddison to join him. "I know some of you haven't met our newest members. This is Noah Seforé and Maddison James. We've discussed their potential involvement before, and I'm happy to say they've come on board. Noah's brother Daniel is the regional liquidator's favorite free agent, so Noah can give us insight we wouldn't have otherwise. This has been the one area we've been lacking in since Gary had to fake his death to continue. If we can't have a liquidator in our group, a family member who's committed to the cause is the next best thing." Several of the others nodded, though Bullard rolled his eyes.

How did they know about Daniel's standing with McCray?

They knew too much. And yet, they didn't know they had a liquidator in their midst?

"If you two would stand there." Ben indicated the far end of the table, and they moved to the end beside Lynn.

"We'll connect and get started." He pushed a button. The sound of ringing vidcoms filled the room. Moments later, the blacked out wall lit up with the faces of eight men, all forty-five or older.

They exchanged greetings, and Noah gathered that these men along with Ben and Billy made up the initial ten who'd formed the Masses.

Beginning from the left, each one gave their location and a number. By the third man, Noah felt his blood chill. Beside him, Maddison stifled a gasp. Like Ben, each one had led a meeting today. They were smaller but scattered throughout the metro area. Altogether, over two thousand people had gathered undetected for the purpose of overthrowing the Elite. It was just enough people to spark a dangerous uprising. And they all waited on one word.

"Well, gentlemen—and ladies—the time has come. Our final pieces are in place, and I can reveal our plan for change." Ben held out a hand to acknowledge Ritchie. "The first phase will begin next week. As you know, Ritchie Callum has been carrying out strategic com interruptions with a group of his peers for the last two years. Six months ago, we began using the focus those hacks draw to hit the Elite in other areas.

"Next Sunday, he and the other college students and teenagers in our group will stage a major hack and protest at the CSE Medical University. If any students from your gatherings would like to join, they are welcome to arrive at the quad at 8:00 a.m. However, any wary students should be discouraged. We expect a reprisal from the government, and these students will be laying their lives on the line to partici-pate in the first wave."

Ben turned to Noah and explained his presence to those joining over com. "Noah, will your brother and the station-ary liquidators retaliate?"

"Yes."

"Would they send for reinforcements to carry out their justice?"

Noah gave a terse nod. "Reinforcements will be sent, whether they ask for them or not. And I wouldn't expect they'll show mercy of any kind."

"Bullard suggested they might record this, do you agree?"

Images of dead students filled his sight. "They may live feed it to the com channels to send a message."

Ben smiled before turning back to the others, and some-thing stirred in Noah's gut.

"Good," Ben said. "We're counting on it. The second phase will start as the liquidators begin arriving on campus. The most faithful of us will filter throughout the metro area wearing these." He held up an exact replica of the liquidator signet ring, and Noah's eyes locked on the familiar black and silver.

"In the name of the Elite, our pseudo-liquidators will destroy hundreds of people in MA-4's local secondary schools, university, and hospitals. Those places the protesters have come from. They will also show no mercy. Every region will be reminded of who the Elite are. And the nation will join us."

Ben stared at each person for a moment. "We will have

to sacrifice. Our fellow citizens will sacrifice, but freedom has always come at a high cost. This revolution is no different. We may not be the ones standing over the potentate's dead body at the Center. But we will be remembered as the region that revealed the vileness of the Elite. The nation will remember our teenagers and students. The images of smoking hospitals and schools will be burned into their brains. Our names may never be touted, but the people will be free. And that is all we are after."

CHAPTER THIRTY-ONE

WATCHING THE FOREST of trees blur by, Maddison felt numb. Like she had been watching someone else mingle with the Masses. Like someone else had heard the madness of their plan. The trembling of her arms and legs increased as Ritchie's face came to mind.

When she'd first seen him, a flash of excitement had run through her. After all, it'd been years since they'd actually spoken. He'd spotted her and sat down to greet her as Lynn left to refill their glasses. She should've followed Lynn.

In secondary school, Ritchie had been passionate, but he'd changed, become angry and vengeful. As he breathed threats toward the Elite, he leaned closer, and it took everything in her not to shrink back. His eyes burned with something dangerous, and she had cast her gaze around for Noah, willing him back to her side. Someone called to Ritchie, stopping him mid-rant, and she breathed a sigh of relief when he stood and joined the person who'd distracted him.

Noah had come striding toward her, and she'd never been happier to see him, wanting to throw herself into his safe embrace. But her fear didn't have time to abate as Lynn and then Ben Yancey met them. She wrapped her arms around herself, remembering the change in Noah's demeanor. The shift had given her chills. Her alarm had increased as Ben spoke to the crowd and turned to horror when he revealed their plan.

They planned to risk other people's lives—no, take other people's lives, at little expense to their own. Their teenagers and college kids, people her age, would die thinking they had been a part of something great. Never to know the adults had used them as pawns, used the MA as pawns, in their own quest for freedom.

Her world had turned inside out. Could anyone, anything, be what she thought? She was dating a liquidator, had been saved by another liquidator, and worked against the resistance. For, it turned out, good reason since she'd been wrong about their position as selfless saviors. They were no better than the Elite.

Even thinking it felt like betrayal.

However, the truth couldn't be denied. Human life meant little more than a bargaining chip, a flint to light the fire Ben and the leadership orchestrated. And those who would die? They would have no more input or warning than the Elite would've given them.

The heat blasted into the car, but it didn't bring feeling back into her fingers or toes. She would never be warm again. For so long, she vilified everyone in the Elite and saw the resistance as the hope of the people. Heroic, good people belonged to a resistance. Evil pledged loyalty to the Elite. She couldn't have been more wrong. Ben, Ritchie, and their leadership were insane—and definitely evil.

She glanced over at Noah, and tears filled her eyes. How could she ever have doubted him? "Thank you."

He stared straight ahead. Red mottled his face. He looked ready to combust. "For what?"

"For being a good man. For making the right decisions."

His white-knuckled hands clenched the steering wheel. Could he exert enough pressure to bend it?

"What are you thinking?"

His head whipped toward her, his eyes on fire. "Does no one value human life? I heard Ben give this great speech about freedom for the future and a better tomorrow, and then he sentenced those students to death. He's using them to make a point. Them and anyone else who happens to be on one of those campuses that day." He banged a hand against the steering wheel. "It's the same thing Marcioni did. Don't they see? Their values might be better, but their methods show how like him they are." His eyes hardened. "At least I'm in a position to do something about it."

She sucked in a breath. She'd seen this intensity once before, the night Callista arrived in town. His warrior persona changed him—his focus, his posture, his tone of voice. "What are you going to do?"

"Well, first I'm going to take you home where you'll be safe. Then I'm going to make myself call Daniel and get him to meet me at the hotel. Someone should be worried about collateral damage."

"Get him to sneak into my house. In case someone's

watching you or him tonight. I'll have Jakob get Taylor out of the house long enough for us to plan."

A low growl rumbled through his chest. "You are not going to be part of the planning."

"I could help. And it'll be less suspicious for you and Daniel to meet there."

"I don't want you to help. I want you to have deniability in case something goes wrong." Switching the car to auto-pilot, he faced her and his expression softened. His mouth twisted. "People are going to die, Maddison, and I'll have to decide who. I won't put you in a position to carry that around with you."

The truth of what he said slammed into her like a tsunami. She didn't want Ben's plan to succeed, but killing them? "Can't you stop them without liquidating anybody?"

He shook his head. "McCray will want all of them dead. I don't know how many I can save. That's why I don't want you there. I need you to let me handle this alone."

"Noah, you—"

"Don't you trust me?"

His words hit their intended target. She willed her voice to respond. "I do. I will."

"Then stay with your brother."

*

Why did he keep hurting her? The pain in her eyes as he dropped her off at the house echoed in him. But she couldn't be a part of this. He knew what this decision would cost—in memories and in nightmares. He'd do anything to save her eyes from looking like his.

A rap sounded on the door, and Daniel's impatient face appeared seconds later. Noah couldn't help but ask, "Were you spotted?"

Daniel gave him a condescending look complete with eye roll. "I've been a liquidator for four years and a rebellious teen before that. I know what I'm doing." Shrugging off his jacket, he looked around the room. "So what's the big emergency?"

Noah pointed toward the information filling the wall.

Daniel paused. "You found it."

"And almost too late." Noah paced.

"Why do you need me? Call McCray and give him the good news."

"It's more complicated than we thought. Things could get messy. I want to give McCray not only his info, but an action plan as well. I need you for that."

Daniel flopped down on the bed, leaning against the headboard, and stretched his arms behind his head. "You know what he's going to say regardless."

"I know. But I figured if I could come up with a plan you agreed with, he'd have to agree as well. I don't want anyone getting hurt that doesn't have to."

"So what's the situation?"

Noah filled him in, pointing out pictures as he mentioned specific people and locations.

Daniel's disinterested look became grave. "A warning won't be enough."

Noah shook his head. "I know McCray's going to say that, but most of those people don't even know what they're involved in."

Daniel sat up, his gaze focused. "No, I meant, a warning won't work with them. They're too well formed and motivated. You could try issuing a warning to those students, but they're idealistic and short sighted. You won't get them to call it off. The leadership won't surrender either. You might postpone their act, but you won't be able to stop it. You need to end it."

Noah's pacing froze. "So, what, we liquidate them for an act they haven't even committed yet? How is that any better?"

"It's better because doctors and nurses don't die because of them. Hospitals aren't burned to the ground. Schools aren't razed with students inside. Children don't die."

"Even if we could arrest them as they arrive next Sunday, what about the others?"

"McCray's going to want them all dead. Or you leave people behind to take the leadership's place." Daniel studied the wall of information again.

Noah's fists clenched. "Some of those are women and children, who don't have a clue what's been planned."

"The women know they joined an anti-government group. That's treason, and it's the way every liquidator will see it. Those under eighteen will be remanded to government custody." He pointed at Noah. "We're going to need help, and we can't trust any of the stationary liquidators here, not with Bullard's defection. There might be more. Ask McCray for at least a hundred young free agents, and they'd better come well-armed."

Noah sank down in the desk chair. "Taking out the leadership is one thing. They're guilty, and I agree they have to be stopped. But killing the rest?"

Daniel shook his head. "McCray won't agree to anything less. Not since he's vying for the minister of justice position. He'll want to make sure he appears in complete control of his territory. Besides, if these people worship Yancey, they'll just raise up another leader to take his place once he's gone. His devoted followers are as dangerous as he is."

Squeezing his eyes shut, Noah pinched the bridge of his nose as the pressure behind it built into a migraine. "But they aren't dangerous now. Liquidating people who might become violent is unjust."

"They've already knowingly broken the law, Noah. Liquidation is the consequence for all acts of treason, violent or not." Daniel's matter-of-fact tone made the situation all too clear. "Look, either you keep this information to yourself for over a week, innocent people die, and then we punish everyone—including the men, women, and children who rise up in protest of the 'liquidator attack'—or you turn all of the adult members in for liquidation now, and no one else gets hurt. McCray isn't going to give you any other option, and I doubt these 'Masses' will either."

Noah wracked his brain for another option. Any solution that didn't doom three hundred plus children to a life like Maddison and Jakob's, but sparing their parents meant risking the lives of innocent and regime-abiding men, women, and children.

. Daniel stood and headed for the door. "When you've made your decision, let me know, and we can talk about at least controlling the way it goes down."

"Wait." Noah's hand shot out to stop his brother. "You're right. I hate it, but you're right." He felt years too old.

"'Bout time you recognized it." Daniel sat back down, spinning the compad toward him. "We have to get the other liquidators here fast but as quietly as possible. We don't want to tip our hand." He typed at a furious pace. "They could all arrive different ways: planes, trains, cars. At intervals over the next two, maybe three days—"

"Doesn't planning people's deaths bother you at all?"

Daniel didn't even flinch. "I'm pragmatic, which is why you called me. You know this plan is the only answer. So what do you expect me to do? Wallow in self-imposed guilt? That's your job. Sit down and let's get this finished, so we can call McCray." His smile twisted. "Then you can take all the time in the world to moan about the hard choices life gives you."

Noah clenched his jaw and bit back a retort, aching to pummel Daniel for good measure.

"We don't have time to go another round. Focus." Daniel searched the financial records of the leadership on the compad.

Noah sank back into the chair, defeated. "So, we get a hundred other liquidators here without being discovered. Then what?"

"This group is too well organized not to have a backup plan in case something happens to derail them." Daniel clicked on another page, smirking as he skimmed its contents. "And I think I found it."

"What are you talking about?" He leaned over to see real estate information on the screen.

"What happens if the group's compromised? Do the last five years go up in smoke? That doesn't fit with what you've told me about Ben and the original ten's careful planning. I think if the organization is found out, if a plan fails, there's a contingency plan in place. A meeting place, a final hurrah before they can all be found and liquidated."

"Makes sense. Ben does seem to have every angle covered. What are you getting at? A spontaneous uprising wherever they are?"

"No." Daniel's smirk grew wider. "Even better. A general meeting place with supplies, some black market arms, and room for everyone to gather. A place that buys them time to go underground or go out fighting." He pointed to a line item on the screen. "And I think this is where it is."

"The abandoned Amtrak station?"

"Several years ago, Tomás Consuelos bought the land it sits on. Isn't he one of the leadership? Why would a retail president buy two acres of land and not do anything with it? I mean, it's prime real estate, and he hasn't even razed the station or the maintenance warehouses. All five of them. And look at the next line item. It's an actual Amtrak train. I bet it even works, archaic or not."

Noah pulled up a satellite image of the property, zooming

in and out to view its surroundings. "It's right in the center of the MA. Anyone could make it to the station within an hour, two tops, if they wanted. And no one would go looking through those warehouses with the electric security fences on the property."

"It's the perfect place to stockpile illegal weapons and supplies and serve as a central meeting place if anything goes wrong. It's a stronghold and escape plan all in one."

Zooming out again, Noah felt a shoot of hope sprout up inside him. "It's separated enough from the surrounding neighborhoods that we shouldn't have to worry about stray bullets. We can contain and deal with them without endangering anyone else."

"Well, yeah, there's that too," Daniel said. "You'll have to confirm it's the place once we compromise them."

Noah crossed his arms. "And how do you propose I do that?"

"We know the leadership is too dangerous to chance them escaping or holing up. I say, on Thursday, we send six pairs of liquidators out to deal with the original ten along with the others in the war room. Once the Liquidation Updates hit the com screens, panic and outrage will set in, and the followers will head for their safe place. All you have to do is call someone who trusts you and pretend to be as distraught as they are—they'll give you the location, not knowing you, me, and the other eighty-eight liquidators will already be there waiting on them."

"I hate the way your brain works," Noah muttered. The tenor of excitement in Daniel's voice, the blasé way he orchestrated the death of so many people, unsettled Noah more than the idea of what they planned.

"But you know I'm right. It's not fool proof but close enough. We deal with all of the resistance in one day with little or no collateral damage. McCray gets his glory. And the other liquidators risk very little themselves as we'll be able to confront people as they arrive at the station."

True. He hated it, but it was true. Noah let his arms fall to his sides. "For a plan I hate, it's not bad."

CHAPTER THIRTY-TWO

NOAH LET HIS head fall back against the chair. It had been tough to convince McCray of their plan. He wanted everything to be drastic and public, even suggesting they liquidate anyone over the age of twelve. A glory chaser made the worst kind of superior, but with Daniel's help, Noah convinced the RL that good favor wouldn't be won by liquidating children. While their plan might not be flashy, it would ensure the complete eradication of the resistance. That's what would matter to the Council at the end of the day.

In a heartbeat, McCray changed his tune. He praised Noah and Daniel's logic and named them liquidators in command for the mission, giving them authority to make whatever arrangements they deemed necessary. They all knew this arrangement handed McCray the soon-to-be-vacant minister of justice title on a silver platter. That was the moment Daniel went off script. He asked McCray if he wouldn't give Noah's girlfriend a pass this one time. As a reward to Noah. Since he was doing so much for McCray.

The smile didn't even drop off the RL's face at Daniel's impertinence. Noah took advantage of the man's good humor and pointed out that Maddison had provided their cause with helpful information, such as the identity of resistance hacker Ritchie Callum.

"Why not?" the RL had responded. "I was pretty hard on you, kid. But you made good on your end of the deal, so I'll honor my end and let you keep your girl."

So magnanimous, that Lawson McCray.

But she was safe. Finally. So he wouldn't complain. He stared at Daniel. "Not that I'm not grateful, but why did you convince McCray to spare Maddison?"

"You didn't expect that, did you?" Daniel smirked. "I wanted to see if I could get him to say yes."

What. "You risked bringing her into the conversation because you wanted to see what you could get him to give you?"

"Well, it worked, didn't it?" Daniel pushed off from the wall he leaned against and walked over to the desk. "I'm hungry. Where's the room service menu?"

"Get out." Noah shook his head and pointed at the door. "Just … get out."

Daniel rolled his eyes but headed to the door. "You're welcome." The door clicked shut behind him.

On a whim. Daniel had risked her life on a whim. Noah shook his head. Didn't matter now. Think about something else. Run through the plan again. The other liquidators would begin arriving tonight from the rest of Coastal South East. They would continue to trickle in over the next four days, giving Noah and Daniel time to stake out the Amtrak station. By Wednesday morning, everyone would be briefed on their responsibilities, That evening a small group would infiltrate the station, securing any arms found and canvassing every inch of its perimeter.

Governing a hundred other liquidators was a weighty responsibility. But the weight crushing his chest had a different origin. He sucked in another deep breath. Tonight, he had condemned hundreds of people to death because they were unhappy with the government. He would sign their death certificates, all because they shared some of the same feelings he had. He grieved the loss of Ben and Ethel, Lynn Walker, even some of the less savory members of the leadership like Billy and John Henderson. They had to be stopped, and he didn't regret turning them in, but the mindless masses would haunt him. His head dropped into his hands. Even now, their faces passed through his mind's eye. Only to be replaced by images of their dead bodies. The image he would help create less than a week from today. An injured groan rose up, unable to be silenced.

He collapsed to the floor, his forehead crashing into the carpet. A fleeting prayer for forgiveness escaped his lips. But God wouldn't hear, let alone forgive, a man who caused more than a thousand deaths.

No amount of good Noah could do in his lifetime outweighed that fact. No great sacrifice existed to undo the blood he had spilled. He was damned.

And he deserved it.

Maddison stood frozen in the doorway, the key Noah'd given her weeks earlier dangling from her hand. Noah's groan made her want to fly forward and comfort him. He knelt on the floor, his hands clenched on either side of his head. The posture was so private, so exposed, it felt wrong to interrupt. She backed out a step, but he straightened.

He swept a hand over his face and cleared his throat. "Didn't I ask you to stay home?"

She sat down next to him and put her hand on his knee. He grabbed it and held on.

"I'm sorry," she whispered. Words wouldn't help. "It's done?"

"Everything will be in place by Thursday morning. That's all you need to know." He seemed to have aged years in the last three hours. His posture stooped. His voice weathered. "We need to talk about where you're going."

She stiffened. "What do you mean?"

"You, Jakob, and Taylor will need to leave Wednesday morning, at the same time you leave the house normally. I'll supply you with official excuses from school and work and arrange permission for you to travel between MAs. We made sure you're safe from the Elite, but the Masses know your face, and I don't want to risk anyone coming after you—to keep you safe or to harm you."

"I'm not leaving you."

He faced her, jaw clenched. "This is not open for discussion, Maddison. If they realize who turned them in, they'll come for you. You, more than anyone else, need to be as far away from here as possible. I'll be worried about you the entire time otherwise. I don't trust anyone else to keep you safe, and I can't stay with you. I have a place in mind, and you can take whoever you want, provided they don't know why until you leave. Or you can choose somewhere else outside of CSE. But I need you to go." His hands squeezed her shoulders, his eyes boring into hers. "For my sanity."

Exactly—for sanity's sake. The members of the resistance wouldn't want to hunt down her alone. And he'd be a lot easier to find—and kill. Why hadn't she thought of that sooner? If she had, she could've called Daniel and made him agree to take his brother out of the equation so Noah could go with them and be safe himself.

He wouldn't have agreed to it. He'd be too worried about the other liquidators' zeal and the innocent who could get caught in the crossfire. He'd put himself in the center of it all for everyone's sake but his own.

If anything happened, she needed to be here, not hours away from him. She needed to have Taylor close by. If they holed up somewhere else, would she even be able to make it back in ... No, she wouldn't think that. She couldn't.

She wanted to argue until he caved, but he looked so defeated already. And if he had to put himself in harm's way, she needed him to be one hundred percent focused. This situation would be dangerous enough without distractions. If saying yes would lighten the load he carried, if it would make him more focused during the arrests and keep him from making a careless miscalculation, she had to do it.

She squared her shoulders. "Where do you want us to go?"

He pulled her closer. "My parents' house."

"MA-16?"

He nodded. "It's in Daniel's name. No one will be there. Once you've secured it, no one but us could get in to you."

"And I can take Josh, Liv, and Sophie, too?"

Noah's shoulders slumped. "I figured you would want them along.... I'll need to lay some groundwork first."

She didn't want to fight with him, not now, but leaving her friends behind wasn't an option. What if someone came after them because they couldn't get to her or Noah? The group had proved capable of it, and grief-filled revenge would only up the stakes. She'd never forgive herself if one of them got hurt because of her. Someone needed to look out for them too. "What do you mean by groundwork? What's the problem?"

He sighed. "Things are going to be very precarious for the next six days. Nothing must seem out of the ordinary. No one should break from our normal routines. No one can breathe a word about what we've learned."

Keeping quiet wouldn't be a problem for her friends, not if she asked. "They won't say anything. We can trust them."

"Removing them from the MA for four days requires telling their parents. That makes the information circle wider than I'd like to consider."

The answer to their problems stared her in the face. At least she could guarantee someone's safety. "So they'll lie to their parents, at least Sophie and Olivia will. Josh's parents wouldn't notice if he didn't come home for a month."

"Fine." Noah's tone made it clear how he felt about lying, but at least they would be alive, right?

She had to confirm. "You'll make the same arrangements for them?"

"Yes." He slid his compad over and made several notes on it. "I'd rather they not know the details until you are on the road, just to be safe. You'll need to stop Josh before he leaves for the agricultural center that morning, and maybe you guys can intercept Sophie and Liv in the school parking lot. I'll let you invent the story the girls give their parents. Will they trust you enough to get in the car without an explanation?"

"No problem, and yes, questions or not, they'll go along."

Noah rubbed one of his temples for a moment before adding to his notations. He fixed his eyes on her. "So you'll go then?"

Arguing with him anymore couldn't have been more unfair, but she couldn't resist pushing back one final time. After all, he would wear the largest target on his back. "I'd rather you go with us." His eyes narrowed, and she sighed. "We'll go."

His whole posture eased, his chest sinking with the deep exhale. He took her face in his hands and leaned close. "Thank you."

The kiss that followed held pain and relief at the same time. When he pulled away, he repositioned himself on the floor beside her and leaned back against the bed frame. His head dropped onto the mattress. "We'll break the news to Taylor on Tuesday night."

His exhaustion awoke her conscience. Noah carried the weight of hundreds of lives in his hands, and instead of supporting him, she demanded he take on three extra lives as well. He deserved better from her. Laying a hand on his cheek, she turned his face toward her and smoothed away the lines etched there. "Whatever you want."

A hesitant smile stole onto his face though the darkness in his eyes remained.

From here on out, she'd do whatever he wanted, whatever would chase those shadows away.

*

When Noah arrived on Wednesday morning, he scanned the dim neighborhood. No one else moved around outside. No curtains fluttered in any of the nearby houses' windows either. He might be able to help Maddison and her family disappear without raising any suspicion.

Taylor exited the house and struggled with a heavy box as she made her way to the back of her Ford SUV. Rushing forward, he took the box from her and wedged it in with the other luggage. The trunk looked like a stockpile for the whole winter.

"That isn't going to get you out of hot water with me, you know." There was no real heat behind her words.

When he and Maddison told Taylor everything last night, she'd been disappointed in them but not as upset as he'd expected. Until she told them she understood because she'd been working with an illegal clinic in UNE before Michael and Tamara's liquidation.

"Well, I'm not about to stand around and watch you wrestle all this by yourself either." He stuck his hands in the front pockets of his dark green hoodie.

"As long as you're here, there's another box in the kitchen."

He nodded and headed for the house. Jakob lugged a hefty overnight bag down the steps, rolling his eyes. "Girls are ridiculous."

Noah swallowed a chuckle. "You'll change your tune one day."

"You aren't the one carrying Maddison's hundred-pound bag. Hey, why aren't you carrying it?" He dropped it at Noah's feet with a grin and headed back upstairs.

Noah hefted it onto his shoulder and grabbed the last box from the kitchen before heading back outside to Taylor. He stacked the box on top of the last and shifted the bag, looking for a place to fit it in.

"If that's Maddison's, it should go in her trunk. It's unlocked already." Taylor pointed to the car in the garage.

He pivoted toward her. "Maddison's taking her car as well? Who's riding with her?"

"Sophie and Olivia, I think. She plans to pick them up at school."

Anxiety crept up his spine. "But you're following her, right? Leaving at the same time, I mean?"

"Of course. What's going on?" She took a step closer.

"I didn't realize you all wouldn't be in the same car. I don't want her … I want to make sure she …" He didn't know how to finish the sentence.

"You wanted to make sure she wouldn't give me the slip and come right back here against both of our wishes?"

He nodded. "I know how stubborn she is. And I want to make sure everyone gets to MA-16 and stays there. Safe."

"I'll be watching her with eagle eyes. We all will. She'll stay with us."

"Thank you. And again, I'm sorry for not being honest." He threw the heavy bag into Maddison's trunk, closing it behind him. When he turned back around, Taylor still stood in front of him, but her face had softened.

"Noah, I want to make it clear," she said, and he braced himself. "You know, I'm not happy with the decisions you and Maddison made. She lied to me, and you put her in danger. I can't overlook those things. There will be consequences when this is finished." She sighed. "However, my opinion of you hasn't changed. I still think you're a good man. I just need you to make better choices for her. Okay?"

"Yes, ma'am."

She waved him off. "Enough with the ma'am stuff. Go see your girlfriend."

"Thank you for another chance. I'll see you on Friday morning."

She pushed him toward the door. "We'll expect you then. Now, go get those two out of the house so we can get going."

He smiled. "Will do."

Jakob's bag lay by the door, and a minute later, he came around the corner, massive sandwich in hand. "We ready?"

"Almost. Your aunt wants you and Maddison to get a move on." Jakob nodded and came to pick up his bag. Noah put a hand on his arm. "Jakob, I need you to do something for me."

"Make sure Maddison doesn't try to sneak away for any reason?" The young man smirked.

Noah bit back a smile despite his fear. "I think she's going to get antsy once you get there. I don't want her making any impulsive decisions. Even leaving the house could be dangerous."

"We'll take care of her." Jakob locked eyes with him. "Whether she wants us to or not. I know how important this is."

Noah sucked in a deep breath and lowered his voice. "If anything happens—"

"Nothing's going to happen."

"This group isn't going to line up to die. I'm afraid it'll be more of a fight than we'd like to believe. I know I'll be a target, so if anything happens to me, I need you to keep her safe. I don't think you'll need extra help, but if you do, you can call Daniel. I know you don't like him, but I'll make him swear to look out for you."

"I promise." Jakob gave him a small shove to the side. "Now if you'll excuse me, I get to go convince Josh to get in Taylor's car."

Noah smiled. "Where's Maddison?"

"Avoiding us, I think." Jakob nodded his head toward the stairs.

Taking the steps two at a time, Noah called out for her. She didn't answer, and when he came around the corner into her doorway, he could tell she'd been crying. He slid a hand out to take hers and pulled her close. "Hey, it's going to be okay."

"If you thought so, you wouldn't have had that little discussion with Jakob." Her arms wound around his waist.

"I'm just being careful." Leaning down, he kissed the top of her head.

"Are you sure you can't go with us?"

Her quiet plea twisted his insides, and he laid his forehead against hers. "No. But as soon as I can, I'll come get you. The minute I can be there, I will."

"I hate this."

"Me too." He ran a hand through her hair.

For several minutes, they didn't speak. When she did, her voice sounded fortified. "I have a condition."

He leaned back. "For what?"

"For me to leave. You have to agree to it, or I don't go."

"Maddison ..." His eyes slid shut, anticipating the fight he'd been dreading all morning.

"Hear me out. I've agreed to leave town because you think it's necessary, and it'll help you stay sane. That's what you said." She leaned back, and he opened his eyes to find her determined gaze staring right into his. "If I am going to stay sane while you're here fighting, I need to know you aren't going to try to save everyone but yourself. That you won't choose to be a martyr. I want you to fight and be careful—no heroics, I mean it."

He sighed, not wanting to lie to her but unsure he could promise to save his own skin over someone else's. He wasn't worth that much.

She poked a finger against his chest. "I'm serious. If I think you're going to go into 'save the world' mode, I can't leave. Because you will get yourself killed. Do your job, protect your brother, but remember you have to come back to me."

He didn't want to deny her. *Please let me be able to keep my word.* "I'll be careful."

An eyebrow arched. "Really?"

"I promise."

She dropped her head back to his chest. "If you aren't, you'll have to answer to me." The softness of her words voided their threat.

"I would expect nothing less." All he wanted, all he needed, was to come back to her. Clutching her tight, he kissed her. She tried to pull him even closer, their lips frantically communicating the words they had to leave unspoken. When he pulled back, tears stained her face.

He brushed them away with his thumbs. Now or never. "I love you."

She reached up and kissed him, the violence from before exchanged for a slow tenderness. "I love you too."

Like cool water to his parched soul, her words spilled into him. Unbelievable. He leaned his forehead against hers. "I wish you didn't have to go."

"Me too." Her lips trembled.

His vidcom buzzed an alarm. Time to get them on the road. He stepped away and pulled her down the steps. He put an unregistered vidcom in her hands. "Don't turn your vidcoms on unless you need to verify your status for a liquidator, okay? I updated everyone's record this morning. No one should stop you or report you missing. If you need to contact me, use this instead. You can use it to call Sophie and Olivia's parents as well."

She nodded. "Okay, I'll tell them to call their parents about the time school lets out. The cover story is that we have a killer group project due in science on Sunday, and we need every spare hour to work on finishing it. None of us plan to leave my house until it's perfect. We had to do something similar last year, so Sophie's parents won't have a problem with it. And since Olivia's parents won't be able to see her face, she should be able to pull it off as well."

Let her be right. If anything went wrong on her end …

Noah squeezed her hand. "Call once you get out of town. And when you hit MA-8, and then MA-12, and once you're all in the house. Okay?"

"That's a lot of calls, mister."

"Okay?" They exited the house, and he paused while she secured the front door behind them.

"I promise."

Taylor's car idled in the street, waiting for Maddison to pull out. They reached her car, and as she opened the door, she turned to face him.

"I'll see you first thing Friday morning."

"As soon as I can make it. I'll steal you away and intro-duce you to my hometown. Just you and me."

"I'm holding you to that, Seforé." She smiled even as her eyes filled with tears.

"You do that, Maddison James. You do just that."

CHAPTER THIRTY-THREE

I T WAS 2:00 p.m. Four hours after the Liquidation Updates aired, and they waited for the first group of resistance members to arrive. Several liquidators, including Brandon, guarded the temporary armory Noah and Daniel had constructed to house the various guns, grenades, and small bombs they'd found in the largest warehouse. They'd positioned other liquidators around the perimeter and in each of the three smaller buildings, including the old terminal. He and Daniel leaned against the left wall of the main warehouse, alert for any movement near the gate on the road.

His thumb spun the dense metal that looped again around his third finger. The ring slid back and forth, feeling heavier for each day it'd been off his hand. He'd grown too used to being without it. It felt as restrictive as it had the day his commander had handed it over to him at the Academy. He wished for gloves and stuffed his hands in the pockets of his leather jacket.

Another cold blast of wind raced between the buildings,

and he pulled the collar up around the back of his neck. Though the sun shone in a cloudless sky, it had no effect on the below freezing temperatures. He shifted back and forth on his feet, trying to keep his blood moving and his body temperature up. Beside him, Daniel stood still and quiet, like a marble statue. The cold seemed to have no effect on him.

"Should be any time," he muttered to Noah.

This time the icy blast ran through Noah's veins. The air felt heavy and ominous. A dark voice inside him whispered. He tucked his head into his chest and gave himself the luxury of one moment to think about Maddison.

It didn't work. The dread remained. He shifted again, almost pacing.

Daniel shot a lazy glance over his shoulder at Noah. "Would you pull it together?"

"Daniel, if things go wrong today, if anything happens—"

Daniel faced him, a threatening look on his face. "Shut up. Nothing's going to go wrong if you keep your head on straight. I'm not going to make plans with you. You're going to calm down and do your job. Got it?"

Across the train tracks came the faint sound of a gate creaking open. It had begun.

*

Laying the older man down beside the other dead, Noah headed for the door. He didn't want to stay a second longer than necessary. As he exited behind another liquidator, the sun slipped behind the trees. He glanced down at his watch. Five thirty had come and gone. The resistance's leadership was taken care of, their children already en route to government foster homes. Five hundred members had arrived in spurts over the last three hours, carrying belongings and dragging their children with them. The ninety children were now ensconced in the largest warehouse and under guard by twenty-five liquidators. Terrified but at least protected from watching their parents be killed in front of their eyes.

The adults lay in the smallest of the warehouses. No longer a threat.

They still had to account for the remaining thousand. And it would be dark within the hour.

Something whistled by his ear, and he dropped on instinct, the hard earth exploding beside him. Other liquidators turned in the direction of the shot, their hands already reaching for the weapons strapped to their sides. Rolling out of the way and back against the wall of the warehouse, Noah pulled his own gun from the holster and surveyed the perimeter.

Every inch moved. Seconds later, heavily armed men and women rushed the fence and gates, rapid firing into the compound. Noah's gut dropped. They had been warned. They were prepared. And more than a thousand approached.

New odds. Each of the seventy-five liquidators would have to take down approximately eighteen people for them to succeed. With night falling fast, it would become hard to distinguish between friend and foe.

Rushing forward, Noah took shots at the men as they

landed on their feet beside the fence. Several went down, but he had to keep moving to keep away from their returning fire. The compound rang out with gunfire, shouts, and agonized cries. Two more shots and a man rushing toward him went down at his feet.

He moved right again, keeping his back to the main warehouse where no threats would be probable. About fifty yards away, he caught a glimpse of Brandon down on one knee, machine gun firing in the direction of the front gate. A bullet hit the warehouse wall to Noah's left, and he refocused, taking another shot before finding cover to reload the clip.

Before he could finish, a young man ran around the corner, screaming and red-faced. Noticing Noah, he plowed forward, and Noah braced for the hit. The man knocked him over. Noah threw him off and to the right, dodging the gun swung at his face. Noah disarmed him, throwing the gun into the growing fray. They grappled back and forth, punches thrown, blocked, and landed, before Noah got the upper hand. A moment later, the man lay dead on the ground.

He jumped back to his feet. The sound of guns firing decreased, and war cries filled in the difference. To his left, several liquidators went down, blood spurting from their chests. The resistance members who shot them were dispatched moments later. Bodies littered the ground. Pairs circled each other in gory boxing stances.

The smell of smoke and blood filled the air.

Behind him, boots rushed forward, and he turned in

time to miss the knife intended for his back. He grabbed his attacker's wrists and twisted. The knife dropped to the ground. He kicked it away even as she landed a foot on his instep. He bit back a groan and pushed her away, but she charged, spewing curses. He pinned her arms to her sides, dodging the head butt she attempted and shifting to hold her arms with one hand while the other snapped her neck.

A searing pain tore through his right arm. Warm blood poured out of the bullet hole. Dropping to his knee, he turned and looked for the shooter. Seconds later, a body collided with his. The heavy man pinned him to the ground, pulled back, and landed a powerful right cross to Noah's jaw before he upset the man's balance and regained some ground. He dodged and punched, feeling the muscles in his right tricep burn with each movement. The blood loss clouded his head. The angry man let out a yell and landed another punch to his jaw before grabbing his throat and squeezing. He used every wrestling move he could recall from secondary school, but nothing worked. As his eyesight began to diminish, the man dropped on top of him, dead weight.

Noah rolled out from under the man and jumped up. Daniel stood yards away, gun still pointed in their direction.

Noah nodded a thank you and took a moment to scan the scene. The numbers on both sides had thinned. Bodies covered the ground so only patches of dirt showed through. The wind blew a cold blast in his direction. And then he smelled it.

He turned toward the main warehouse. Flames licked up the side and front of the building, smoke growing and billowing up in the wind. He shot a panicked look in Daniel's direction and saw a similar look on his brother's face. Their eyes connected for a moment.

The children.

He took off running, not heeding the angry voice of his brother yelling after him. The wind drowned out Daniel's words anyway.

Shielding his face, Noah ran through the flames into the open doorway and dropped to his knees to escape the black smoke. He yanked his t-shirt over his mouth. The heat singed his hair and scorched the leather jacket. His eyes shot down to his sleeve. It'd caught fire during his entrance. As he jerked the coat off, the signet ring slipped away as well. He slapped away the embers glowing on his sweater before crawling toward the children.

As he stumbled over several dead bodies, it occurred to him. No liquidators had come rushing out from the flaming building. He heard no faint cries or smoke-induced coughing. Quickening his pace, he reached the corner where the children should be.

It was empty.

A cold draft blew across his face, and he made out the silhouette of the open back door. They'd escaped. Or been freed by someone. The flames raced toward the new supply of oxygen.

He had to get out.

He stood and ran the final seven steps. The heat burned through his clothing. He cleared the door and continued running away from the building. Not a soul moved on this side of the compound.

The world exploded.

He was thrown into the air, and chunks of concrete and debris flew by him. The sky lit from the ground up as the building erupted in flames and shrapnel. As quickly as the blast had picked him up, it threw him down, all his weight on his right leg. Bones shattered upon impact. Pain unlike any other raced through his body. He couldn't breathe. His head thudded against the packed dirt. A heavy, hot weight landed on his left shoulder, and he cried out as fire seared his skin and muscle. He rolled out from under the slab of wood and concrete, and the pain deepened before deadening—nerve damage.

The blaze still raged, claiming more ground, and his eyes darted around for a refuge. A storage building stood several yards away, unscathed. Pulling himself on his right arm, he ignored the blood seeping from it and groaned with each inch gained. He'd crossed half the distance when he froze. He hadn't heard himself groan. He paused and listened. Nothing. Not even a faint throbbing.

The heat hit him again, and he gritted his teeth. *Keep moving.* Dirt and grass grated against the cuts and burns on his arms and hands as he dragged himself forward. If he could make it the last foot and get inside the storage building, it would be cool and dark there. That would ease the searing burns and pain radiating through his body.

Once he'd pulled himself into the building, he collapsed and shifted to find a position that didn't hurt. No such position existed. His useless right leg throbbed. The edges of his left shoulder and forearm burned, though the center seemed numb. His right arm seeped blood from around the bullet wedged in his arm. His ribs ached with every moment and screamed with each cough and sputter from his smoke-filled lungs.

As he lay still, the pain intensified, making it hard to think. The edges of his sight dimmed. But if he lost consciousness, he wouldn't wake up again.

He fought to stay awake, to think of Maddison, of introducing her to his hometown, of growing old with her. The heaviness dragged him under still. He wouldn't be able to keep his promises to her.

Another vow broken. Another wrong to add to the never-ending list. He wished for more time. He wasn't ready to meet God.

He needed another chance—to earn forgiveness. In that moment, he realized he needed to make peace with God more than he wanted to see her face one last time. *Would You even hear me?* The idea of staying silent sent desperation racing through him. He had to try.

As the darkness began to encroach, he choked out the few words his mind provided. "God, I'm sorry. Please help me."

Too inadequate but all he could muster.

The fuzziness receded, and he felt something digging into his left thigh. He traced the edges of a box in his cargo pocket. The silver box! Ignoring the pain, he rolled onto his right side, plunging his hand into the pocket and pulling out the box. He fumbled the latch open with one hand, grasped a miraculously undamaged vial, and jammed it into the syringe as the darkness began to overtake him. He drove the needle into his thigh as the pain crescendoed, and consciousness slipped away.

CHAPTER THIRTY-FOUR

MADDISON PROWLED THE one-story house like an angry tiger, pacing from the living room to the sunroom and back again. Instead of sleeping, she spent the night waiting for Noah's arrival, calling his vidcom, and plotting ways to slip away. Her friends had made escape difficult though. Josh slept slumped against the front door, and Jakob lay in front of the sunroom door.

The girls hadn't even let her go to the bathroom alone by midday yesterday. It made her anxiety worse. Sophie and Liv had given in to sleep just two hours ago, one on the couch and the other in the recliner in the den. Taylor was in the master bedroom down the hall. Silence filled every inch of space.

A clock chimed from the kitchen—five tones. He should have been here twenty-two hours ago, which meant one thing.

Something was terribly wrong.

And they wouldn't let her go help him. She pushed open the vidcom clutched in her hand and voice commanded his number again. Straight to voicemail. For the thirty-fifth time. Resisting the urge to throw it against the wall, she slapped it closed again, his recorded voice dying away as the cover snapped shut.

She had to find him. She marched toward the front door, pushed Josh's sleeping form aside, and began to punch in the security code. A hand landed on her arm. She shook it off.

"You're not going anywhere." Josh nudged her away from the security panel and it timed out, the system remaining armed. He stood fixed between her and the door.

"I have to find Noah. Something's wrong—don't you know that? Why doesn't anyone else care that he's late?" The tones of her voice pitched higher and louder as she pushed at him. "Just because you don't care whether he's alive or dead doesn't make it true for everyone else."

"Maddison." Sophie rose and walked over to them. "No one wants Noah to be hurt. But he made it plain we all have to stay here until he or ..." Her voice died away as Maddison shot a glare her way. "Until he comes."

Josh stood statuesque against the door, his arms crossed in front of him. Jakob and Taylor stood feet away, probably drawn to the living room by her tirade. Their expressions were wary as though they faced an actual caged animal ... or a person experiencing a psychotic break. Sophie shared their look.

Olivia walked over and put a hand on her arm. "We know you're scared, Maddie. But it doesn't—"

"I'm not scared," she yelled. "Do I look scared? No, I'm angry. I don't know how you could be this heartless. And I'm angry at him for keeping me waiting. When he shows up, I'm going to kill him."

"Fair enough." Taylor inclined her head toward the kitchen. "In the meantime, why don't we all get dressed and have some breakfast?"

She crossed her arms. "I don't want to eat." *And no one can make me.*

Taylor imitated her crossed-arm pose, eyebrows raised. "Well, maybe we do." She headed for the kitchen. Jakob and the girls followed.

When she turned around, Josh took a step forward. "You can stop anytime, you know. We're here to help, regardless of how much you rant and rave." He moved closer. "Because we love you and because it's what he wants us to do."

"How do you even know what he wants? You barely tolerate him." She stared at him, daring him to defy her.

Josh took a deep breath. "He hurt you." He held up a hand as she opened her mouth. "I'm protective. It's been my job to look after you and Jakob for most of my life. I didn't want to hand it over. And, I guess, I felt a little jealous that you could replace me so fast.

"But Sophie set me straight, and I know now how much he's done to protect you." She must've looked confused because he shrugged and kept talking. "Jakob and I had a long talk on the way down. Noah's going to do everything he can to get back to you. But you have to be here for that to happen, okay?"

Tears welled up in her eyes. "I'm scared, Josh."

Josh pulled her into a hug, comfortable and safe. "I know."

Tears overflowed. Her mind filled with everything horrible her imagination had concocted in the last three days. Josh patted her back at an uneven rhythm and with a light pressure, as uncomfortable with her tears as always. The normalcy of it settled her emotions a smidge.

She pulled back, distancing herself from the fears. "I should go clean up, so I'll be ready when he gets here."

"Sounds good. I'll make sure Taylor saves you some breakfast."

*

She opened the bathroom door with a clean face and her hair pulled back into a braid. Quiet conversation filtered down the hallway, but she turned toward Noah's room. Put a hand on the doorknob and twisted. Maybe just one peek without him.

The security system deactivated from the outside.

Noah.

She ran down the hall and stopped cold. A lone figure stood framed in the doorway.

Daniel, dust covered and haggard, stared right at her. She began to shake her head. He took a step toward her. Dust shimmered like an aura around him, and blood stained his clothes. Cuts and abrasions marred his face.

"No," she whispered. "No. No. No."

Behind her, she heard the movement of her friends, but

no one said anything as Daniel entered, closing the door behind him.

"Maddison." His voice croaked. "We need to talk."

She backed away from him, reaching behind her for something stable, something to keep her bound to reality. Her hand found Jakob's, and he came to stand with her, bolstering her.

"Where's Noah?"

"You should sit down."

"Is he parking the car?"

Daniel shook his head and winced.

"The hospital then? They admitted him for observation? That's why he sent you?"

"Maddison, sit down."

"Tell me where he is."

Daniel stepped further into the room. The determination in his eyes frightened her. Were his hands ... trembling? "During the fight, someone set fire to a warehouse. A warehouse we'd taken the children to, to keep them safe. Noah ran in to save them." He swallowed. "The building exploded." Another swallow. "It exploded with him inside."

Someone let out a soft cry behind her, but she felt numb. "I don't believe you."

Jakob said something. She shook him off.

"No, he promised me no heroics. He promised he wouldn't try to save the world or martyr himself or do anything stupid. He wouldn't have done that. He couldn't have."

"I saw it happen," Daniel said, his own tone lifeless.

"He must've had a plan then." Her hand flew to the

ring around her neck. "Was there a back door? Maybe he got out before it exploded? Did you search the whole area? What if he's lying somewhere hurt, and you didn't search hard enough?" She put a hand on her hip, pushing down the desperation flooding through her. "He can't be dead. Hurt maybe, but not dead. He said I couldn't lose him. He said it. That means he's not dead. I don't believe you."

Daniel's jaw clenched, torment written in every feature. "I found his … microchip." He clenched his fists. His arms shook and the color drained from his face. His hands unfurled. "We unearthed his ring along with the partial remains of the other twenty-five liquidators we knew to be in the building."

Daniel reached into his jacket pocket then extended his hand. A twisted piece of platinum and onyx sat in his red, scarred palm.

The truth crashed into her, dragging her down. The words echoed through her soul. The air rushed out of her lungs, and her hand flew to her mouth. Images cemented in her mind. The burned out building.

The charred body.

She slammed her eyes shut.

"Maddison."

Her eyes shot open to meet Daniel's. Rage welled up inside her. She rushed forward, hurling her open palms against his chest. "You feel guilty? Well, you should." She pushed him again. "You were supposed to keep him safe." She slapped his chest. "You're his brother. It's your job." A fist pound. "He wouldn't have even been fighting if it weren't for you." Her blows rained harder. "Didn't you try to stop him? Him and his death wish? His martyr complex? Why didn't you knock him unconscious to keep him out of that building? Why didn't you go in after him? You should've dragged him back out. He's dead, and it's all your fault."

His right arm pinned her wrists against his chest, but she continued her verbal assault. Hot tears ran down her face. "The one time it really mattered, and you didn't protect him. Why? This time mattered, Daniel. Do you hear me? It mattered, and you let him die."

She collapsed against him, sobbing, and his arms went around her waist, holding her up. But his shoulders shook too, and moments later, they both slid into a heap on the floor. Moisture trickled into her hair. His broken whisper repeated, "I know. I'm sorry. I know …"

EPILOGUE

THE DAY BEFORE

ISAIAH SLID THE Bible closer to the electric lantern on the small desk. Its light provided just enough illumination for the desk's surface area. His elbows found the edge as he hunched over, seeking wisdom in the one place he could trust to find it. Skimming the page, he found the place he'd left off yesterday.

Luke chapter four, verse sixteen. After all these years, reading the gospels remained a habit. His anxiousness to know more about the One who'd freed him from his guilt had not waned.

"'The Spirit of The Lord is upon me.'" He read verse eighteen aloud, his deep bass echoing through the little room. "'Because he has anointed me to proclaim good news to the poor. He has sent me to proclaim liberty to the captives and recovering of sight to the blind, to set at liberty those who are oppressed.'"

He paused, reading over the words again, letting them

sink into his soul. "Thank You, Jesus, for setting us free, for giving sight to those of us stumbling in darkness. Please help me to remember, help us to remember though we are oppressed now, it is temporary. We will not always cower underground. I look forward to that day."

His eyes fell upon the solitary picture frame on the desk. The smiling faces of his wife Cara and daughter Abby stared back at him. "To see them again. To see You for the first time. I pray it will not be long."

The blare of a compad in the room next to his interrupted him. The problem with buying items on the black market was that they had to take what they could get, including a compad stuck on the highest volume possible. It belonged to the community, but Isaiah guessed Mark Battais had possession of it now. The fourteen-year-old devoured news of any kind. Isaiah couldn't fault him. It was difficult for such a young man to be buried in an underground bunker when he should be running across football fields and basking in the sunlight.

It must be 7:00 a.m. Through the thin walls, Isaiah heard the local newscaster introduce the top stories. The anchor began with an explosion downtown. Liquidators had arrived on site to process the scene and determine the cause of the blast. MEs and cremation specialists from the surrounding metro areas assisted MA-4's staff in clearing the area of bodies. Over two thousand dead in total. Such a waste.

Go there.

Go to the scene? Why? Twelve hours had passed since

the explosion. His medical skills could be of no help at this point—illegal citizenship aside.

I am not willing that he should perish. Go there.

Isaiah would not question a second time. Rising from the chair, he removed his reading glasses and set them on top of the book. He grabbed his jacket and headed for his door and then the surface.

He passed Christianna on his way to the entrance. Her bright eyes asked him no questions, trusting his leadership without disillusionment. Such a childlike faith the twenty-year-old had, so like his Abby's. She wished him safety and went on to her family's quarters, her curly blonde hair bouncing behind her. He smiled at her retreating form, grateful for young ones like her who believed with abandon.

Raising the opening, he stared into the barren cornfield, but there were no signs of movement. He climbed out, stood, and took a deep breath. Fresh oxygen rushed into his lungs. He sucked in another gulp, thankful for a chance to be out of the stale air if but for an hour.

With quick and practiced movements, he re-covered the entrance with dirt and dead plant stalks and made his way to the farmhouse, staying alert the entire time. William and Sue would already be in the barn at this time of day, but they left a spare set of keys to the ancient truck under the stairs of the back porch.

The engine caught on the third try, and he sighed a prayer of thanks as he headed into town. Being a weekend, few cars traveled with him into the heart of downtown, and he managed to make it near the explosion site within the hour.

Red tape cordoned off the area, and cremation specialists in dark green uniforms worked along the eastern side of the compound. A pair of liquidators guarded the front gate. News vans sat idling along the side of the road by the entrance. Driving down a side street on the west, he circled the old station and grinned.

Providence smiled down on him today. The small back gate was unguarded and propped open. Shutting off the engine, he waited to hear the sound of approaching voices or vehicles. None came. He stepped out into the cold air and pulled his coat closer around him. Exposure to this temperature wouldn't be good for anyone wounded.

"Did I hear You right?" He walked through the back gate, anxious to pick up the sounds of any moving feet, but the surrounding area lay quiet and still. No answer came, but the urgency remained.

The sun spilled over the buildings, highlighting the carnage. Debris and rubble lay in a wide arc around the blackened circle of what had been the main warehouse. Dirt lay in random piles throughout, littered with shell casings and bullets. Deep red puddles stained the ground around his feet. He had never seen anything like it.

"No one could be alive here, Lord." His gut churned as his mind concocted images from the news report and the desecration before him.

In the darkness.

What darkness? Light covered everything. Even shadows were few and far between at this time of day. He moved forward, trying not to look down at his feet as he moved.

He scanned the area. Did God want him to dig through the pieces of rubble at the building's base? The debris' arrangement in ordered rows made plain that someone had searched the area once already. Then, on the edge of the property, he spotted it.

A small storage building, not six feet wide. Running faster than he had in many years, he reached the shed and swung the door open.

In the corner lay a body, curled up against the cold. He stepped inside, but the young man did not move. Blue lips. Burns. Blood stained the floor. Isaiah's ER training clicked into gear. He hadn't practiced more than first aid in almost ten years, but he knew what his eyes told him. This man couldn't be alive—he'd suffered without treatment too long.

"Why did You bring me here?" Still he knelt down to take a pulse, instinct needing to confirm it. Isaiah's breath stuttered out. It was thready, but against all odds, the pulse throbbed on.

The stranger lived.

STATE V. SEFORÉ – BOOK TWO:
HUNTED

Safe underground, Noah heals from his injuries. He finally gains freedom from his demons and a future apart from the Elite. However, Maddison and Daniel don't know that. All they know is—Noah might be alive, but he hasn't returned home.

As they search for Noah and his assumed kidnappers, the pair discovers they're being hunted as well. And after a series of dangerous encounters, Maddison is left wondering if Daniel really is the villain she thought. While Daniel realizes he might not be immune to his feelings after all. But where does that leave him when they find his brother?

Coming Winter 2014

Want State v. Seforé news, bonus scenes, and extras first?
Become a newsletter subscriber at
www.charitytinnin.com.

ACKNOWLEDGMENTS

To the Author and Creator, thank you for giving me this small story in the midst of Yours.

Amanda G. Stevens, I don't even have words. Thank you for loving Noah so much, for editing and proofing several times, for begging me to write *Hunted*, for endless brainstorming, for praying and encouraging and loving not only the story but me. And thank you especially for these last eight weeks—where you've fielded at least one phone call, three e-mails, seven to ten text messages, and endless gchats a day. If the copy is clean and my characters deep, it is because of you. I cannot wait until we do this for Marcus and Lee.

Jessica Keller, my YA BFF, I'm beyond grateful to walk the YA indie journey with you. Thank you for having a heart for stories that matter. Thank you for keeping me sane and launching a month before me so all the kinks were worked out. ;) Thank you for sending me pictures of cute guys, offering to make a Team Seforé shirt, and running FictionCrush with me. Thank you also for celebrating and crying with me during the last two years. I'm trusting God for a whole lot more of the former for us both!

Erynn Newman, thank you for challenging me to stop hiding my fiction in a notebook or in a fan fiction forum and DO something with it. I will always be grateful for those first two years and what God taught us both. Thank you for reading a chapter a day during NaNoWriMo to keep me on track. Thank you for being the friend who not only fixes my copy but pulls me out of the crazy, over-analytical plotting place; your humor is always what I need in those moments.

Edie Melson, thank you for befriending me at Blue Ridge. Your encouragement made my first writers' conference so much easier. I'm excited we get to be critique partners now and can't wait to get my hands on more of your fiction. Thank you for supporting my move to indie pub.

Speaking of going indie, Susan Kaye Quinn, I don't know that I would've ever considered indie publishing were it not for you. Getting to watch your journey throughout the years has been inspiring. Thank you for being transparent and prolific in talking about indie. Thank you also for championing me through the first NaNo draft in 2010. And for all that microchip info—even if it did put a huge wrench in my plot. Several times. Throughout the series. ;)

Lauren Bielick, if Noah and Maddison seem like they have any medical knowledge, it is a direct result of your advice. (If they don't, I blame myself.) Thank you for answering my patient care questions, sharing insights about life as a medical professional, giving me nursing textbooks, and looking at an illustration of Noah's back to assess the burn damage. The *Metro Seven* reference? That's for you.

To my male beta readers, you guys rock. So hard. Especially you, Seth Gardner. Thank you for giving me detailed thoughts on *Haunted* from a high school guy. If Noah ever gets rid of his Mustang, it's all yours. Chris Hamblin, thank you for signing off on Noah, Daniel, and Jakob's dialogue and encouraging me to beef up those fight scenes. Michael Noto, thank you for caring about the name of my fictional country, for the financial support you and Rachel gave me, and for letting Rachel use your facebook to promote me. I don't take that lightly!

Chloe Ross, you are a discerning YA reader, so thank you for liking my first fifty pages and wanting to read more. I hope you enjoyed it all. Rachel Noto, thank you for challenging me to show Noah and Maddison's journeys more clearly and for being my cheerleader and self-proclaimed #1 fan. I needed it during the dark days of editing. To everyone else who critiqued *Haunted*: Jen Grady, Halee Matthews, Lisa Carter, Hope Dougherty, Melanie Dickerson, Kristen Heitzmann, and Jessica Kirkland—each one of you added something special to the series, whether it be automated car details or Daniel's score fixing, and I'm so grateful. Thank you for investing in Noah's story enough to make it better.

Mary Weber, Kim Vandel, Kristi Chestnutt, Melanie Dickerson (again), Jessica Keller (again), Kiera Cass, and Ally Carter—YA authors rock! I am so glad to know most of you personally and benefit from the awesomeness of all of you. Thank you for caring about the stories you write and interacting with teen girls in such a positive way. Jacque Alberta, thank you for being an advocate for the best YA stories; *Haunted* is a better book because of our fifteen-minute appointments at ACFW.

To Adree Williams, Staci Ball, Miranda Beal, Beth Rakel, and Tonya: you ladies were the first to read my fiction, fan or otherwise, and I continued writing because of your encouragement and enthusiasm. Noah might never have existed were it not for your love of my original muses.

To Stephanie Roberts, my Treasuring Christ Church community group, the staff at Christ Baptist (I'm looking at you, Jane Brown and Andy Duke), and my Missionary Ridge family (especially Janet Lawson, Rachel Holland, Gwendolyn Epley, Travis Hill, and my high school students), thank you for endless prayers, numerous questions about how the writing is going, and promises to buy the book even if you aren't sure you'll actually read it.

Mom and Dad, thank you for investing in my spiritual growth and my dreams in so many tangible and intangible ways in the last thirty-two years. This book would NOT exist without you. To Mom, Dad, Faith, West, and Hope for voting on my country name, discussing male/female dynamics, the downfall of the White House as we know it, and whether or not Maddison should be the girl every guy falls for, you have my undying love, but then you had that already. ;) To my Hendrick and Tinnin families, thank you for all of your support and excitement; I am grateful to belong to you.

My readers (squee!): thank you for buying *Haunted,* for reading it, for telling your friends, for sharing on social media, and for reviewing on Amazon/GoodReads [I'm thanking you in advance because it'll be hard to do afterward ;)]. You guys are the reason I write YA. Your support allows me to continue to do what I love. Seriously. I couldn't do this without you.

So thank you. All of you. Yes, you reading right now, I'm thanking you!

CHARITY TINNIN

Charity's fascination with dystopian lit began in high school with *Brave New World*, and she's been devouring the genre ever since. Now, she mentors high school students at her church, works as a freelance editor, and lives in the foothills of North Carolina—a terrain very similar to a certain series. When she's not editing for a client or inventing new ways for Daniel to be delightfully snarky, she spends her time reading YA and discussing the merits of Prince Charming and Captain America online.

Speaking of the interwebs, Charity loves to talk about YA fiction, TV, and the State v. Seforé books. Find her on Twitter (@CharityTinnin), Facebook (www.facebook.com/Charity.Tinnin), or her website (www.charitytinnin.com) to start the conversation.

22656751R00226

Made in the USA
San Bernardino, CA
16 July 2015